Illegal Goodbye
by
Angela Chapman

1

"Illegal Goodbye" by Angela Jobe Chapman ISBN-978-0-9845362-1-4

Published 2010 by Fire Pit Creek Publishing, 31208 E Heidelberger Road, Buckner Mo 64016 US © 2010 Angela Jobe Chapman. All rights reserved. No part of this publication may be reproduced, stored in a retrieval system, or transmitted in any form or by any means, electronic, mechanical, recording, or otherwise, without the prior written permission of Angela Jobe Chapman.

Book Design: Brady Jobe & Angela Chapman
Edited by: Candy Myers
First Print 2004

Manufactured in the United States

To: Brady & Brittney—your ongoing ambition has inspired me to turn my dream into reality.

CHAPTER ONE

Kari glanced at her makeup in the visor mirror while her sister, Kelli, parked the sporty blue Sunfire alongside the curb of the Eastside Shopping Center.

"This is just great—I don't even have to cry and my mascara runs." Kari ran her finger underneath her eye to wipe away the smudge and flipped the visor back to its normal position. She flung the passenger door open and climbed out. She pushed the back of her seat forward so her best friend, Jill, could crawl out. Kari leaned back inside the car, resting her knee on the seat and her hand on her hip. "Don't forget to come and get us at five," she told Kelli.

"I won't, as long as Gary lets me off work on time."

Kari reached across the seat and gently patted Kelli's shoulder. "Sorry you have to work today and can't go shopping with us."

"At least I will be *making* money instead of *spending* money." Kelli rolled her eyes and brushed Kari's hand off her shoulder.

"You're jealous and you know it!"

"You just better be here at five or I'm not waiting for you," Kelli replied.

"I'll tell Mom!" She grinned and quickly slammed the door before Kelli had time to respond. The highlight of Kari's life was teasing her sister.

4

Kelli was not only Kari's sister but her twin sister, born only a few minutes apart, with Kelli being the oldest. They had recently celebrated their sixteenth birthday two months earlier, on September 1.

They had a few similar traits, but mostly they were as different as day and night with the exception of their looks. If it weren't for their hairstyles, they would be almost indistinguishable. Kelli wore her sleek red hair shoulder length and flipped up on the ends, while Kari hot-rolled her waist-length red hair every morning. They both had a few freckles sprinkled across their high cheekbones, and reddish-brown eyebrows that curved perfectly over their sky-blue eyes. Their lips were thin, but having perfectly straight teeth made up for the minor flaw.

Kari didn't mind that Kelli was the brain of the two; the one that always made straight A's while she had to struggle just to make the B honor roll. She didn't mind because she knew she was the one that the popular guys flirted with.

Kari wasn't sure what year it was when she became popular; it seemed like the boys were chasing her as early as kindergarten. She was certain that she was born boy crazy. Even at four years old, she could remember always wanting to go next door to play with five-year-old Jimmy Skiles on his red swing set. She had told her family she was going to marry Jimmy when she grew up. She vaguely recalled babbling about her husband-to-be to everyone who would listen. Kari had been crushed when Jimmy's father had taken a different job out of state and moved away.

Kari smiled silently when Kelli flipped her middle finger up and squealed her tires as she pulled away from the curb. She waited until Kelli glared back in her direction, and then Kari waved at her, grinning broadly. She loved her sister dearly, but couldn't resist bantering with her.

Kari laughed aloud and spun toward Jill. "I just love to give her a hard time."

"I noticed. You two are terrible!" Jill tossed her sun-streaked blond hair back and giggled. "But I have to admit, you both know how to keep me entertained."

5

"We do have fun. It's a good thing she's a good sport, or I'd probably be dead meat." Kari locked arms with Jill as they headed in the direction of the mall. Jill had been her best friend for seven years and was like part of the family. *Poor Jill,* Kari thought, she always had to be in the center of all of her and Kelli's quarrels.

Kari nodded toward the entrance doors. "Don't let me forget what entrance we're going in."

The mall was the core attraction in Leewood, Michigan, besides the Douglas College. The peaceful town had fewer than ten thousand people and most of them were college students. Besides the activities at the college, the shopping center was the only realistic place for teenagers to hang out. A theater in Centerside, a nearby city, served as entertainment for a lot of the college students, but most of the high school students preferred to loiter at the shopping mall.

They entered the bustling mall, and Jill immediate paused to peek through a window at a short-waisted leather jacket. Her eyes lit up. "Let's go in there."

"Do you care if we check that place out on the way out? I'm anxious to get to Sears; they're supposed to be having a huge clearance sale." Kari knew by experience if you didn't get to the sales early, all the favorable clothes would be picked over. She was hoping to find a new sweater at a reasonable price to wear to Jenny's party next weekend.

"Okay, let's go," Jill said.

Kari glimpsed through the store windows at the latest fashions as they hurried toward the escalator. She never could understand how the trendy outfits always fit so much better on the mannequins. It has to be their slender waistlines, she decided, glancing toward the flat stomach on a motionless brunette dummy.

It was particularly crowded for a Saturday afternoon. Kari continuously bumped into people as she made her way to the escalator. A line of people was already waiting to get on the escalator. Kari folded her arms across her chest and tapped her foot in rhythm as she waited. She loathed going shopping when there was a crowd. It always seemed like everyone was in a

6

hurry to get to where they were going; they would run right smack into you and never utter a word of an apology. She assumed the upcoming holiday season was the reason for the hasty crowd.

The line ceased after a few seconds, and Kari and Jill stepped onto the congested escalator. Standing directly in front of Kari was a long-legged, muscular, dark-haired hunk. Kari thought he resembled a younger Ricky Martin. She guessed him to be a local college student, because he appeared more mature than the usual high school boy. She suddenly recalled the words of Shelly Bell, an eight-year old neighbor girl, who she used to baby sit—when Shelly chattered about a cute guy in her second grade class, she would refer to him as a hottie. Kari smiled—that was the perfect word for this guy—a hottie!

Jill playfully shoved Kari toward the fellow while making a face like she was whistling. Kari giggled louder than she had anticipated, and the guy spun around and smiled. Kari's pulse quickened; she beamed flirtingly back at him. She ran her fingers through her hair, pulling her long bangs behind her ears; a nervous habit she had picked up when she grew her bangs out three years earlier.

They reached the bottom of the escalator and the young man turned right, the same direction Kari and Jill were headed. Suddenly, the guy whirled around. "Excuse me, are you girls familiar with this mall?"

Kari was flabbergasted. "Yes, we are," she stuttered. She instantly noticed the embedded dimple in his left cheek. His avid eyes were dark, and he had a smooth tan complexion. He wore his thick black hair somewhat long and layered on the sides, and his tight blue jeans couldn't fit him any better. He definitely resembled a Latin dancer. Kari had had many boyfriends, but not one of them measured up to this guy. She silently thought how exciting a relationship with him would be.

"I'm new here. I'm looking for a photo place to get some film. Would you know where one would be?" he asked.

Kari thought his sweet nature was alluring. He had an intelligent, sophisticated manner about him, unlike the juvenile boys she was used to hanging out with. She glanced toward Jill,

7

who only shrugged her shoulders. "I think there might be a photo place around the corner." Kari pointed in the direction she believed the photograph shop was located. She scuffed her shoe against the floor a couple of times as she racked her brain, searching for something sensible to say. "Do you go to college here?"

"Yeah, I do now. I went to Lincoln last year, but I decided to transfer here because I couldn't afford Lincoln." He extended his hand to shake Kari's. "I'm sorry for not introducing myself first. My name is Doug—Doug Parker."

"Hi, I'm Kari Raker."

"I'm Jill Jackson." Jill shook Doug's hand.

Doug tucked his hands in the back pockets of his jeans. "I don't know very many people in this town. It feels good to meet someone my own age." He glanced from Kari to Jill. "Are you two from here?"

"Yeah, we both go to Leewood High School," Kari said softly. She prayed that her age wouldn't make Doug reconsider socializing with them.

Doug's eyebrows furrowed. "You're kidding! I thought maybe you were both in college—you both look older."

"Actually, I just turned sixteen a couple of months ago." Kari blushed. She noticed Jill was gazing at another couple kissing and wasn't paying any attention to the conversation. She nonchalantly elbowed Jill. "*Jill* will be sixteen next month."

Jill's eyes darted back to Doug.

"Oh really? That does shock me. I would have guessed you both to be around eighteen." Doug pointed to the crowded snack bar a few feet away. "Hey, would you two like to get a soda with me—my treat?"

Kari was surprised that Doug was interested in their company. Her fortunate cookie last night at China Wok was right; it said her luck was about to change for the better. But she never dreamed this was what it meant. She nervously pulled her bangs behind her ears. She didn't want to sound too willing, but she desperately wanted to hang out with the gorgeous college guy.

8

She tossed Jill a swaying glance, but Jill turned toward the clock hanging down in the center of the food court. Kari ignored Jill's gesture; she knew Jill was trying to hint that they should be hurrying to the clearance sale. Kari's keen eyes traveled to the snack bar and then back to Doug's magnetic, chocolate-colored eyes. "Sure, that sounds great."

"Great. You two find an empty table, and I'll go get the sodas. Do you both want Cokes?" Doug asked.

"I do," Jill said somberly.

"That's fine with me too. Thanks." Kari smiled.

"I'll be right back." Doug strolled toward the food counter.

Kari quickly spotted an empty table and zigzagged through the other tables toward it. She sat down on one of the high spinning stools and immediately started fidgeting with the buttons on her long-sleeved, green-striped blouse. She wished she had worn her low-cut peach sweater. It emphasized her figure so much better than the blouse that just hung loosely on her. Not that she thought her chest was anything to brag about. Although her bust size had increased from a 36A to a 36B this year, but she had also gained ten pounds. This time last year, she had only weighted one hundred and twenty pounds. She imagined all the snacking at Sonic while she worked was the reason for the extra pounds. Her sister hadn't gained but two pounds over the summer. Of course, Kelli never had to worry about her weight; she ate like a pig all the time and hardly ever gained.

Kari had started working at the local Sonic in May, and Kelli started shortly after that. They had both worked countless hours of overtime to save extra money to buy a decent-looking car—a 1997 two-door midnight blue Sunfire.

They worked out a reasonable schedule to share the car between them, rotating weekends and school days with the agreement they would give each other rides when needed. Kari thought the schedule was working out conveniently; it hadn't caused any major conflicts yet.

Kari smiled silently; she was happy that Kelli didn't have the right touch when it came to guys. Who cares if she has brains? She still can't catch a hunk like Doug. She smoothed the

9

wrinkles on the front of her blouse with the palm of her hand. She knew that one hundred thirty pounds on her five-foot, five-inch frame still looked desirable; she still had all the right curves in the right places.

Kari's mind raced back to Doug. She spun her stool toward Jill. "I hope you don't mind us having a Coke with him."

"No, not really. I just thought you were in a hurry to get to Sears." Jill's eyes narrowed in a good-humored gesture.

"I know, I know, but what can I say—he's so gorgeous! I can't believe he talked to us."

"He is cute," Jill admitted.

"I hope you don't like him, too." Kari twisted to stare at Doug's backside while he paid for the drinks. "I've got to have him!"

"Okay. I won't go after him; he's all yours." Jill's face turned solemn. "Seriously, Kari, don't you think he's a little old for you?"

"I don't care—he's way too cute to ignore." Kari lowered her voice as Doug walked toward them. "Now, don't embarrass me."

"I ought to—for Kelli," Jill hissed.

"You better not or I'll..." Kari's voice faltered as Doug approached the table; he carefully set each of their sodas in front of them.

"Thanks." Kari melted as his eyes met hers.

"Yeah, thanks," Jill added.

"You're welcome. So, how long have you two lived here?" Doug slid onto the empty stool and handed the girls each a straw.

Kari ripped the paper off her straw and wedged it into her drink. "I've lived here all my life—Jill hasn't, though."

"No, I moved here in fifth grade," Jill said.

"Well, it seems to be a nice town. So far, I like it." Doug's eyes lingered on Kari as he lifted his drink.

"There's not much to do around here except shop and do homework." Kari bit her lip, annoyed at her choice of words.

"Really? Would you believe that's what I'm working on today—homework? I'm researching the history of this town. It's a school project." Doug's eyes locked with Kari's. "That's why I'm looking for film."

10

"What kind of project?" Kari was more fascinated with his mesmerizing looks than with his actual project. She hoped she wasn't imagining him flirting as he spoke.

"It's a history assignment. The professor wants us to research as much as we can on the history of the town. He wants to see how many different historical sites we can find. I'm going to go around taking pictures of different spots today."

"That sounds fun!" Kari said.

"Well, you're welcome to come along and show me around." Doug flashed his flawless teeth at Kari.

Kari rested the palm of her hand over her stomach; it was in major turmoil. She was thrilled that he had asked them to hang out! How could she resist that captivating smile? She nervously swallowed a drink of her soda and spun toward Jill to see what kind of reaction she had from his invitation.

"I'm sorry." Doug reached across the table and patted the top of Kari's hand. He shook his head. "That was rude of me. I know you two have come to shop. It would be boring hanging around with me taking pictures all day."

"Oh no, I don't think it would be boring at all. It sounds fun, doesn't it, Jill?"

"Yeah, sure." Jill shrugged. "We can go shopping anytime."

"Are you sure?" Doug asked.

"We're sure," Kari said as she glanced uneasily at Jill. She instantly detected the fake grin from Jill. She knew Jill as well as she knew her own twin—Kari could read every concealed expression. She could tell easily that Jill wasn't interested in going in the least. She was certain Jill was just agreeing to tag along because she knew how much it would mean to Kari.

"Great! I would really appreciate it. I didn't know where to start." Doug finished his Coke in one slurp.

"No problem. We have some old historical homes and churches in this town." Kari said, trying to portray intelligence.

"That is what my professor said. Hey, if you two want to finish your sodas, I'll run over and grab the film I need, and be right back."

11

"Okay, that's fine with me." Kari turned toward Jill, who nodded her approval while noisily sucking the last part of her Coke through her straw.

"I won't be long—don't leave me." Doug waved and disappeared into the crowded shoppers.

Kari felt as if she was floating on a cloud. She couldn't believe that Jill's little jousting shove had led to this. She waited until Doug was out of view and then excitedly pounded her fists against the table. "Can you believe this? I am in love! You don't really mind that we go, do you?"

"No, I guess not, but you owe me." Jill sighed.

"I promise we'll do anything you want this weekend."

"How old do you think he is, anyway?"

"Who cares? When you look that good, you can be any age." Kari giggled.

"Our parents would be furious with us for going with him."

"Don't tell them." Kari tilted her head sideways. "You've been hanging around Kelli too long; you're starting to sound just like her." She whacked Jill gently on the arm. "Loosen up and enjoy life. We live only once."

Jill's grave face relaxed. "Well, someone has to watch out for you when Kelli isn't around."

"Whatever!" Kari had known it wouldn't take much to coax Jill into going. "You don't mind if I ride in the front seat, do you?" A devious grin spread across Kari's face.

"You know, you guys could just drop me off at home, and then you two could be alone."

"No way. Please, stay with me," Kari begged. "I'm too nervous to be left alone with him. Besides, he probably doesn't even like me." She puckered her lips as if she was pouting. "Remember, he just wants us to help him with his assignment."

"Well, I think he *does* like you. I see the way he keeps staring at you."

A few minutes later Kari spotted Doug rushing around the corner toward them. "Shhh—here he comes." Kari noticed he was carrying a brown paper sack and assumed he had found the film. She quickly pulled her fallen bangs back behind her ears as

12

he charged toward the table. "Did you find what you were looking for?"

"Yeah, I did. But I'm so absent-minded." Doug smacked his forehead with the palm of his hand. "I just remembered I left my camera at home on the counter. Would you girls mind if I swing by there first and pick it up?

"Sure, that would be fine. We're ready if you are." Kari stood.

"I think this is all I need. Let's go back this way." Doug nodded toward the escalator they had recently come down. "The entrance I came in is up there." He hesitated and then added, "I think." He laughed and glanced awkwardly around at his surroundings.

Kari felt like she was in a footrace, trying to keep up with Doug's pace. She glanced down at his Nike shoes. She had always heard people with big feet walk faster, but his feet seemed to be of normal size. By the looks of his body, Kari guessed he was into total fitness; that's probably why he liked to walk fast.

She elbowed Jill and pointed to Doug's backside—Kari fanned her face. Jill giggled, and Doug twisted around to smile at them. He was quiet as he led them out the entrance doors. Kari wondered if she should try to start up a conversation. She suddenly had a sinking feeling; she hoped that he wasn't already regretting asking them to go with him. "Do you live far?" she asked.

Doug grinned. "No, not at all. It won't take us long." He pointed to a glossy black Mustang in the back row of the parking lot. "There's my joyride."

"Wow!" Jill and Kari said simultaneously.

"That's an awesome car! I love it!" Kari said.

"Me too." Jill glanced at Kari with raised eyebrows.

"Thanks." Doug circled around to the passenger side of the car and unlocked the door.

Jill scrambled into the back seat, and Kari climbed into the front seat and fastened her seat belt.

Doug slammed the door and hurried around to the other side of the car. He quickly slid behind the steering wheel. He glanced

13

awkwardly toward Kari while starting the car. "Where do you live at?" He jerked the car in gear and peeled out of the parking lot.

"I live a few miles from here on Delaware." Kari secretly wished he had taken the time to fasten his seat belt. Her dad's words echoed in her head, 'they should revoke people's licenses if they're caught driving without a seatbelt. Maybe then they would take the law more seriously.' Kari knew her dad would be furious if he found out she was riding with someone like Doug. On the other hand, there was no reason for him to know about Doug; she would keep this a secret just like she did the time she snuck out after curfew to meet Craig Parker.

"Delaware Street?" Doug kept his eyes glued to the road. "Do you have any brothers or sisters?"

"Yes, I do. I'm a twin. I have a sister named Kelli." *Unfortunately, she didn't get the chance to meet you today,* Kari thought. She couldn't wait to rub it in to Kelli.

"A twin, really?" Doug glanced at Kari in surprise. "Her name is Kelli—I like your names—Kari and Kelli. What did you say your last name was—Raker or something like that?"

"Yeah, that's right. It's Raker." Kari stirred and shifted her eyes awkwardly back out the passenger window. She wondered if he did like her.

Doug glanced in the rearview mirror at Jill. "And you, where do you live at?"

"I live on the same street as Kari, a couple of houses down."

"Oh, you two are neighbors." Doug momentary glanced over his shoulder at Jill. "I do remember your name. It's Jill Jackson." He pressed a CD into the CD player. "Are you an only child?"

"No. I have a little brother, Timmy. He's only five, though."

"I see." Doug turned up the volume on the CD, and Cher's electrifying voice filled the car. He glanced at Kari and winked. "Is your sister as pretty as you?"

Doug's words stunned Kari. She was sure her cheeks were flaming red; she was known to flush easily. She was utterly speechless. Usually she wasn't so reserved around guys, but this one had caught her off guard with his stunning looks. She smiled at him while reaching to pull her hair behind her ears, but

14

suddenly stopped and placed her hands back in her lap instead. She wished she didn't have the annoying habit.

Kari was definitely convinced that he liked her now! *He did wink at me,* she thought. *And it wasn't a wink like 'you're a cute kid' either; it was definitely flirtatious.* And how bizarre was it that Cher was one of her favorite singers too. She would never doubt the words in a fortune cookie again.

She gradually focused her eyes out the window as Doug's rousing words stumbled through her head. She had a feeling she would never forget this day.

CHAPTER TWO

As they rode in silence, Kari wondered where Doug lived. He had said it wasn't far, but they were almost on the outskirts of the town now. If he drove too much farther, they would be completely out of the city limits.

Doug finally pulled down a dusty gravel road that Kari was unfamiliar with. After a few miles, the houses started thinning out. "Do you live this far out?" Kari asked, while silently reading a road sign named Willow.

"Yeah, I guess I do. It doesn't feel like that far to me, though. I guess I'm just used to driving the distance." Doug glanced in his rearview mirror and then at Kari. "It's not much of a place, but it'll do until I finish school." He sped down another adjoining gravel road, leaving behind a trail of dust. "It's not much further now."

"I probably should have stayed at the shopping center. I forgot my mother wanted me home early today." Jill yawned.

Doug made another sharp turn to the left. "I won't keep you girls long, I promise. I'm sorry for asking you two to help me today. I should have let you shop."

"Don't worry about it. We don't mind, do we, Jill?"

Jill hesitated. "No, we don't mind."

Kari glanced toward a burnt-out barn in a vacant field. They past several fenced pastures. A small pond was nestled down at the bottom of a slope, and Kari assumed there were cows nearby.

After another five miles on the potholed gravel road, Doug pulled down a narrow, single-lane driveway leading up to a spacious metal building sitting in the middle of nowhere. Three luxurious cars were parked outside the building.

Kari gawked at the expensive cars—a black Cadillac, a mint-green BMW and a sleek silver Porsche.

She glanced toward the extraordinary metal structure. It looked more like an aged warehouse, heavy silver metal with a horizontal black-tire top for the roof. Wide double barn-like doors were in the front center of it and there were numerous windows on the sides. Kari guessed it could have been converted into an apartment house. However, it wasn't one that she would have chosen to live in. *If the attendants could afford luxurious cars, why couldn't they afford something nicer to live in?* Kari wondered. *And who in their right mind would want to live without neighbors anyway?* She would go insane. She hated even to be left alone in her own house. She never understood how Kelli could hide away in her room for hours reading books. Kari would rather be talking on the telephone or entertaining friends.

A trail of leafless trees behind the isolated building led to a patch of thick woods, and countless rows of plowed corn stalks surrounded the building on the other two sides. Kari didn't see another house in sight anywhere.

"I know it looks bad on the outside, but it's actually exquisite on the inside. It's all been remodeled. Come on, I'll show you." Doug flipped off the ignition and stepped out of the car.

"Is this an apartment house?" Kari crawled out of the car and held the front seat up for Jill.

"I'll just wait here for you guys," Jill said.

"Oh, you got to see my place and my amazing fish! Come on in." Doug glanced back at Kari. "This place has been converted into three different apartments." He nodded in the direction of the parked cars in the driveway. "These men all have money, too. They more than likely just wanted the peace and quiet of the country that you can't find in town."

"I don't mind waiting out here," Jill continued.

"Come on, Jill." Kari stared pleadingly while holding out her hand to help Jill out.

17

"We won't stay long, I promise." Doug added, "You two can look around my place while I load the film in my camera."

Jill reluctantly climbed out of the car. She followed Doug and Kari up to the double doors.

Doug politely held the door open while the girls entered the building.

Kari nodded thanks and walked awkwardly into the huge room with Jill close at her heels. She slowly took a few steps forward and gaped around at the enormous room. It didn't look anything like an apartment building; the room was massive with a concrete floor and an eight-foot high ceiling. There was a rectangular rusty folding metal table sitting in the center of the room with a laptop computer on it and newspapers scattered across it. Six metal folding chairs were sitting upright, nearby the table. Kari glanced to the four wooden doors leading to different rooms along the sides of the bleak gray wall. She wondered if Doug's apartment was behind one of the doors. She didn't think it could be a very spacious apartment if it was. She decided it was probably a tiny one-bedroom apartment.

The door slamming behind her startled her—she jumped, whirled around, and caught Doug locking the door. "You scared me!" Kari clasped her hands over her heart. She was curious why he was locking the door when they were way out in the middle of nowhere. Surely, he didn't think it was unsafe out here. She instantly sensed something was wrong.

Jill suddenly let out a shriek, "I'm getting out of here!"

Kari spun back around to see what had frightened her friend. She stared in disbelief at five dark hair men with dark complexions and dressed in fancy suits. Two of the men were carrying guns. *They must have come from behind one of the wooden doors,* Kari thought. Dazed, she searched Doug's vacant face for an answer. "What is going on here?"

Doug's face was sober; he was no longer smiling. Goosebumps emerged on Kari's arms as she glanced from Doug's empty eyes back to the men holding the guns.

One of the stout men, brandishing a row of yellow teeth, shouted forcefully at the other men in a language she didn't recognize. The other four men quickly spread out over the

18

immense room while the man who had given the orders strutted toward Kari and Jill. He was middle-aged with greasy-looking jet-black hair that was cropped and spiked on top; a line of gold earrings dangled on one ear while the other ear had only two. As he neared them, Kari could see the bristly stubble on his unshaven face, and the aroma of whiskey stung her senses. His forehead was drawn tightly into fine lines; his cold, black, piercing eyes were uncanny, as if he could easily slice you up and never think twice about it. Kari could feel his chilling eyes gazing up and down every inch of her body. She shivered as fear engulfed her.

Jill suddenly scrambled for the door, but Doug's muscular body stood blocking the way. "Let me out of here!" she screamed.

The man grabbed Jill by her arm and yanked her around so she was facing him. His eyes hardened. "You'd better be good," the man yelled powerfully in English.

"Let go of me!" Jill twisted her body, trying to pull away from the man's tight hold, but his grasp was too tight. She lifted her leg and kicked her foot into the man's abdomen.

"You bitch!" The man slapped Jill across the face with such force she stumbled backwards.

Kari watched in horror. Everything was happening so fast, she couldn't believe it. She immediately lifted her arms to shove Jill's attacker, but one of the other men sensed her motive and quickly approached her, pointing a gun to her head. She froze; she was too scared to move another muscle.

None of this was making any sense to Kari. Out of the corner of her eyes, she saw Doug, who stood silently watching—she could have sworn he was the one for her. Not even a hint of remorse was revealed in his face. What the hell was she thinking? She should have known that it was too good to be true. Why would a college guy want a sixteen-year-old high school girl?

Another man silently crept up behind Jill, grabbed both her arms, and held them behind her back so she couldn't move. The face of the man who had smacked her was mere inches from Jill's. "You listen to me, bitch." He abruptly turned to Kari and

19

shoved his finger under her nose. "You, too! If you two give me any fucking trouble—I will punish you both so bad—you both will wish you had listened to me."

Jill didn't weaken, she screamed again. This time it was a loud, long, high-pitched shriek.

The man smacked her across the face again, twice as hard, sending blood out her nostrils. "Shut the fuck up! I will tape your mouth shut if you scream anymore! Do you hear?"

Kari was surprised to see Jill display such boldness. For a petite girl who was only five-foot two and a hundred pounds—she sure was being courageous; Jill was usually frightened of her own shadow. Kari was usually the daring one while Jill was more vulnerable.

Any other time, Kari might have appreciated Jill's bravery, but she was terrified that these men might kill them. She had to somehow get Jill to calm down. "Jill, please don't scream," she said assertively.

Jill fell silent as her frightened eyes met Kari's. The other man still had Jill's arms pinned behind her, and the blood from her nose was dripping onto her bottom lip and then splattering onto the concrete floor.

Kari watched in dismay as the man who spoke English gave orders to the other men in his foreign language. The burly man continued to angle the pistol at Kari's head. The other man, who had Jill's arms pinned, released her arms, while a different man approached Jill, pointing a gun to her head.

***

Doug silently followed Vaar up to the table where the laptop computer was and waited for him to sit down. He shoved his trembling hands into his jean pockets. He hoped Vaar didn't notice his edginess. "Did I do okay, Vaar?"

Vaar chuckled and shook his head. "You did get some damn rowdy ones!"

"I'm sorry. I didn't know." Doug just wanted to get his money and get the hell out of there. Vaar had agreed to pay him five thousand dollars for two girls with either blond or red hair,

20

fair skin, and anywhere from fifteen to nineteen years old. Doug had brought him just what he wanted—Jill was a blond, Kari was a redhead, and they both were sixteen or close to it. All he was told to do was to get their names, their address, and any other information that he could and deliver them to Vaar and his men at the warehouse.

Vaar lifted his eyes from the computer screen toward Kari and Jill and then back at Doug. "They are pretty." A slow, cunning smile spread across his aging face as he eyed the girls. "I will definitely make some big money now!" He grinned at Doug and drew a cigarette from his pocket. "You did good. You get names and addresses?" His eyes rested on Kari. "If not—I'm sure I can persuade the girls to tell me."

"Yes—I did—the redhead is Kari Raker," Doug began in a quivering voice. He waited as Vaar typed the information into his computer and then he continued, "She lives on Delaware Street in Leewood. The blond is Jill Jackson; she's on the same street." He waited for Vaar to stop typing. He breathed steadily, trying to calm his nerves. "Kari has a twin sister named Kelli, and Jill has a five-year old brother named Timmy." He casually glanced toward Kari and Jill. Kari was staring at him with a devastated look. A sudden guilty feeling overwhelmed him. He couldn't believe he was doing this; he had never done anything like this before. But he needed the money to surprise his lover; he had wanted to do something special for their anniversary. A friend of his who had gone down the wrong tracks in life had helped him land the job.

Doug immediately shifted his back toward Kari. *For crying out loud, what was he thinking? What if the police found out about this? Jay would never forgive him.*

Doug's tongue darted over his dry lips—he knew it was too late now. He couldn't change the past, so he wasn't going to dwell on it any longer. *Sometimes we have to do unwanted things to get ahead in life,* he thought—*it's just the way life is.* Besides, this time tomorrow he would be sitting on the beach in Hawaii, drinking something with a little umbrella sticking in it. He smiled silently at the comforting thought.

21

Vaar typed in the last of the information, picked up the cigarette from the ashtray, and took a long drag off it. He exhaled the smoke slowly while reading silently what he had typed. He suddenly stubbed the cigarette out and glanced toward Doug. "This is good. Your money is in the case over there." Vaar turned and nodded toward a folding chair sitting directly behind him. "Go ahead and check it."

"That's okay. I trust you." Doug just desperately wanted to get out of there before he felt any more guilt for what he had done. He quietly walked over to the case and bent forward to pick it up by its handle. Suddenly, Jill's screams startled him, just as a loud thud came crashing down on the back of his head. An intense sharp pain shot through his head as he fell to his knees. He clutched the back of his head—blood spilled through his fingers and soaked his shirt. He could hear Kari crying as the room went black and he fell forward onto the cold hard floor, unconscious.

***

Kari screamed and covered her eyes with the palms of her hands. *Oh God, we're going to be killed,* she thought. She slid her hand a few inches just enough to peek to see if Doug was moving—his body was stiff except for his chest; it was slightly inflating.

She was more frightened than she had ever been in her life. She had witnessed more violence than she had wanted to see. One of Vaar's henchmen had snuck up behind Doug and hit him in the head with a club, and Doug had crumbled to the ground with blood gushing out of the back of his head.

Kari bowed her head to the floor; she couldn't stop bawling. Vaar had just sat there on his computer typing, as though he didn't hear anything. Kari was sure he had ordered the man to do it. She didn't know why she cared anyway after what Doug had done to her—but she did. She didn't want Doug to be killed.

Kari now was more petrified of what Vaar was going to do with her and Jill than anything. She had listened warily as Doug willingly shared with Vaar all the personal information about her and Jill. She had heard Vaar say he could make money off her and Jill. Kari's immediate thought had been he was going to try to turn them into prostitutes. Just the thought gagged her. She had to fight back the nausea she was feeling.

Kari's sobs slowly ceased. She pulled her bangs back behind her ears and folded her arms across her chest. The man holding the gun to her head didn't budge. She watched the two remaining men pull Doug by the arms out the back door, leaving a trail of blood behind him. She could only imagine what they were going to do with him next. They had lied to him about some money, and he had been gullible enough to believe it. Although she felt he was just as guilty of this ghastly crime as the other men in the room, she still felt sorry for him.

She glanced over at Jill; she wished she could embrace her frail friend and comfort her—she looked disorientated. Kari knew it was her own fault for getting them into this mess. Jill hadn't even wanted to come. *Oh dear God, what have I done to my best friend,* she thought. Kari realized if she wasn't so boy-crazy, none of this would ever have happened. Kari squeezed her eyes shut; she was feeling horribly guilty about the chaos she had created.

Kari's eyes flew open at the unmistakable sound of footsteps. Her body trembled as Vaar quietly neared them. He slowly paraded around them, observing their youthful figures with his probing eyes. He suddenly stopped in front of Kari and crouched low enough so he was looking directly into her eyes. He grinned callously and ran his hand smoothly over her hair. She cringed and shifted her eyes toward the floor.

Vaar chuckled and yell orders to the remaining two men. The men lowered their guns and hurried to stand near Vaar. All three men laughed continuously and talked in their foreign language as their eyes darted up and down the girls' bodies.

Kari could tell by the men's bearing and the heartless glare in their eyes that they were capable of any vicious act. She thought she heard Vaar call his colleagues by name. She believed the older man with sprinkled gray hair, thin mustache, and rounded beer belly was called Masory, and the shorter, slimmer guy with the receding hairline was called Ivan.

23

She was too scared to glimpse at Jill, but Kari was glad she was being quiet.

Vaar rambled off something else to the men, and Ivan grabbed a hold of Kari's arm roughly, while Masory grasped Jill's arm.

Vaar calmly placed his finger under Kari's chin and lifted her face so she was staring into his dark, furtive eyes. "You do as you are told and you will not get hurt." He paused to glare at Jill. "If you fucking scream anymore—you're going to get hurt. If you try to leave—you will be killed." Vaar's eyes drifted back to Kari's while he slowly ran his index finger across the front of her blouse where her breasts were. "You understand me?"

Kari's face paled and her knees weakened. The stench of bad breath mixed with alcohol filled her nostrils—she tried to shut out his image as she focused on the chip missing from his bottom tooth. She squeezed back the tears as she nodded her head in agreement.

Vaar dropped his hand, turned, and shouted crossly at his men. The men pushed Kari and Jill toward one of the wooden doors. Ivan unlocked the door with a key while Masory shoved the girls through the door. He slammed the door shut fiercely and locked it.

Kari only saw darkness at first, because there wasn't any light in the room except for a small ray at the top of the door. It took her a few seconds for her eyes to adjust so she could focus on Jill.

Kari instantly wiped at the tears spilling down Jill's terrified, bloody face. She wrapped her arms around her friend's slender shoulders and drew her close to her. "I'm so sorry, Jill. I won't let them hurt you any more—I promise. I'll find a way for us to get out of here somehow."

Jill buried her head into Kari's shoulder and sobbed.

Kari glanced up at the only window in the room, distant high upon the bare wall while Jill clung to her, crying. The room was small, a little larger than a kitchen pantry. An old, brown plaid area rug covered part of the concrete floor. The walls were dirty beige. Her eyes shifted to the two unmade beds across from each other. Sheets were folded and lying on top of them. In the corner

24

was a small faded wooden table with a bowl of water, two cups, and a glass pitcher full of water on it. An isolated toilet stool was positioned against the far wall with a roll of toilet paper sitting on the floor beside it. Kari thought the room resembled a prison dorm. Then she realized that that was what they were— prisoners. She couldn't fight the tears any longer. She held Jill close to her as tears spilled down her own cheeks.

Kari hugged Jill tighter. She struggled to swallow the lump enlarging in her throat. She knew she had to portray courage — she didn't want Jill to know how scared she actually was. She needed to stay focused if she planned to save both of them. She closed her eyes and fought to control the painful tears. "Please God, help us," she whispered.

CHAPTER THREE

Kelli spotted a parking space close to the entrance door of the shopping center and whipped the Sunfire into the empty spot. She flipped the ignition off and stretched her arms out in front of her. It had been a long, drawn-out day at work; one of the car hoppers had called in sick, and Kelli had to work like crazy to keep the orders circulating out to the customers. And to top it off, a elderly lady had became irritable because she had ordered mustard and pickle on her sandwich and when she got her sandwich, it had ketchup and onions on it instead. Of course, the woman blamed Kelli and bawled her out in front of the whole parking lot. Kelli had wanted to crawl under the car and hide.

She glanced at the clock—she was a few minutes early, so she pulled out her History book and started reading while she waited for Kari and Jill. Every few minutes, Kelli peeked toward the entrance doors to see if they were coming out. With annoyance, she glanced down at her clock again—it was 5:10 p.m. She didn't have much patience when it came to waiting—especially if it was Kari she was waiting for. She guessed it was possible that Kari had lost track of time; she knew how ditzy Kari could be—either that, or she was busy flirting with a bunch of guys—more than likely, it was the latter. Kelli irately pushed her seat back and propped one of her knees on the steering wheel.

She whirled her hair around her finger as she read a few more pages of her assignment. She glanced toward the clock—it was

26

5:25 p.m. She wondered if Kari had hitched a ride home with a friend and hadn't bothered to call to let her know. They only had one cell phone between the two of them, and whoever had the car, also got the phone. It was still inexcusable, Kelli thought; she could have used a pay phone.

She reached for the cell phone in her purse, dialed her home phone number, and waited. She knew her mom and dad would be home. Her mom usually stayed home and cleaned house on Saturdays while her dad worked out in his shop. Her father was a self-employed construction worker, and her mother worked for a local insurance office three days a week.

After the fifth ring, Frances Raker answered the phone. "Hello."

"Mom, it's me. Has Kari come home from shopping yet?"

"No. I thought you were supposed to pick her up."

"Yeah, I am. I'm outside the shopping center now waiting, but she hasn't come out. So I thought that maybe she got a ride home with someone else."

"No, she hasn't been here. She probably lost track of the time; you know how her and Jill are when they go shopping."

"But it's almost 5:30. She was supposed to be out here at 5:00. I'm not going to wait much longer!" Kelli twisted the key back and fiddled with the radio knob.

"Yes, you are! Don't you dare run off and leave her." Frances sighed heavily. "She'll be there soon. I haven't started supper yet anyway."

"Okay. We'll be home as soon as I find the *loser.*"

"Be nice, now—she'll be there soon."

Kelli hung up the phone, disgusted. She was really going to let Kari have an earful when she found her. She had more important things to do than wait for Kari to finish dawdling around. She glanced back down at the clock. It was 5:35 p.m. *Damn, I was hoping to get cleaned up and catch the library before it closed,* Kelli thought. Flustered, she climbed out of the car and slammed the door. She figured she might as well go inside to see if she could find her.

Once inside the mall, Kelli ventured around the surrounding area near the door, but there still wasn't any sign of Kari or Jill.

27

Finally, annoyed, she collapsed down on a wooden bench and gawked at the people coming in and out of the stores. She couldn't imagine what could be taking Kari and Jill so long. After awhile, Kelli pulled her phone out of her purse to check the time—it was 5:55 p.m. She visualized the conversation that she and Kari had earlier. She was positive that Kari had said to pick her up at five.

Kelli noticed an information desk near the entrance and hurried toward it. She smiled politely to the salt-and- pepper haired woman sitting at the desk. "Hi, I was wondering if you have a way of announcing names across the intercom. I'm looking for someone."

The lady peeped over the rim of her glasses. "Yes, we do, but if the person you are looking for is inside a store, he might not hear it."

"Okay, I understand. Could you please try calling Kari Raker and Jill Jackson?" Kelli waited as the elderly woman announced the names across the intercom. "Thanks a lot," she told the lady.

Kelli wandered back over to the bench to wait. She watched the people climbing off the escalator for a while, but there still wasn't any sign of her sister. She checked the time—it was 6:20 p.m. Kelli's concern was increasing more every minute; this was so unlike Kari. She wondered if they could have gone to Jill's house. She quickly dialed Jill's house.

Tom Jackson answered the phone in a hoarse voice, "Hello."

"Hi Tom—this is Kelli. You sound sick."

"Hello Kelli. I have a cold. How about you—school keeping you busy?

"Yes—very much so. Hey, I'm looking for Jill and Kari. I was supposed to pick them up here at the shopping center, and they're not here. Are they there, by chance?"

"No, they're not here. I was just asking Julie where our daughter was, and she told me that she was supposed to be home by 5:30, and it's after 6:00 now."

"Well, I've been here since a few minutes before five, and they haven't shown up yet." Kelli roamed over to gaze outside the entrance doors.

28

"Jill must enjoy being grounded all the time." Tom chuckled. "Those two probably got to goofing off like they do and not paying any attention to the time."

"Yeah, you're probably right," Kelli said, although she had her doubts.

"Have her call home as soon as you find them, would you, Kel?"

"You bet. I'll be here at the West entrance waiting—if they happen to call you. Do you have my cell number?"

"Yeah, we got it. Thanks, Kel. Let us know if you hear something."

"I will."

Kelli disconnected and plopped back down on the bench. She crossed her legs and rested her elbow on her knee. Her stomach was rumbling. She didn't know if it was from hunger, or because she was disturbed about the situation. It was probably a combination of both. She didn't know what else to do besides sit and wait. She was scared that if she started searching for Kari and Jill in the stores that she would end up missing them. The phone ringing made her jump. She was certain it was Kari apologizing for her irresponsible behavior.

"Hello," Kelli sputtered.

"Kelli, it's your mom. Where are you gals?"

"Hi Mom," Kelli's chin dropped as she moaned, disappointed. She was no longer furious at Kari, but worried sick about her. "I still haven't found Kari or Jill."

"You're kidding! It's nearly 6:30. Where could she be?"

"I don't know—but Mom—I'm really starting to get worried."

"Kelli, what entrance are you at? Your father and I are driving down there to see if we can find them."

"I'm at the West entrance by the Cheese Factory."

"Okay honey, don't leave. We'll be there in a few minutes."

The knots in Kelli's stomach were getting worse—she sensed that something was dreadfully wrong. She knew Kari would never deliberately pull a stunt like this.

Kelli silently prayed that Kari wasn't hurt. Although Kari's constant teasing ruptured Kelli's nerves sometimes, she still

29

didn't know what she would do if anything were to happen to Kari.

Kelli was connected to Kari not only in a physical way, but also spiritually. They were closer than any other two sisters she knew. Kelli's throat grew dry. She fought back the tears forming behind her eyelids. She wasn't going to panic yet—*Kari has to be here somewhere.* She was confident that her parents would find them.

Kelli could recall only one other time that Kari had been sidetracked and lost track of time. Kari had met some boys from another town at a basketball game, and Jill and her had gone to Sonic with them after the game—she had been so engrossed with flirting she missed curfew by a half an hour.

Kelli stood and stretched, trying to relax—it was probably the same scenario this time. Kari and Jill most likely hooked up with some guys from school and were riding around. Kelli couldn't comprehend why Kari was so infatuated with guys. If she cared about books even half as much as she did boys, she would definitely make better grades, Kelli decided.

Suddenly, an idea surfaced; Kelli dug a picture out of her wallet of Kari and hurried toward the information desk. "Ma'am, I'm sorry to bother you again. Could you please look at this picture and tell me if you have seen this girl today? She's my twin sister."

The woman glanced up from her paperwork and removed the pencil from her mouth. "Sure." She held the picture up to the light and studied it closely. "I'm sorry. I don't recall seeing her today. Would you like me to call her on the intercom again?"

Kelli disappointed, reached for the picture. "Yes. I would appreciate it."

"What were the names again?"

"It's Kari Raker and Jill Jackson." She momentarily glanced at the picture of Kari before tucking it back in her purse.

"Okay. I'll try again."

Kelli waited for the woman to finish calling the names on the intercom. "What time do you close?"

"We close at eight on Saturdays."

"Okay, thanks." Kelli sighed, rested her hands on her hips, and scanned the crowd. Not seeing Kari or Jill, she lowered her eyes to the floor, and walked slowly back toward the bench. She dug her cell phone out to check the time. It was 6:50 p.m. Her parents should be coming any time. Kelli's house was only three miles from the shopping center. She propped her arm across the back of the bench and stared toward the entrance doors—she figured she would have more luck finding her parents than she would her sister. Again, she fought back the tears that were threatening to break.

A few minutes later, Kelli caught sight of her dad and mom shuffling through the doors. She rushed toward them. "They still haven't showed up," she spat.

"Oh no! Where are those girls?" Frances covered her mouth with her hand.

Bill wrapped his arm around his agitated wife and glanced uneasily around the shopping center. "Okay gals, let's not overreact now. They have to be here. Let's break up and look around. "Honey," Bill gently positioned his hands on Frances's shoulder, "you wait here in case they show up."

"Oh, Bill, what if they've been in a car accident or kidnapped?" The usually radiant glow in Frances's eyes suddenly vanished. "Should we call Jill's parents and let them know we're looking for them?"

"I already called them earlier. But it has been a while, so maybe I should call them back and let them know we still haven't found them," Kelli said.

"That would be a good idea. They might want to come down and help us search for them." Bill shoved his hands in his jacket pockets and shifted his weight nervously from one foot to the other while searching through the crowd.

The next few hours were an inconceivable nightmare for Kelli; she had never felt so powerless in her life. She had finally broken down and cried several times. Jill's concerned parents had driven to the mall to help with the search. They all had desperately searched until the shopping center was ready to close. All the stores had agreed to look in the stores after they

31

closed, but none of them had had any luck. There was still no sign of Kari or Jill anywhere.

Kelli's dad notified the police, and they immediately came down to the shopping center to make a police report. One of the police officers suggested the girls might have run away, or taken off with their boyfriends. Kelli's dad became upset with the accusation and chewed the officer out in front of all the bystanders.

The police performed their routine duties, including asking all the people walking to their cars if they had seen anything unusual. There wasn't anyone that had seen anything out of the ordinary.

It was close to 11:00 p.m. when Kelli finally ducked through the front door of her own home. Her mom and dad, along with Jill's parents, had gone to the police station to fill out more papers, and Kelli had driven her car home in a depressed state. She was clueless over what she could do to help find her sister.

Kelli's stomach ached; she had sharp, intense pains in the pit of it. She didn't feel like eating anything, but she was scared she would be sick if she didn't try. She hurriedly fixed a ham sandwich and a glass of ice, and grabbed the bottle of Coke on the counter. Her hands shook as she poured the Coke in the glass—twice she spilled it on the table. After wiping up the spilled pop, she grabbed her plate and glass and headed toward the stairs. She carefully carried it up the narrow flight that led to her bedroom at the back of the house. She suddenly slowed as she passed Kari's silent room. *What if by some miracle Kari had come home and was in her room asleep*, Kelli thought. "Boy, are you going to be in trouble if you're in there," she said aloud.

Kelli rushed toward her own room and stumbled through the door. She quickly lowered the glass and sandwich down on the desk, not bothering to wipe up the soda spilling over the side of the glass. She dashed back to Kari's bedroom door. Her hand trembled as she grasped the doorknob—she hesitated for a brief second, inhaled deeply, and carefully turned the knob. The door eased open slowly—the nightlight on the end table was still on, making the room completely visible. She stared in dismay at the empty, unmade bed.

32

Kelli's emotions stirred as she stepped into the room. She gradually glanced toward her sister's personal belongings. Her eyes lingered on the photograph sitting on Kari's TV—it was of her and Kari with their arms wrapped around each other, smiling up at the camera. They both looked so happy—it had been taken two months earlier—the day they had turned sixteen and passed their driver's test. Kelli's eyes grew misty as she remembered how excited they had been. She recalled Kari singing 'it's my birthday and I'll cry if I want to' and then Kari had burst out laughing while waving her driver's license slip over her head. She then changed her tune and sang, 'nothing can make me cry today.'

Kelli's eyes drifted to another picture hanging on the cluttered wall. It was Kari dressed up for homecoming last year; she looked beautiful in her blue silk dress and long red curls. And Ryan, her date, was about as fine as they come—in his black suit and tie, and golden blond hair.

Kelli smiled—Kari never did have trouble getting dates with the good-looking guys; she had always been the popular one in school, the one to make football cheerleader and drum majorette. Everyone who knew Kari loved her spontaneous personality; she was witty and fun to hang out with.

Kelli shifted toward another panel and stared into an oval mirror suspending on the wall. She traced the image in the mirror with her index finger in a dispirited manner. Although her eyes were puffy and swollen, the reflection reminded her just how different she was from Kari. She was shy and mostly enjoyed being left alone in her room to read. She wasn't even close to being the social butterfly Kari was. Kelli had always been too timid to try out for any activities other than the academic team and the science club.

Sometimes she was envious of Kari because of her admired reputation. But she didn't value the fact that Kari was a little slow when it came to scholastics. All through the years, Kelli had continuously bailed Kari out of the misfortunes she had fallen into. And for some reason, trouble always seemed to follow Kari.

33

Kelli scanned the remaining pictures on the wall—her heart aching for the company of her sister. Now all the bitterness she had ever felt suddenly vanished as tears surfaced. She ambled around the room picking up sentimental items that reminded her of Kari.

She spotted Bono, a raggedy stuffed monkey, crumbled on the floor. Kelli scooped up the memorable animal and hugged it tightly against her body. It was Kari's when she was a little girl—she always had to take Bono with her everywhere she went. She raised the monkey up to her nose and sniffed; she could smell Kari's Curve body power on the stuffed monkey. She imagined Kari still slept with Bono for a sense of security.

Kelli threw herself on the familiar twin bed and sobbed. She clutched Kari's feathery pillow to her chest and cried aloud, "Please come home, Kari. I love you so much! Please come back home. I'm sorry for all the times I've been mean to you." Kelli rolled over and beat her fist wildly on the bed. "I will find you, Kari." She wiped at her nose with the back of her sleeve. "I will protect you just like I have always done. I'm going to find you, Kari, if it takes me the rest of my life." Kelli pulled the pillow closer against her body. "Oh Kari, don't give up...wherever you are. I'm going to find you, I promise!"

CHAPTER FOUR

Kari paced the floor while Jill remained on her back on the bed, staring up at the ceiling. Kari didn't know how many hours they had been locked up in the cramped room—Jill had left her pocket watch in her purse in Doug's car. Kari hadn't even brought her purse; she'd had Jill stashed her cash in her purse before they left for the mall.

Kari glanced toward Jill, relieved to see that her friend had calmed down—she had been an emotional roller coaster the first hour or so. Now for the last few hours, Jill had remained silent with her fingernails clinging to the mattress and her disoriented eyes fixed on the ceiling. Kari was concerned that Jill was in shock, and she didn't have any clue how to help her.

Kari crossed over to the pitcher of water and poured some in the cup. Her stomach growled from hunger; she hadn't eaten since breakfast. She guessed it to be after 9:00 p.m. Her parents, more than likely, were looking for them by now. Kari didn't know how they would ever find them, though—she was sure Vaar's men had killed Doug by now.

Masory had been in once to check on them. He had snapped a couple of pictures and immediately left the room without commenting. Kari wondered what he planned on doing with the pictures. If this was a premeditated kidnapping to get hold of some hard cash—Vaar had made a huge mistake, because neither she nor Jill's family had much money. However, for some reason, Kari didn't think that was the circumstance at all. She

35

wasn't sure yet what the reason was, but she had a feeling she would find out soon.

She glanced up at the window, trying to estimate how far up it actually was; she had racked her brain trying to figure a way that they could get out of the unpleasant room. "Damn, it's too high up," she muttered. Even if she climbed on Jill's shoulders, she still wouldn't be able to reach the window. At least now she was finally able to see—someone had turned the light on from outside the room.

Kari studied the area, searching for a device that might be taping them. She didn't see anything that resembled a camera. She glanced toward Jill again; she still hadn't moved.

Kari marched over to sit on the edge of Jill's bed. She reached for Jill's hand and spoke softly, "Jill, are you okay?"

"I want to go home!" Jill remained in a trance-like state.

"I know you do, honey, and so do I. We will, soon." Kari smoothed Jill's damp hair back off her forehead. "Are you as hungry as I am?" Kari detected puffiness around Jill's sad eyes. She waited for Jill to answer—there was no response. "Jill, are you hungry?"

"No."

"We have to try to stay focused and try to think of a way to get out of here. Can you do that for me, sweetie?"

"How?"

"I don't know yet, but we've got to keep thinking about it. I think..." Kari words cut off as the door to the room opened.

Masory entered and placed a loaf of bread down on the table. He pointed his stumpy finger toward the bread. "*Ekmek.*"

Kari glanced uneasily at Jill. Jill's eyes didn't flicker; they remained on the ceiling. Kari pulled her hair behind her ears and gazed back toward Masory. She hadn't a clue what he had said.

Masory glared at Kari for a few seconds, shrugged his shoulders, spun his rounded body toward the door, and left the room.

Kari sashayed toward the loaf of bread. She flipped it over, examining it closely. She lifted a piece up to her nose and inhaled the fresh aroma while wondering if it contained poison. However, she immediately dismissed the thought; she realized

36

that Vaar could have just shot Jill and her if he wanted them dead.

She took a sizeable bite of the bread. She couldn't remember ever being so hungry; it tasted superb. She grabbed another piece and carried it over to Jill. She clasped Jill's hand. "Sit up, Jill. You need to eat. You're going to need your strength."

Jill didn't respond at first, so Kari shoved the piece of bread into her hand.

"Okay. Okay. I'll eat it." Jill pulled herself up and folded her legs into an Indian-style position. She took a bite of the bread while watching Kari cram the rest of her piece into her mouth. Jill's eyes widened. "Hey, slow down. I don't need you choking to death on me and leaving me here all alone."

Kari was glad to see Jill still had her sense of humor. She hoped that was a positive sign. Kari tried to smile through a mouthful of bread. She reached for the cup of water to help wash it down. "Would you like some water?" Kari ran her hand over her stomach. "Boy, I didn't know bread could taste so good. I'm starved."

"Yeah, I'll take some of your famous firewater."

"What happened to you? Your mood has suddenly changed." Kari hurried over to pour Jill some water.

"I don't know. I just decided if I was going to have to share a room with you for the rest of my life—I had better try to make the best of it. Besides, I'm all dried up—I don't think I have any more tears to cry." Jill reached for the cup that Kari was holding out.

Kari's face turned serious. "We need a plan to get out of here or leave some kind of clue in case they take us somewhere else.

Jill swallowed the water and glanced up at the window. "That's too high up, isn't it?"

"Yeah, I think so. There's got to be something else we can do."

"How about we leave an article of our clothing somewhere in here? Then if they move us somewhere else, maybe someone will find the garment."

Kari glanced around at the diminutive room. "Where would we hide something that those guys wouldn't see?"

37

Jill took a bite of bread while gaping around the room. "I don't know, but there's got to be somewhere."

"I know." Kari suddenly dropped down on her hands and knees and glanced under Jill's bed. "We could put a pair of our socks in between the mattress and the springs."

"Hey, great idea." Jill jumped to her feet. "We better just put one pair of socks, though. Or they will be curious why we both weren't wearing socks in this weather."

"I'll put mine up under my bed since I haven't put the sheet on it yet. I'll tuck the ends of the sheet under the bed loosely so they won't have any reason to lift the mattress when they pull the sheet off." Kari quickly slipped her shoes off and peeled both of the blue striped socks off.

Jill rushed toward the door. "I'll listen in case someone comes." She pressed her ear firmly up against the rigid door.

Kari hurriedly lifted the mattress, stuck the socks in between the mattress and springs, and then dropped it back down. She quickly made up her bed with the spare sheet. Kari motioned to Jill that she was done. "It's cold in here," she said, rubbing her arms.

"I was wondering about that myself. I'm freezing."

"I guess I could sleep in my shoes." Kari crawled up on the bed and tucked her feet underneath her.

Jill grabbed a couple more slices of bread and handed one to Kari before returning to her own bed and climbing onto it. "What do you think they're going to do with us?"

"I've thought of a hundred different things, but I really don't have a clue.

Jill chewed on her bottom lip. "Do you think," she hesitated, "they will rape us?"

"I thought of that, but don't you think they would have already done that if that was their intention?"

"Yeah, you're probably right." Jill shrugged. "What then? What could they possible want from us? A kidnapping for money?"

"No, I don't think so. I think they would have been more selective and picked girls who had more money," Kari said.

38

"Boy, you have thought this through. I'm glad one of us is thinking."

"Well, there's not too much else to do."

The sound of the door opening silenced both the girls. Masory entered the room carrying two green army blankets; he threw one on the end of each bed. He didn't bother to speak this time; he turned on his heels and left the room.

Kari listened as he locked the door. She kept hoping that one time he would forget to lock it. All she needed was one lucky break, and she was sure that she and Jill could escape. If she could get out of the complicated corn maze that she and Kelli used to go through when they camped at the lake, then she was sure she could find her way out of the countryside in the dark. She had always been a pro at hide-and-seek too, which could pay off if they got a chance to flee.

Kari quickly grabbed the blanket and spread it over her legs. "Well, at least we get covers. I can go without a pillow."

The room suddenly turned dark. Both girls fell silent.

Jill whispered softly, "Why do you think they turned out the lights?"

"I don't know. I guess they want us to go to sleep now."

"I'm too scared to go to sleep," Jill said in a shaky voice.

"Don't worry—I'm a light sleeper. I will wake up if I hear the door open. Go ahead and go to sleep."

"Are you sure?"

"Yeah, I'm going to lay here and think awhile anyway."

"Aren't you scared?" Jill asked

"Yeah, I am," Kari admitted. "But I'm sure our parents and the police are looking for us. They'll find us." Kari said, trying to sound convincing. "Besides, Kelli can't go too long without giving me a hard way to go, right?"

"I bet you really miss her."

"I do." Kari swallowed, trying to keep her voice steady. "I promise I'll never get angry at her ever again."

"Good night, Kari." Jill sniffed.

"Good night. Try to get some sleep. We'll need all of our energy tomorrow in case we get a chance to escape."

"Okay, I'll try."

39

Kari folded her arms under her head as she stared up toward the ceiling. *Please, God, help us get home, and I promise I will forget about boys until I graduate,* she prayed.

After a few minutes, Kari rolled over, turning her back toward Jill—she stared at the dull wall. She knew it was going to be a long night because she hadn't any intention of sleeping. She wasn't going to take any chances with Vaar's men. However, she couldn't let Jill know just how frightened she really was.

***

The sound of the door opening startled Kari; she bolted straight up in bed. The light was already on in the room. She glanced up toward the window and noticed the sun was starting to peek through. It must be morning already—she must have ended up falling asleep after all and slept soundly through the entire night.

Kari glanced over at Jill, who was beginning to stir. Jill's eyes slowly fluttered opened; she squinted at Kari and then followed Kari's gaze to the door. Masory was entering the room carrying a fresh loaf of bread and a pitcher of water. He replaced the remaining bread on the platter with the fresh loaf, took the empty pitcher, and sat down the other pitcher of water. He spun and left the room, locking the door behind him.

Kari threw the covers back and stumbled out of bed. "At least, they don't want us to starve. Too bad it's not bacon and eggs, though." She grabbed two pieces of bread and handed Jill one. Kari poured them both a fresh glass of water.

Jill sat up on the bed and ate the bread hungrily. She crossed her legs tightly. "I need to go to the restroom, but I keep thinking that there's a camera watching me every time I go."

"I know what you mean. I thought the same thing yesterday." Kari finished eating the slice of bread and eagerly grabbed another slice.

They were both sitting on the beds plotting their next stratagem when the door sprung open. This time when Masory entered the room he wasn't alone. Vaar glided into the room wearing an unbuttoned floor-length black leather coat.

40

Underneath it, he had on a blue flowered silk button-up shirt and tight-fitting black leather pants. He wore a thick shimmering gold chain around his neck and several hoop earrings in his ears. A lit cigarette dangled from his left hand while the other hand pushed his coat aside and rested on his hip, revealing a shiny black pistol tucked in the top of his pants. Kari thought he resembled a pimp she had recently seen on a NYPD Blue show.

Kari stared in awe as a highly fashionable lady followed Varr into the room. Her beauty was undeniable. She had silky black hair that was piled high upon her head. She wore a pair of stylish, silver-framed glasses over her dark cinnamon eyes. A touch of rose blush on her cheeks and a reddish-maroon colored lipstick highlighted her smooth bronze skin. Kari guessed that she stood close to five-foot eight inches in her high-heel shoes. She was dressed in black slacks and a suit jacket that flattered her curvy figure. She wore a diamond necklace with matching earrings, along with huge diamonds rings on most all of her fingers. Kari thought she was the prettiest foreign lady that she had ever seen.

Vaar smiled deviously. He sucked a long drag off the cigarette, dropped it on the floor, and squashed it with the heel of his boot. He slowly exhaled the smoke from his mouth as he glanced from Kari to Jill. "I hear you two have been behaving." He removed his hand from his hip—letting the coat fall over the gun. "This is good."

Kari couldn't wait any longer. "What do you want with us?" she asked in a strangled voice.

Vaar's smiled turned to a frown as he glared at Kari. "You do not ask questions. I do the talking—understand?"

Kari glanced at Jill, who was being solemnly quiet. She was glad that Jill was being cooperative. Kari glanced back toward Vaar and nodded.

"Good." Vaar's eyes shifted toward the lady. "This is Sahre. She also speaks English." He pointed to Kari while speaking to Sahre, "The one with the outspoken tongue is Kari Raker." He proceeded on to point toward Jill. "And this is Jill Jackson."

Sahre didn't smile at the girls, but instead looked at them cautiously. "Get up," she said rudely.

Kari and Jill quickly jumped to their feet.

Sahre slowly strutted around both of them, gazing up and down their bodies. She stopped in front of Kari, studying her face closely.

"Hold out your hands," Sahre demanded.

Kari quickly extended her hands in front of her.

Sahre examined Kari's hands, turning them over to inspect them further. She did the same to Jill's hands. She spun back toward Vaar. "Both have good hands." She hesitated as her eyes lingered on Jill. "This one could use some meat on her, though." She patted Jill on her backside, indicating her slender hips and rear. "But she will do."

Vaar beamed proudly. "I am pleased." He edged his body between Kari and Jill. "Listen to me carefully." He glanced from one to the other." You both will be escorted on an airplane with Sahre. You are to talk to no one—you are not to speak English. Understand? No English whatsoever." He waited until the girls nodded their heads. "You will show this passport only when Sahre tells you to." He held up two passports with their pictures on them. "If anyone tries to make conversation with you—do not answer. Sahre will do the talking for you." Vaar moved within inches of Jill's face. "If you try anything funny or do other than what I have just told you--there will be great consequences." He reached for his wallet and pulled out two pictures. He scooted toward Kari and held up a picture of Kelli climbing out of the Sunfire at their house. "My men will be near her the whole time you are on the plane—if you make one wrong move, I will order my men to kill her." Vaar paused is if he was letting his words sink in. Then he slowly turned to Jill and held up a picture of Timmy playing on the swing set in her back yard. "If you screw up—my men will kill him."

Jill gasped aloud, her eyes filled with tears as she stared at the picture of her little brother. "Please don't hurt him. I promise I will do everything you say."

Kari didn't know if she was capable of concealing her fear any longer. She chewed nervously on her lower lip. She didn't want Vaar to know how scared she was and the last thing she wanted was for him to see her crying. She had almost lost it,

42

though, when she had seen the picture of Kelli. The picture was taken after dark under the light post in front of her house. They must have taken the picture late last night, because Kelli still had on the Sonic uniform she was wearing yesterday.

Kari cringed at the thought of Vaar's men circling around her family. She now realized how unsafe they all really were. Before, she had been fearful for her own life, but now she was terrified for her sister's life. She could never live if something happened to Kelli—she was her other half. She wasn't going to take any chances on jeopardizing her sister's life. After seeing what the men did to Doug—she was sure Vaar meant every word he said.

Sahre snatched the bag out of Masory's arms and set it on the bed. She pulled out two dresses. One was a blue flowered, knee-length dress with long sleeves; the other one was a green, knee-length long-sleeved dress. She flung the flowered dress at Jill and the green one at Kari. "Put these on as soon as we leave the room." She grabbed two pairs of dull brown leather slip-on shoes out of the bag and dropped one pair on the floor at Jill's feet and the other pair at Kari's feet. She then reached back in the bag and continued to draw out more things; she pulled out panties, bras, and socks along with a toothbrush and hairbrush. "Leave your other clothes on the bed."

Vaar waited until Sahre had finished displaying everything out on the bed. He glanced from Kari to Jill. "Do you both understand what I have told you? Do you plan on behaving?"

Jill nodded, and Kari whispered softly, "Yes."

Vaar's voice boomed loudly, bouncing off the walls. "What? I can't fucking hear you!"

The girls stiffened. "Yes," they said simultaneously.

Vaar didn't lower his voice any. "Remember, if you try anything funny there will be death in both of your families." Vaar didn't wait for a reply this time; he spun around and left through the door with Masory following him.

Sahre folded her arms across her chest and paced back and forth in front of Kari and Jill. "I want you both to be dressed and ready to go when I come back shortly." She stopped pacing, placed her hands on her hips, and looked directly into Kari's

43

eyes. "Just so we understand each other—I will not tolerate any funny business." She pulled back the collar on her jacket collar to reveal a black star tattoo with different color points. "Do you see this?"

Kari nodded.

"Each colored tip represents a person I have killed."

Kari stared at the star; it had nine colored points. The woman was more violent than what she thought. She nervously pulled her hair behind her ears. "Don't worry, we'll do what you tell us."

Sahre released the collar. "That would be the smart thing to do." The firm sound of her heels clicking against the floor as she walked toward the door proved how self-confident she was. She shouted back over her shoulder, "Now hurry and get dressed."

Kari waited until she heard the door locking and the footsteps fading away before she spoke. "I can't believe this is happening to us!

Jill's tears turned to whimpers. "What do you think they're going to do with us and where could they be taking us on an airplane?"

Kari tenderly put her arms around Jill. "Calm down, we can't fall apart. We have to do everything they say for now, so they don't hurt Kelli and Timmy. We'll have other chances to escape." Kari picked up the hideous green dress. "Let's just get dressed."

Jill stopped sniveling briefly and picked up the blue flowered dress. "Okay, but I don't trust that woman at all."

"We better hurry before she comes back."

Jill bravely sobered up and undressed rapidly. "Why did they give us a toothbrush? How the heck are we supposed to brush our teeth without a sink?"

Kari already had the green dress on and was pulling on the socks. "I guess we can just spit into the toilet when we rinse."

"Alright."

Kari and Jill grew silent.

Kari's mind raced with upsetting visions of what the future could have in store for them. She hadn't been prepared for the news that Vaar had just delivered to them.

44

Kari's previous getaway plans subsided. All that was left was pure agony—she didn't think anything could be worse than the nightmare she was living right now. If she could only turn back time, she would have never talked to Doug yesterday. She would have gone about her business and shopped instead of flirting with Doug. She would be home right now with her family if she weren't so damn gullible.

Kari used the back of her hand to dab at her eyes—she shifted her back to Jill. She knew if Jill saw her crying she might turn hysterical herself. Kari couldn't handle Jill falling apart again, not at a time like this. Somehow, they were going to have to try to stay rational, so they didn't put their families in any more danger.

Kari wondered where they could possibly be flying. Vaar had held up their passports for them to see—which explained the pictures Masory had taken yesterday. However, Kari was certain they had to be fake passports, because she knew they couldn't have real ones returned that fast.

Kari's first thought had been that maybe Vaar was going to sneak them into Mexico. They did have dark complexions like Mexicans had, but Kari didn't think you need passports to go across the Mexican border. But she wasn't positive—Kelli would know. Kari cursed under her breath for having a dense mind.

She was curious why Sahre had wanted to see their hands and why she had said Jill needed meat on her bones. What could they possibly want with them that would matter what their bodies and hands looked like? Kari finished putting on the repulsive shoes. She was also curious why Sahre was having them dress in such unstylish clothes.

Kari closed her eyes, fighting back the tears—she prayed a silent prayer for strength. She couldn't imagine how she was going to stay stable when she felt like she could crumble at any moment. She glanced over at Jill, who was busy brushing her teeth. Jill was so frail—Kari knew she had to stay sane for her.

Kari suddenly thought of Kelli and her heart sunk. She wondered what Kelli was doing—any other Sunday Kelli would be soaking in a hot tub of water, and then she would make a

45

plate of cinnamon rolls to eat while she watched *Sister Sister*. But Kari was certain that this particular Sunday wasn't the case. She imagined that her family and Jill's family were out searching for her and Jill. For the first time, Kari realized just how precious life really was. She thought if she survived—she would never again take life for granted.

CHAPTER FIVE

Kelli quickly showered and threw on her favorite blue Levi jeans and a lightweight pullover sweater. She hadn't had much sleep during the night. She had tossed and turned, and awakened in a troubled state several times. When she did sleep she'd had disturbing life-like dreams of her and Kari when they were young. The dreams had seemed so real.

Kelli was eager to get out of the house and find Kari. She quickly slipped on her brown leather loafers, grabbed her purse and jacket off the chair, and hurried out of her room. She didn't slow down in front of Kari's room this time. She moved rapidly down the stairs, gripping the rail tightly, and skipping every other stair. Kelli briefly imagined how miraculous it would be if she walked into the kitchen and Kari was sitting at the kitchen table, being scolded for pulling a stunt like this. But she knew that wasn't going to happen.

Instead, her parents were sitting at the kitchen table—still dressed in the clothes they were wearing the night before. Kelli glanced from one to the other—her father's usually perky eyes seemed to sag while her mother's were red and swollen. Her mom sipped her coffee as she stared out the window; her eyes seemed to be locked on the tree house that Kelli's dad had build when they were younger. "Have you two gotten any sleep?" Kelli asked.

Bill looked at his wife tenderly and then back at his daughter. "Your mom and I were scared the police might try to call with information, so we decided to stay awake."

Frances wiped her nose with a tissue and reached for the coffeepot. Her hand shook as she tried to pour coffee into her cup. "I've called them four times now and there's still no word from Kari."

"Here, honey, let me do that." Bill retrieved the coffeepot from his wife and poured the coffee. He reached for the rag on the end of the table and proceeded to wipe the spilled coffee.

"Well, I'm going back to the shopping center to see if I can find out anything else." Kelli hurried around to the side of the table to plant a kiss on her father's cheek.

Frances's jaw dropped, "No, you mustn't. I want you to stay here. I don't need something else happening."

"But Mom, I've got to help try to find her. I'll be fine."

"Honey, you can't keep Kelli locked up in the house." Bill reached over, grasped Frances's hand, and massaged it gently.

"Oh, I know. I'm just so worried, and besides, the shopping center isn't even open yet," Frances glanced toward the circular clock hanging on the wall.

"That's okay—I'll wait for it to open. I've got my cell phone with me, so call me if you hear anything."

"We will." Bill stood. "Maybe I should go down there with you."

"No, Dad. I think mom needs you here."

Bill glanced toward his wife and nodded in agreement. "You're right. You be careful and call us if you find out any little thing."

"I will." Kelli kissed her mother on the forehead.

The drive to the shopping center didn't take long—there wasn't much traffic because it was Sunday. Usually during the week the traffic was a lot more congested. Kelli knew it was too early to get in the shopping center; it was only ten, and the center didn't open until ten-thirty. She whipped into the McDonald's drive through and picked up her favorite breakfast—a cinnamon roll and an orange juice. She pulled into a parking space right outside the mall; the same entrance she had dropped Kari and Jill off.

She bit into the roll—it tasted like cardboard, unlike the sweet, gooey cinnamon roll that she was used to. She assumed it was because she didn't have much of an appetite. She took another bite and then stuffed the rest of the uneaten roll back in the brown paper bag. It didn't matter how hungry she got, nothing would taste good until Kari was found.

Kelli calculated the various employees hurrying into the center, searching for anyone that looked suspicious of committing a violent crime. By the looks of them, they seemed to be just average people, rushing to get to their jobs on time. It was just another ordinary day to them.

Tears blurred Kelli's eyes as she glanced around the parking lot, searching for anything unusual. She didn't see a thing other than the usual parking lot trash: a candy bar wrapper, a pop can, and a Winston cigarette package. She finished her juice and climbed out of the car to get a closer look. She slowly scanned the parking lot, not sure just what she was looking for.

After a few minutes, Kelli still hadn't spotted anything abnormal. She decided to peek inside the windows of the empty cars. She wasn't sure what she could possibly find that would lead her to Kari. But she once saw them doing the same thing on the Law and Order series.

She crept up to a parked car, cupped her hands, and peeped through the tinted window. Not seeing anything other than a Dr. Pepper can and some loose change, she went on to the next car. She continued on to each of the parked cars. She was advancing toward the back of the parking lot when she noticed two men sitting in a silver Porsche. Kelli blushed, realizing how silly she must look strolling around the parking lot, picking up empty trash, and peering into vacant car windows. She hoped they weren't undercover policemen thinking that she was trying to steal a car. She quickly discarded the possibility—she didn't think police officers would be driving a Porsche.

She pretended not to see them. She tucked her hands into her jacket pockets, whistled a simple tune, and headed inside to wait for the stores to open. She sat on the same bench she had sat the night before. She dug the recent picture of Kari out of her purse—tears formed, but she fought for control. She had to remain calm enough to follow through with her plans.

Kelli waited until the stores opened, and then went in and showed Kari's picture, and asked the employees if they had seen her sister.

After a long two hours, she still hadn't had any luck in finding anyone that had seen Kari or Jill, and she had been in nearly every store.

Kelli's throat was dry, so she decided a cold drink might perk her up. She climbed on the escalator and rode down to the food center to grab a Coke. It was lunchtime and the lines were long; she had to wait ten minutes to get a soda. The two ladies behind the counter didn't seem to care about the extended line—they continued to work at a snail's pace. The plump lady that waited on Kelli spoke in a deep, rough manly voice; she briefly glanced at the picture of Kari before saying that she'd never seen her before. Kelli thanked her but the rude lady just shrugged. Kelli had to bite her tongue to keep from telling the lady what a crappy employee she was.

Kelli snatched the Coke off the counter and found an empty table to rest. She gawked at the people standing in the food line. She wondered how the hell the lady could know if she ever saw Kari with so many different people going through the line every day. Kelli decided the lady actually had no clue if she had seen Kari and had lied to brush Kelli off more quickly.

She took a sip of her pop while watching an elderly, white-haired lady cleaning off a table. The lady smiled, and Kelli returned the smile.

The lady hobbled toward the table next to Kelli and picked up the empty cups. Her eyes rested on Kelli. "You didn't find what you were looking for yesterday?"

"Excuse me?" Kelli asked, puzzled.

The lady stooped over to wipe a rag across the table. "It's hard to hit all the sales in just one day, isn't it?"

"What?" Kelli sat her cup down. The woman had her full attention. "Did you see me here yesterday?"

"I'm sorry—I didn't mean to be nosey. I just recall seeing you yesterday with that handsome guy and stunning blond." She tucked the rag in her apron as she straightened. "I like your haircut."

Kelli felt as though someone had just stuck her with a sharp pin. She almost knocked her Coke off the table as she jumped to her feet. She held out the picture of Kari to the woman. "That was my twin sister you saw—she was here yesterday. Please, tell me everything—we can't find her."

"Oh my. I didn't realize you weren't her. Well, let's see." The lady thumped lightly on her wrinkly forehead with her fingers. "She was sitting over there." She pointed to an empty table a few feet from them. "She was with a young girl about the same age with blond hair, and a nice-looking young man with dark hair. They all seemed to be laughing and having a good time."

"Anything else? What time was it? Were they eating lunch?"

"No, it was before lunch time. I'm not sure of the time, but I do know it was earlier in the morning. I cleaned up the table after they left, and they just had drinks—I think. I didn't see which direction they went."

"You're the first person who remembers seeing them! Can you tell me more about the guy and what he looked like?"

"I noticed him right off because of his exceptional handsome features." She smiled, revealing several missing teeth. "I may be old, but I still recognize a nice-looking man. After sixteen years of working in this hellhole—I tend to enjoy watching people. It seems to make the time go by faster." She glanced uneasily toward an open closet door disclosing shelves full of supplies. "Speaking of men—I better pretend to be busy or my boss will can me for slacking off." She grabbed her broom off her cart and swept around the table. "The guy was tall, probably six feet and built muscular. He could have been a college student; I'm not sure. I do recall that he was wearing a dark green sweater—only because I remember thinking it would be a nice sweater during the holidays. I don't know if he was wearing slacks or jeans."

Kelli again waved the picture in front of the lady's face. "Are you sure it was her?"

"Yes, I am positive," she said, nodding.

51

Kelli grabbed a pen and a piece of scrap paper out of her purse. "Could I please get your name in case the police needs to ask you some questions?"

"Sure. I'm Agnes Camp and my phone number is 983-5278. I hope you find her. She'll probably show up soon—that good-looking man probably just swept her off her feet. I know he would me." Agnes winked before empting the dustpan into the trashcan.

Kelli's hand shook as she scribbled Agnes's phone number down. "Would there be anyone else that worked here yesterday that might have seen her?"

"No. I was the only one working down here yesterday. Everyone is either asking off or calling in sick on Saturdays, so I'm stuck working every weekend. I don't mind, though—I have nothing better to do…"

"Thank you so much for your help," Kelli interrupted. She had a feeling the lady was on the verge of telling her whole life story. And as much as Kelli appreciated her help, she didn't have time for chitchat.

"You're welcome. Good luck finding her."

"Thanks." Kelli took one last swallow of her pop before tossing it in the metal trashcan and hurrying toward the escalator.

Tears oozed down Kelli's cheeks as she gritted her teeth and dug her fingernails into the side of her purse. She was furious with Kari—she couldn't even go a day without flirting with a strange guy. Hard telling what kind of creep they had been mingling with—a gush of revolting images filled Kelli's head.

She knew she had to let the police know right away about Agnes. She believed if they could find out who this guy was, maybe then they could find Kari and Jill.

Kelli headed toward the entrance door, barely aware of the people swarming around her. However, out of the corner of her eye, she caught sight of two middle-aged gentlemen sitting on the same bench she had sat on earlier. She didn't know what it was about the two dark-haired men that seemed peculiar, but for some reason, they seemed familiar. They looked like foreigners. They both seemed to be engaged in reading their newspapers.

She quickly dismissed her inquisitiveness; she didn't have time to fret over the men and where she knew them from—she needed to get to the police station immediately. She staggered out the entrance door as she tried to dial her parents' phone number. The line was busy. "Damn," she muttered as she dug the car keys out of her purse.

She was unlocking her car door when she noticed the same two men exiting out the door. Kelli was sure that it was just a coincidence that they were leaving the same time. Nevertheless, she crawled into the car and locked the doors while keeping her eyes fixed on the men.

She concentrated on the men as she dialed her parents again. "No wondered they looked familiar," Kelli said aloud as she recognized the silver Porsche they were climbing into. She shuddered and wondered if they were following her.

She suddenly shook her head in disbelief at the ludicrous thought; she was letting her imagination escalate.

Kelli waited for her parents to answer the phone while watching the silver Porsche pull out of the parking lot. She didn't think any more about the strange men.

"Hello?" Frances answered anxiously.

"Mom, its Kelli. I wanted to let you and Dad know that I found someone who saw Kari and Jill yesterday."

"Thank God! Who was it? Do they know where Kari is now?"

"Calm down, Mom. No, all she saw was Kari and Jill with a boy getting a soda down in the food center. That's all."

"What boy?"

"I don't know. That's all I know right now." Kelli could tell by her mom's voice that she was disappointed that there wasn't more news.

"Oh, I wonder what we should do now." Frances asked, more as a thought out loud than a question.

"I'm going down to the police station now to give them this information. Do you and Dad want to meet me there?"

"Yes, we'll meet you there. See you in a few minutes. Please, be careful, honey."

"I will."

***

Hank spat his gum into an empty wrapper, wadded the paper up, and hook shot it into the wastebasket. He grabbed the report off his desk and skimmed over it; it was the file on the missing girls, Kari Raker, and her friend, Jill Jackson. Raker and Jackson had disappeared from the Eastside Shopping Center yesterday. He figured that they probably ran off with their boyfriends.

Kari Raker's parents were on the way down to the station to talk with him. He studied the picture of the girl with long red curls and freckles—trying to recall if he had ever seen her before. Not recognizing her, he tossed the picture back on his desk and turned to check his own reflection in the oval mirror hanging on the wall. He flashed his slightly yellowish teeth to make sure he didn't have any of the bagel from earlier stuck between them.

He was satisfied with what he saw. After fifty-two years of living, he still had the looks of a thirty-five year old stud. Not a hint of gray streaked his stubby black afro. Although he couldn't see the rest of his body, he knew it looked fit on his five-foot, eleven-inch black frame. All of the late night workouts consisting of lifting weights and running a mile and half had paid off over the years. There had been some nights when he was too exhausted to exercise, but he always pushed himself to do it anyway. He was glad he did.

The phone rang—it was the clerk at the front desk letting him know that the Rakers were there to speak with him. Hank shoved the open drawers shut on his desk and hurried out of the office. He immediately spotted the trio huddled together at the front of the station. He motioned them back to his office.

"I'm Hank Catron. Please, have a seat and make yourself comfortable." Hank pointed to the empty chairs sitting around the room before turning to shut the door. He reached across his desk and handed each of them a business card. "I will be working on this case, so if you have any questions—don't hesitate to call me."

54

"Thank you. I'm Bill Raker." Bill extended his hand to shake and then pointed to his wife, who had already sat down. "This is my wife, Frances." Bill proceeded to point to Kelli. "And this is one of the twins, Kelli."

Hank picked up the picture of Kari off his desk. "I can definitely see the resemblance in the picture." He smiled. "Would you like a Coke?"

"No thanks." Kelli sat down in the chair next to Frances while Bill took the seat on the other side of Kelli.

Hank rubbed his hands together and turned toward Bill and Frances. "How about you two—a cup of coffee or a cold drink?"

Bill glanced toward his wife, who shook her head, and then he spoke for both of them. "We're fine. We're full of coffee."

For the next hour, Hank asked a series of routine questions about the proceedings that led up to Kari and Jill's disappearance, and the talk Kelli had with Agnes. This was the first Hank had heard about another guy being seen with the girls yesterday, and the first time he had considered the possibility that maybe the girls hadn't run away.

Hank rubbed his chin with the back of his hand, trying to make logic out of the situation. "Would you excuse me? I'll be right back."

"Sure," Bill said.

Five minutes later, Hank returned to the office with a photograph in his hand. "This may be a long shot and not have any connection to your daughter. However, a college student here in town called this morning and reported that his roommate never came home last night. We just assumed he had probably stayed out all night drinking and had slept over at a friend's house. His roommate came in while ago to bring us a photograph, and he informed us that his roommate didn't drink and had never stayed out all night." Hank held up the photograph of the boy for Kelli and her parents to observe. "Do any of you recognize this boy?"

Frances and Bill immediately shook their heads no. Kelli took her time studying the picture and then glanced up at Hank. "I have never seen him before, and I'm positive he's not a friend of Kari's or Jill's."

55

Hank remained holding the picture out while searching Kelli's face, trying to detect if she was covering up for her sister in any way. The corners of her mouth were drawn tight as she spoke, never faltering on her words, and her vibrant eyes met his gaze evenly. "Well, his name is Doug Parker. He's from North Dakota. He goes to college here and lives with a guy by the name of Jay Madison. We have contacted his parents, and they haven't heard from him either. There's a chance there might be a connection somehow."

Hank settled back down in his leather computer chair and studied the picture of the boy in detail—he was a handsome, well-groomed, mature guy. But the one thing Hank had learned after all these years on the job was that looks could be deceiving. He was deeply hoping this case didn't turn out to be foul play.

Hank tapped his pencil on his notepad several times. He noticed Frances was having a hard time coping—every few minutes she was sobbing into her tissue. He thought the father and the other twin were holding up pretty good under the circumstances. "Kelli, can you think of anything at all that happened yesterday or today that was unusual that you haven't already told me?"

"No, not really. I went to every store at the shopping center today—showing Kari's picture, and no one had seen her except for Agnes." Kelli hesitated and then added, "There was a silver Porsche in the parking lot, and I thought the men in it were following me. But I think it was all in my head."

Hank suddenly straightened. He glanced up at Kelli as the pencil slipped out of his hand. This was the clue he had been searching for. "A silver Porsche? Can you tell me anymore about it?"

"Well, it was probably nothing, but when I first got to the center, I was walking around the parking lot looking around, and I noticed a silver Porsche sitting in the parking lot with two men in it. It felt like they were watching me, so I just went into the mall. And then when I was leaving, they were sitting by the entrance door reading a paper. I didn't think too much about it, but I did notice they left out the door right after I did. However, they pulled out of the parking lot before I ever did, so that's why I thought it was probably just my imagination."

Frances covered her mouth in a surprised gesture. "Kelli, why didn't you tell me? I don't want you going there again. All I need is to..." Frances's voice drifted off.

Bill wrapped his arm around his wife and pulled her close to him; he let her sob into his coat jacket.

Hank grabbed a couple of Kleenex off his desk and handed them to Frances. "I know this is very hard for you guys, and my heart goes out to you. You must believe I am going to do everything I can to bring your daughter home safely." He turned back toward Kelli—he didn't believe she was holding back any information. "Could you describe these men for me?"

"They were around forty or fifty years old, I guess, dark hair and dark tan skin. They looked like foreigners. They were both rather short, but one was heavily built while the other one was thin. That's all I can remember."

Hank scribbled some notes down on his pad. "Did you happen to see the license plate number on the Porsche?"

"No, I didn't."

"Well, that's fine. There can't be too many silver Porsches in this town. I'll have some of my men check it out. In the meantime, I want you people to go home and try to get some rest. I know it's hard, but you will need your strength. I promise I'll let you know if anything turns up." Hank stood.

Bill stood up and extended his hand again to shake Hank's. "Thank you very much for your help. We are just devastated over this. Our daughter would never run away."

"I understand, and we'll do our best to find her. I'll be talking to Jill's parents this morning also. We will let you know if anything else turns up." Hank opened the office door. "Don't forget to call me anytime."

"Thank you." Frances dabbed at her nose with the tissue.

"Yes, thanks." Bill added.

"You're welcome. And Kelli, call me if you think of anything else."

"I will. Thanks." Kelli grinned.

Hank closed the door, plopped down in the chair, and scratched his head. He propped his elbow up on the desk and sat his chin in the palm of his hand. At first he had been skeptical about the case. He assumed it was just a couple of girls that had run away. In the last few years, the runaway cases had increased drastically.

However, now that he had gathered more information, it sounded like abduction could be a possibility. He hoped that wasn't the case, but in his line of work, he knew he had to be prepared for anything. He just had a hunch that this Doug guy was up to no good since Kelli was certain her sister didn't know him.

He reached over and picked up the picture frame on his desk of his fifteen-year-old niece. He would absolutely die if it were her that was missing. What a beauty she was, he thought, as he stared fondly at the picture. His brother, Chip, had married Kristin, a beautiful Caucasian woman, and together they created the prettiest baby. Leila, his niece, now a fine young lady, had lustrous olive skin, eyes dark as coal, and a charismatic smile. Not only was she a beauty, she also made straight A's, was the president of her class, and was a football cheerleader. The gal had a lot going for her, he thought, as he placed the picture back on his desk. Hank knew if anyone ever hurt Leila, he would break all the laws and blow the guy away. There wouldn't be any trial to deal with—except maybe his own.

He picked the picture of Kari back up and then Jill's. He shook his head—the cases kept getting tougher for him. He didn't know how much longer he could keep doing this job. He thought he might have to retire early. The last two cases he'd had ended up being murder cases—dealing with broken hearts in the families was the worst job of all.

Hank did enjoy catching the bad guys, and saving lives was a rewarding feeling. But unfortunately, there wasn't always a happy ending. He sure hoped this case didn't end in the same sad way the last two cases had.

***

58

Kelli drove her own car home while her parents traveled in their vehicle. She thought the meeting with Hank Catron had gone quite well. She believed he was committed to his job and would do everything in his power to find Kari. At least, that was the impression she got from him. She felt confident that they were on the right track to finding Kari and Jill—she thought it was just a matter of time now.

Right now, however, she felt her parents needed to get some rest. Her father looked drained, and her mother was a basket case. Kelli figured her mom would probably have to take a sleeping pill. One way or another, she had to get them in bed before they collapsed.

Kelli figured that once her parents fell asleep she could concentrate on her next plan. The only way she could be certain if that silver Porsche had been following her earlier was to return to the shopping center and wait. If they were following her, they might show up again. Kelli knew her mother wouldn't agree to her going back down to the mall, so she decided to wait until they had fallen asleep. She decided she would leave a note just in case they woke up while she was gone.

She was also considering visiting Jay Madison, Doug Parker's roommate—if she could locate the address in the phone book. She thought that maybe Jay could tell her more about Doug Parker. She knew that she shouldn't be interfering with the police investigation, but she couldn't wait—it may be too late if she did.

Kelli never did have patience—Kari was always telling her when God handed out endurance he left her out. And Kelli would argue back that she had more patience than Kari, at least she had enough patience to sit and read a book. But deep down, Kelli knew Kari was right. She smiled as she suddenly remembered all the junk she had shoved under her bed earlier in the week when her mother had asked her to clean her room. A bad habit she had started as a young child. Her mother always wondered why it took Kari so long to clean her room and it didn't take Kelli any time. Kelli suddenly felt guilty.

She pulled up in front of her house and pulled the emergency brake on. She pulled the picture of Kari out of her purse and set

59

it on the dashboard. "See, Kari, we're getting closer. I told you: I'm going to find you." She grabbed her purse before locking her car and hurrying toward the house.

Kelli was so anxious to get inside the house, she didn't notice the silver car, two blocks up, parked on the opposite side of the street.

CHAPTER SIX

Kari nervously pulled her hair behind her ears as the Dodge van pulled up in front of the building to pick her and Jill up for the ride to the airport. Vaar and Sahre climbed in the back seats with Kari and Jill, and Masory rode in the front with the driver. Kari soon understood why they had chosen the van: most of the windows were covered with curtains so that she and Jill couldn't see out. Only the back window was visible for the driver to see. Kari and Jill rode quietly while the other three spoke in their foreign language.

The drive was long. Kari had hoped they were going to be flying out of the nearby airport in Centerview so that someone might recognize her. However, too much time had passed for them to be going there. Kari guessed they had been on the road at least two hours, and she hadn't a clue in which direction they were going. She wondered if they were heading toward Canada. She knew that would be the logical thing for Vaar to do—if he was trying to cover up a criminal act. However, there was also an airport in Drury, which was located on the northern tip of Michigan.

Sahre eyed the girls suspiciously. "Remember, do not talk to anyone on the airplane. Pretend you do not know English. Your country of origin will be Germany. I will do all the talking."

Kari nodded her head. Germany? Kari didn't believe that Vaar and his men were from Germany. A friend of Kari's mother, Faustine Straus, was originally from Germany, and on a few occasions when she had been at their house, she would scold her two-year-old daughter in German. It didn't sound anything like the way these men were talking. Kari was more confused than ever.

Vaar reached in his jacket and pulled out the two passports. He handed one to each of the girls. "Show this only when you see Sahre holding hers up, and she nods to you. Do not talk to each other or anyone else. You will be allowed to go to the restroom once we get to the airport. If you must go to the restroom once you are on the plane, hint to Sahre by yawning and covering your hand with your mouth." Vaar pulled out the pictures of Kelli and Tommy from a pocket inside his coat and held them up for Kari and Jill to view. "I will have other men on the plane watching you two. If one of you decides to try to be a hero and speak to someone—well, I shouldn't have to say it again: you know what will happen to your families."

Kari's stomach weakened; she glanced at Jill, who was gnawing nervously on a fingernail. She had asked Jill to restrain from crying in front of Vaar if she possibly could.

"Also," Vaar continued, "Sahre will be timing you from the time you get up to go to the restroom until the time you come back. If you are gone any longer than five minutes—she will contact me to follow through with my plans." He paused. "Do you both understand what I am saying?"

"Yes." Kari said as Jill nodded.

"Do either one of you have any questions?" Vaar glanced from Kari to Jill.

"If we do everything you say—will we be seeing our family soon?" Kari asked softly.

Vaar leaned forward and grasped Kari's cheek with his thumb and his finger; pinching her cheek, he jerked her head so her eyes met his. He glared at Kari. "Just remember this, my fucking clever girl: if you don't do what I say—you will definitely never see your family again. Do you comprehend me, now?"

"Yes," Kari said boldly, although the pain was stabbing at her cheek and shooting down the side of her face. She was determined not to display how scared she really was.

Vaar viciously released hold on Kari's cheek while cursing under his breath. He reached for a cigarette and lit it. He yelled in his language at Masory.

Masory quickly reached for a glass and the Vodka bottle to mix Vaar a drink.

Kari watched nervously as Sahre and Vaar exchanged annoyed looks and spoke to each other in words she didn't understand. She wished, more than anything, that she had taken some foreign language classes in school. She might at least have been able to recognize what language they were speaking.

Vaar's cold eyes suddenly shifted to Kari and his language changed back to English. "I will be seeing you when you get off the plane." His voice hardened, "I sure hope Sahre has a good report to give me about the flight."

Kari's eyes narrowed. "You won't be having any trouble out of either one of us. Right, Jill?"

"Yes," Jill muttered.

"You don't know how glad I am to hear this—because killing people tends to be a messy job—if you know what I mean." Vaar chuckled.

Kari hated this man with every ounce of energy she had. He was the cruelest person she had ever met in her life. She knew that once she and Jill got off the plane, they were going to have to find a way to escape. Otherwise, it was hard telling what would end up happening to them.

The driver pulled the van up in front of the airport. Sahre and Vaar swapped words before Sahre turned toward the girls. "When we get out I want you both to follow me. We will go into the restroom, and then we will go to the waiting area. Masory will get our tickets for us. Remember, there will be no talking from here on out. I want you to follow me and show your passports only when I tell you to. Any questions?"

Kari and Jill exchanged curious glances before shaking their heads no.

"Okay, let's go." Sahre waited for the driver to come around to open her door. She gracefully stepped out.

Jill climbed out of the vehicle after Sahre. Kari positioned her foot down on the pavement to step out when suddenly Vaar

63

clutched her arm tightly. "Don't forget our conversation." He grinned ruthlessly.

Kari glared into Vaar's malicious eyes and waited for him to release her arm. She quickly followed Jill and Sahre into the airport without once turning to look at Vaar.

Kari immediately glanced around at her new surroundings, trying to figure out the name of the airport. However, Sahre was walking extremely fast, and it didn't give Kari much time to search. Kari did notice Masory had followed them in.

She was relieved to get to go to the restroom; she'd had to go for quite some time. The restroom was nearly empty except for one young woman washing her hands and a cleaning lady who was filling the paper towel holders. The woman finished with the paper towels, turned, and smiled at Jill and Kari before glancing toward Sahre and continuing out the door.

Jill and Kari disappeared into separate stalls. Kari thought she heard Sahre's familiar heels tapping across the floor and into a stall. She wished she had a pen that she could write 'help' on the walls with, or an article of clothing she could take off and stuff in the sanitary napkin box. Kari couldn't think of any clues that she could leave behind. If only Kelli was here—she'd know what to do, she thought. She cursed silently, irritated that Kelli had been given all the brains.

Sahre and Jill were already finished and standing near the door by the time Kari moseyed out of the stall. Sahre waited for Kari to wash her hands, nodded to the girls to follow her, and hurried toward the waiting area.

The vicinity was rapidly filling with people—Sahre chose three chairs that were further away from the crowd. After a few minutes, Masory returned and handed Sahre three tickets.

Kari noticed that some of the people were already loading onto the plane. She leaned to see the flight information sign, but a hefty man blocked her view.

Sahre spoke quietly to Masory before leaving him in the waiting area. She motioned the girls to follow her up to the short line of people waiting to check their carry-on bags. She quickly laid her purse down on the conveyor belt, hurried through the metal detector, and down to the other end of the belt to retrieve her purse.

Jill and Kari followed close behind her—neither had anything to be scanned, so they hurried on through the metal detector. Sahre turned toward the entrance of the plane and handed the young gentleman all three tickets. He barely glanced at the girls before giving Sahre directions to her seats on the plane.

Kari's jaw dropped as she passed the sign saying: JFK airport in New York. She now understood why they didn't have to show their passports. She couldn't imagine, though, why they were going to New York rather than another country, like she thought Vaar had planned.

The seats they were assigned were in the last row of the plane. Kari assumed that Vaar had chosen the seats so there would be fewer people observing them. Kari purposely staggered down the aisle coughing—in hopes that one of the passengers would take notice of her and Jill, but they were all too busy loading their carry-on bags.

Sahre shot Kari a warning look. She stopped at the last row of three seats, and motioned to Kari and Jill to crawl into the seats toward the window while she took the aisle seat.

The flight lasted an hour and forty-five minutes. The flight attendant came back only once to serve them peanuts and a soda. Sahre ordered the drinks for the girls, and the attendant didn't give Kari and Jill a second glance.

The plane landed and the girls followed Sahre off the plane.

Jill and Kari grudgingly trailed behind Sahre down the packed walkways. After a short time, they arrived at another busy terminal, and Sahre maneuvered through the crowd toward the front desk to purchase more tickets.

Kari caught a glimpse at the flight sign: Istanbul, Turkey. Her heart rate increased as she glanced toward Jill's bewildered expression. Suddenly, it made sense; Kari had totally forgotten that international flights always flew out of New York. She shook her head, baffled—no wonder she didn't recognize Vaar's language—she had never heard anyone from Turkey speak.

Sahre moved ahead to another location and placed her purse on another conveyor belt. The purse slid through the conveyor

65

belt, and a homely man with acne scars picked it up and opened it, glanced inside, and laid it back down. Sahre retrieved the purse, and the three of them proceeded through the metal detector. Sahre hurriedly dug her passport out of her pocket and nodded to the girls to do the same.

Kari nervously wrung her hands together; she wanted to flee. She knew if she grabbed Jill's arm and yelled for her to run that she would follow. She was certain that any of the employees at the airport would help them. The police would come, and Sahre would be arrested. But Kari was afraid it would be too late to save Kelli and Timmy, and she couldn't risk taking that chance. Although she was petrified to be whisked away to a faraway country like Turkey—she felt there wasn't any other alternative. She wasn't going to jeopardize Kelli's life in any way.

Sahre casually glanced over her shoulder at the girls as they neared the elderly, bearded man that was checking the passports. Sahre held hers up for the man to check. He nodded and Sahre glided on through the passageway—she instantly glared at the girls. Her deceitful eyes showed no compassion.

Kari reluctantly flaunted her passport in hopes that the man would recognize that it was fake. But the man just nodded his approval and continued on to the next passenger. Kari hesitated and then followed Sahre and Jill onto the plane.

It was an enormous airplane, the biggest one Kari had ever seen. It had seats in three sections; the middle section had eight seats in it, and the aisle seats had three. Kari wasn't surprised that their seats were located in the back. Again, Sahre stood aside so the girls would sit in the inner seats near the window.

While the plane was loading Sahre pointed to the restrooms in the back, indicating to the girls to go ahead and use the facility. Jill and Kari both eagerly squeezed by Sahre. Kari noticed Sahre didn't hesitate to glimpse at her watch as soon as they stood up. Kari recalled Vaar's terms—that they only had five minutes to be gone. Any longer—Sahre would call Vaar, and he would go ahead with his plans.

Kari and Jill exchanged silent, troubled smiles before entering into separate cubicles. Kari found it difficult not being able to speak to Jill. She glanced around the cramped area. There was

66

hardly enough space to turn to sit—only a stool and sink. She again struggled to think of something that she could leave behind that could be traced, but again she was clueless. She sighed helplessly and returned to her seat. Jill was already in her seat, fastening her seatbelt.

Kari thought the men sitting in the middle section of the back row were Vaar's associates, because they kept staring their way. The men resembled Vaar. However, as Kari glanced around the plane, she noticed that most of the passengers were Vaar's nationality.

Kari leaned her head back against the seat and squeezed her eyes closed as the plane glided into the air. Shortly after takeoff, the pilot's voice boomed over the intercom—he explained it would be a ten-hour flight, and that they would be offering movies and meals. He mentioned that the flight attendants would be passing out pillows for everyone.

An attractive blond flight attendant stood in the front of the plane and explained the safety rules.

An hour after the flight was in progress a flight attendant made her way down the aisle and asked Kari and Jill what they would like to drink.

Sahre quickly responded, "We all want Coke, please."

The flight attendant quickly made a glass of Coke, handed it to Kari, and then made one for Jill. "Is this you girls' first time going to Turkey?"

Kari and Jill exchanged puzzled glances.

Sahre immediately spoke. "They don't speak English; they're from Germany. Their school in Wiesbaden is paying their way to go to the USA, Turkey, and then Spain to study the variety of cultures before returning back home. I am their guide and interpreter."

The flight attendant handed Sahre a Coke. "Well, that sounds fun. My name is Brittney and if you need anything—don't hesitate to let me know. It's going to be a long flight, so try to relax and enjoy it." Brittney rolled her cart over to the next aisle and proceeded to push her cart down it, offering drinks to the other passengers.

67

Kari had hoped that Brittney might be leery of the situation, but she acted as if she believed Sahre's phony story.

Kari knew time was critical—she needed to cogitate up some kind of strategy that would help them escape when they reached Turkey.

She leaned her head against the window and gazed out at the soft, fluffy white clouds. She glanced down, thinking she would see land, but all she could see was blue from the ocean. They would be going through a time change soon, and the sky would grow dark. Kari was glad it would be nighttime soon, and she could relax some without Vaar's men watching every move she made. She sure wished she could talk to Jill to pass the time. She had almost slipped numerous times and spoken to her.

Kari stared out the window, absorbing the tranquility of the floating clouds. She thought they resembled melted marshmallows—like the ones she and Kelli used to roast over the fire when they would go camping with their parents. Kari visualized her and Kelli as small girls, fighting over the sticks that her father would sharpen for them to roast the marshmallows. Her mother would finally have to hide one in each hand behind her back, and then they would have to pick which hand they wanted.

Kari grinned silently as she swallowed the lump in her throat; her eyes stung from the unshed tears. It seemed like an eternity since Kelli had dropped her and Jill off at the mall.

She suddenly remembered the science report her and Kelli were supposed to turn in on Monday. She recalled Kelli promising her that she would help her with it. She wondered if Kelli was working on the paper now, or if she had decided not to do it at all.

It was almost dark out, and the clouds were fading.

Kari stretched her legs out in front of her, leaned her head back against the seat, and closed her heavy eyes.

She enjoyed the flashbacks of her family. Kari figured the longer she could keep them in her mind, the closer they would be to her heart. Besides, the only thing she had left of her family was the precious memories.

68

A single, lonely tear oozed down her cheek and splattered onto her hand.

CHAPTER SEVEN

Kelli didn't have any trouble finding Jay Madison's address in the phone book. He lived on Maple Street which was only a few blocks from her own house. She decided she would go there first before going to the shopping center.

She slipped the phone book back under the phone and fiddled with the channels on the TV, pretending to be interested in finding a talk show program. She kept glancing in the kitchen, patiently waiting for her parents to go to bed.

She had been worried that her dad wouldn't be able to get her mom to lie down. However, he finally coaxed her into taking a sleeping pill, and a short time later, her mother fell asleep and her dad followed.

Kelli left a short note on the kitchen table, explaining that she had to run a few errands and would be back shortly. She didn't expect her parents to be up before she returned, but she left the message just in case.

She tiptoed to the bottom of the stairs and listened for any sound of commotion coming from the upstairs—it was quiet. She was sure her parents were sleeping.

Kelli quickly grabbed her purse and car keys off the kitchen counter and quietly sneaked out the front door. "Crap," she muttered as she stepped out on the porch. She forgot to grab her jacket and hesitated whether to go back in to get it. She decided she didn't want to risk waking her dad up. She crossed her arms, tucking her hands under her armpits as she hurried down the sidewalk. She paused outside of the Sunfire and looked in her purse to make sure she had her cell phone. She still believed that Kari might call.

Kelli started the cold engine, waited a few minutes for it to warm up, and pulled away from the curb. She shivered from the chill in the air and flipped the heat on high. She tried to recall if Kari had been wearing a coat. She didn't think she'd had one on; she prayed Kari and Jill weren't stranded somewhere in the cold.

Her eyes quickly filled with tears, and she turned on the radio to help clear her head. She sure didn't want to be an emotional wreck when she spoke to Jay Madison. She was particularly edgy about going to some strange guy's house and probing for answers. She realized it could be risky. She decided if Jay appeared even a little bit dangerous, she would pretend she was asking for donations for a charity.

The cream-colored house Kelli pulled up in front of was newly built and fashionably decorated. On one side of it, under the front bay window, a row of silk flowers hung out of stone vases, and on the other side of the house, stone statues of deer, rabbits, and a baby raccoon filled the yard. A little wooden bench sat among the animals next to a white birdbath. The sidewalk leading up to the door was created with thousands of various-sized colored pebbles. Kelli stared up at the incredible house; she knew it had to be expensive.

She pulled the address out of her purse to double-check the numbers. She couldn't imagine a college guy living in such an exquisite place. Most of the college students she knew had to live in cheap, run-down apartments.

Kelli took a fleeting look at herself in the mirror. The reflection that she saw was ghastly; her eyes were not only puffy, but bloodshot. Her hair looked as though it had been through the spin cycle on a washing machine. She had brushed it earlier in the morning, but she had skipped washing and curling it—and it showed. Usually she flipped the ends up, but now the red strands hung loosely and unevenly around her neglected features. Her face seemed pale without the usual makeup, and a few new pimples had popped up on her forehead. She sighed at the horrid reflection and climbed out of the car.

71

She hadn't prepared what she was going to ask Jay about his roommate. She just knew she had to learn more about Doug Parker, and this was the only way she knew how. She caught glimpse of a red Eclipse parked in the driveway and continued to gaze over her shoulder at the extravagant car as she walked toward the door. *These guys must have a lot of money,* she thought.

Kelli pressed the doorbell and waited. After a few seconds, a tall, lean blond-haired guy wearing thick-lenses glasses answered the door. "Yes?" he asked.

"Are you—are you Jay Madison?" Kelli stuttered.

"Yes, I am." Jay's eyebrows creased as a half-smile spread across his face.

"Hello. My name is Kelli Raker." Kelli thought he looked civilized—he didn't look like a mass murderer. "I heard your roommate was missing, and so is my sister." She hesitated as she studied his stunned expression. "I was wondering if you've heard anything from him yet."

Jay's smile faded. "No, I haven't heard a thing." He opened the door further. "Would you like to come in?"

"Thank you." Kelli was skeptical about entering his house. *What the hell am I doing here?* she thought. But she stepped into the house regardless. She entered the hallway and glanced around at the well-kept place while Jay shut the door. She nervously followed him into the newly modeled, sunken living room. A warm fire was glowing in the stylish oval-shaped fireplace. Jay motioned for Kelli to sit on the white leather sofa. The huge room had plants hanging from the ceiling, and trendy candles decorated the round glass coffee table. An enormous aquarium was located on the left side of the room with striking colored fish swimming around.

Kelli was indeed impressed with the house and the immaculate cleaning that she observed. "This place is really nice."

"Thank you." Jay nodded toward the aquarium. "Those are Doug's fish. He loves his fish." He removed his glasses and rubbed his eyes. "I can't imagine where he could be. I've tried contacting everyone I could think of."

"Have you talked to his parents yet?" Kelli asked.

"Yes. They haven't heard from him and didn't seem too concerned about it either! Of course, Doug always said they could care less about him." Jay sat down on the sofa next to Kelli, leaned back, and crossed his legs. "He doesn't see them much. They usually just send him some money once a month for school and that's about all the communication that they have." Jay hesitated, then rose, and walked nervously across the room to the bar. He reached for an ashtray and drew a cigarette out of the package that was lying on the counter. He lit one and then held the package up. "Would you like one?"

"No, thank you."

"Doug hates it when I smoke in the house, but I've been so worried about him—I haven't thought twice about it." Jay inhaled a long drag off his cigarette and blew the smoke out slowly. "Did you say your sister is missing, too?"

Kelli felt sorry for Jay—she could tell that he was truly missing his friend. He seemed terribly disturbed about Doug's disappearance. "My sister was seen at the shopping center yesterday with a male that could have been your roommate. Her name is Kari Raker—she is my twin sister. She was with a girlfriend named Jill Jackson. Have you ever heard either of those names before from your roommate?"

"No, I'm sorry, I haven't." Jay's eyes drifted toward the fish tank as he stared sadly at the lively fish. "Doug's not just my roommate—he's also my lover." He hesitated before glancing back toward Kelli. "Doug's gay, and seriously, I don't even know if he has any female friends."

"I see." Kelli blushed. "Do you know if he was at the shopping center yesterday?" She thought the situation was getting even more confusing—if Doug was the one who was involved with Kari and Jill's disappearance.

"Yes. He did say he had to stop by there and pick up a few things. He said he had a lot of different errands to run before he could tell me about my surprise." Jay reached for a Kleenex on the end of the counter and gently blew his nose. "Last night, he was supposed to take me away somewhere special for a few days, but he wouldn't tell me where. It was sort of like an

73

anniversary present to me. We were going to skip a few days of school and get away from it all. But now..." Jay's voice quivered. "He told me to pack and be ready. So, I waited and waited—the hours slipped by and still there was no sign of Doug. I stayed up all night waiting for him and when he didn't show up I knew something was wrong." Jay strolled over to the window and stared out. "I called the police station this morning, but they didn't take me too seriously. They just thought he might have been drunk and slept over at someone else's house. However, Doug rarely drinks, and I knew he wouldn't have stayed with anyone else. I took a picture of him by the police station this morning, but I don't know if they're trying to find him or not. They said they would get back with me if they hear anything." Jay turned back toward Kelli. "I'm sorry. I'm just rambling on and on, and you're grieving over your sister, too. I just don't see how there could be any connection between your sister and Doug."

"Maybe not, but we might as well check it out to make sure. Do you have any extra pictures of Doug? I met a lady at the shopping center that saw my sister with a young man yesterday. If I could take the picture to her, maybe she could tell us if it was Doug or not."

"Yeah, sure. I'm willing to try anything at this point. I'll be right back." Jay hurried toward the bedroom.

Kelli glanced at the oil-painted pictures hanging behind the couch. She gazed at the forest scenery with the colorful flowers and plants. She squinted to read the signature, and it looked like it read: Doug Parker. Her eyes darted to the next picture. It was a vast ocean scene with sailboats and an orange-red sunset. The signature read the same—he was definitely a gifted painter.

She was surprised to learn that Doug was gay. It didn't make any sense for Doug to be involved with Kari and Jill's abduction. There had to be more to the story, or maybe, Doug's absence wasn't even connected to Kari and Jill.

Jay entered the room and handed Kelli a wallet-sized picture of Doug. "Would this do? All our other ones are in frames."

Kelli reached for the picture and glanced down at it. Hank had showed her the exact same picture. A professional

74

photographer had developed it—Doug was leaning back against a tree trunk wearing khaki slacks and a striped sweater. The pose revealed his muscular body and his incredibly handsome face. She could definitely see Kari being attracted to him. It seemed like ever since Kari started watching Ross Blum on a soap opera, she had become infatuated with college men. "This would be perfect." Kelli slid the picture into her purse. "Well, I appreciate all your help. I think I'll run down to the mall now to see if that lady is working and show her the picture."

Jay ran his fingers nervously through his wiry hair. "Would you mind if I ride with you? I just can't take this sitting around—waiting. I am truly going nuts!"

"No, not at all. We can keep each other company. That may be the only way we can keep sane." Kelli moved toward the front door.

"I think I'll grab a jacket. Be back in a sec." Jay disappeared down the hall. He returned carrying a lightweight black jacket. "Okay, I'm ready." Jay opened the front door. "Do you want me to drive?"

"I don't mind driving unless you just really want to."

"No. I don't think I feel much like it. I'm so edgy—I would probably wreck."

Kelli unlocked the passenger side door. "It's not the prettiest car, but it gets me where I'm going." She glanced toward the red Eclipse.

"Oh, I like it." Jay waved his hand in the air. "Hey, it doesn't matter to me what I ride in." He waited until Kelli had crawled into the driver's seat, and then he pointed to the Eclipse. "I wouldn't have that car right now except my parents bought it for me for my birthday. As a matter of fact, Doug and I wouldn't be living in such a nice place if it weren't for my parents. Doug's parents do send him a fairly large check every month, but my parents are the ones that shower me with money and gifts all the time."

Kelli buckled her seat belt and pulled away from the curb. "Boy, you're lucky."

"I guess I am. They weren't always like that, though. However, as soon as they found out I was gay, they started buying me everything. It's as though they feel sorry for me or something."

"But you say Doug's parents are distant from him, but they still send him money?"

"Oh, yeah. His parents are loaded with money. They sent him to some rich military boarding school when he was growing up. He said he only went home on holidays, so he wasn't really close to his parents." Jay reached for a cigarette in his pocket. "I'm sorry, do you mind if I smoke?"

"No, not at all. Here's the ashtray." Kelli pulled out the ashtray.

"Thanks. Well, anyway…" Jay lit his cigarette and blew out a stream of smoke. "When he told them he just wanted to go to college here instead of some big expensive college, they had a fit. And then when he told them he was gay and moving in with me, they really hit the roof. They couldn't believe they had a son that was gay." Jay cracked his window. "So they slowly stopped calling and visiting, but they do continue to send Doug a check for school and expenses. Oh, it isn't a superb amount, but it pays the bills, including his car payment and his school expenses. He sometimes runs a little short on money toward the end of the month, but I always insist on helping him out. He doesn't like it, though, when I do. But what can I say—I love him." Jay chuckled and stared miserably out the passenger window.

"Well, it sounds like you two have a good relationship."

"Oh, we do. What about you and your sister? Are you two close?"

"Yes, very much. We give each other a hard time a lot, but we both know we're only kidding around. She has always been so much fun to hang out with. We used to fight a lot when we were younger, but not anymore." Kelli grew quiet, in fear she would start crying.

"What about your parents?" Jay asked. "Are they easy to live with?"

"Oh yes, very much. My poor mother is a mess over all of this." Kelli pulled into the shopping center and parked in the closest spot to the entrance doors that she could find.

76

The shopping center was bustling with people shopping, and Kelli and Jay had to stick close together to avoid being separated. Kelli immediately caught a glimpse of the back of Agnes' white hair as they descended the escalator; she was busy clearing trash off a table. Kelli pointed her out to Jay. "There she is over there—she's really nice."

"I wouldn't want her job." Jay said.

"Me neither—not with this mob." Kelli slid up next to the table that Agnes was cleaning off and waited until she glanced up. "I know you're busy, and I'm sorry to bother you, but this will only take a minute."

"No problem. What can I help you with?" She smiled at Kelli, glanced at Jay, and nodded before turning back to Kelli. "You just missed Hank Catron. He was here asking questions."

"Well, then you might have already seen this picture?" Kelli reached in her purse and pulled out the picture of Doug. She held it up so Agnes could get a full view of it. "Do you remember if this could have been the guy you saw with my sister yesterday?"

Agnes glanced at the photo. "Oh yeah, that's him. That's the same photo Hank showed me, too."

Jay's eyes widened. "Are you sure that's the guy you saw with the girls?"

"Yes, I'm sure. I remember him distinctly, because he's such a nice-looking boy."

"Yes, he is." Jay bowed his head and stared at the floor.

"Well, I guess Hank Catron is ahead of me," Kelli said.

"Yes, he is. I guess you haven't heard anything, either." Agnes's eyes depicted concern.

"No, nothing." Kelli nodded toward Jay. "This is Jay. He's Doug's roommate." Kelli didn't think she needed to say how close Doug and Jay actually were. The older generation generally didn't accept those things too well.

"Hello." Agnes held out her hand to shake Jay's. "I'm sorry about your roommate. I hope he turns up soon."

"Thank you."

"Well kids, I hate to be rude, but I took up too much time talking with Hank, so I better get back to work before my boss starts griping. You would think he would appreciate me showing up to work—but no—all he can do is complain."

"Sure. I understand. Thanks so much for all your help," Kelli said.

"Yeah, thanks," Jay added.

"You're welcome. Good luck, kids. I hope you find them." Agnes turned toward another empty table and bent over to pick up the trash.

Jay didn't speak until they were in the car pulling out of the parking lot. "I'm just dumbfounded! I can't believe this is happening. I don't understand why he was with your sister and her friend."

"I'm confused about this whole mess myself." Kelli pulled up to the stop sign and turned on her right blinker light. She casually glanced in her rearview mirror. "Oh my God! I don't believe this," she exclaimed. "Don't look now—but the car behind me is the same one I thought was following me earlier today." Kelli quickly shifted her eyes back on the road. She waited for her turn to go, turned the corner, and glanced back in her rearview mirror to see if the car was still following her. It wasn't—it had gone straight.

"Can I look now?" Jay asked.

"Yeah, it's the silver Porsche that's heading north."

Jay quickly turned around. "Are you sure they were following you earlier? They're not following you now."

"Well, I'm not positive, but it sure seemed like they were. I think I'll give Hank Catron a call when I get home."

Jay stared out the passenger window for a few minutes. He suddenly reached for a cigarette and lit it up. "I think I'll call down to the police station when I get home, too. I'll check my answering machine first and make sure they haven't been trying to contact me."

"Thanks for riding with me to speak to Agnes." Kelli felt bad for Jay—he looked so worried.

Jay smiled. "No, thank you for letting me go with you. I'm so glad you came by today. I really could use a friend through this."

"If I hear anything at all on this, I will call you. Will you do the same, if you hear anything new?"

"You bet I will." Jay grew quiet again and stared back out the passenger window.

They both rode in silence the rest of the way back to Jay's house.

Kelli pulled in front of the house and shifted the car into park. She left the car running while she dug in her purse for a paper and pen. She scribbled her home phone and cell phone number down on the scrap of paper and handed it to Jay. "Here's my phone numbers. I already have yours—I got it from the phone book earlier."

"Thank you so much, Kelli. Oh, I hope Doug comes home soon before I go crazy!" Jay hesitated before climbing out of the car. "Don't forget to call me—and come by anytime. We can cry on each other's shoulders. Oh wait," he tore a piece of the paper that Kelli had given him and scribbled a number. "Just in case I am outside or something when you call, here is my cell number. Please call—anytime."

"I will. Thanks."

"Bye." Jay gently closed the car door and dug his keys out of his pocket. His head was bowed as he toddled toward the front door.

She waited until he had gone inside before pulling away from the curb. She kept glancing in the rearview mirror, expecting to see the silver car—but she never did.

Kelli's mind was playing too many tricks on her lately. She was starting to wonder if she had just imagined that the silver Porsche had been following her this morning. If Kari were the one that was kidnapped, why would they be following her around anyway? *That didn't make any kind of sense,* she thought. *Of course, this whole mess doesn't make any sense. What would a gay guy want with Kari and Jill?* She didn't think it would be likely that he would kidnap the girls—maybe, if he wasn't gay and had rape on his mind, he would.

Kelli assumed Kari and Jill didn't have any clue that Doug was gay. Agnes had said they were all happily socializing while drinking their sodas. Therefore, they had to have met at the shopping center sometime yesterday morning. *Why would Doug want to hang out with Kari and Jill—that is if he truly was gay?*

79

Kelli couldn't stop asking herself that question. Jay sure seemed like a nice guy—but Doug was the one she was concerned about. The situation was getting increasingly difficult to follow. Kelli wished she had asked Jay what kind of car Doug had. She decided she would call him and find out.

She glanced at the picture of Kari still on her dashboard. She hit the dashboard with her fist. "Where the hell are you?" she mumbled. Her mind was cluttered with unanswered questions.

Kelli didn't feel like going home; she was too depressed. She drove toward the City Lake and parked her car where she could see the water and the geese. The trees were already bare, as the upcoming winter months were approaching. Kelli thought the leafless trees looked the way that she felt—lonely and empty. All of the colorful leaves had already fallen to the ground and were wet and muddy from the earlier rains.

She patiently watched two geese playing together. The geese instantly made her think of Kari. They probably loved each other unconditionally—the same way she and Kari did.

Kelli let the tears fall. She was tired of fighting the sensation that had been building up. She sat and bawled for what seemed like forever. She finally noticed the sun starting to set.

She glanced down at her gas gauge; it was getting low, so she decided it was time to head for home. She briefly thought about her mom and dad and wondered if they could have awakened yet. She glanced at her clock and was surprised that it was nearly five; she hadn't planned on being gone so long.

Kelli shifted the car in drive and glanced in the rearview mirror to make sure it was clear. A cold chill shot down her spine when a streak of silver flashed in the mirror. She quickly looked over her shoulder and spotted a silver Porsche leaving the top of the hill behind her. They were following her—Kelli was sure of it now. They had probably been following her ever since she left the mall—they had been sitting up there the whole time, watching her.

She quickly reached for the button to lock her doors and then hurriedly pressed on the gas pedal. Suddenly, Kelli felt a sense of fear like she had never felt before. The thought of someone sitting up there watching her while she bawled her eyes out was too freaky. She couldn't imagine what the men wanted, but she was sure it had something to do with her sister's disappearance.

The lake was completely empty; she didn't see a single car anywhere. She pressed harder on the pedal—it felt like she was barely moving. Suddenly, the lake seemed eerie as the naked branches from the trees cast shadows across the lake. The noisy geese had disappeared. Kelli continued to glance uneasily in her rearview mirror until she reached Main Street where there was other traffic. She could hardly wait to get home, call Hank Catron, and tell him the latest. There was no doubt in her mind that she was being followed, and she was sure these strangers could lead her to her missing sister.

Kelli pulled up in front of her house and hurriedly pulled the parking brake on. She grabbed her purse out of the back seat and pulled the keys out of the ignition. She glanced at Kari's picture and assured her sister aloud: "So help me God, Kari: if they've hurt you in any way—I'll kill them." She hurried out of the car and glanced up and down the street before rushing inside the house.

CHAPTER EIGHT

The plane finally landed, and Kari couldn't have been more relieved. As much as she didn't want to be in Turkey, riding in the airplane any longer would be pure torture. It had been a long, tiresome flight. Sahre hadn't let Kari and Jill watch any movies because they weren't supposed to understand English—Kari assumed that that was the reason, anyway. Kari and Jill had spent most of the time napping.

The pilot had said Turkey would be seven hours ahead of the United States. He had announced that the airplane would land at 5:45 a.m. Turkish time—he was right on the nose.

Kari and Jill stood to follow Sahre off the plane. Most of the passengers that were chatting among themselves spoke Turkish. The few that did speak English, Kari assumed were tourists.

The airport wasn't quite what Kari imagined. It was more modern than she thought it would be. She had always heard that Turkey was less civilized than the United States, but you couldn't tell by the looks of the airport. Windows bordered the colossal building, and skylights filled the ceilings. Everything was painted white, including the escalators.

They had to show their passports again before being permitted to exit through the gates. Sahre pushed her way through the crowd of people, occasionally glancing back over her shoulder to make sure the girls were trailing.

Kari and Jill tailed Sahre out the exit doors.

Kari shivered as the frigid air hit her in the face. It was still slightly dark, with the threat of the early sun starting to break through the clouds.

Kari rubbed her hands over the goose bumps emerging on her arms. She wondered why Sahre hadn't brought any luggage—not even jackets. However, her curiosity didn't last long when an expensive, oversized black car pulled up and Masory jumped out to open the door for Sahre.

Kari's mouth flew opened in disbelief. Her stomach suddenly cramped as she climbed into the back seat of the car and came face to face with Vaar. She couldn't imagine how he and Masory could have gotten there before them. Seeing Vaar again only reminded her of the painful memories of the last two days. However, the question as to why they were in Turkey was still hanging in the air. She kept praying that she would wake up from the terrible nightmare.

Vaar greeted Sahre in Turkish and then glanced at Jill and Kari. Changing his language back to English, he addressed Sahre, "Did these two give you any trouble?"

"No. Luckily, they behaved properly," Sahre said.

Vaar's overpowering eyes remained on Kari while he continued his conversation with Sahre. "The boys will be disappointed. They were hoping they would get to execute someone. You would think that they would have had enough fun getting rid of that Doug character—but I guess not."

"Don't you think you should call and let them know we're here, so they can get the hell out of that town before the police start snooping around?" Sahre pulled a tube of lipstick from her purse and a pocket mirror. She carefully applied the lipstick.

"In time, dear." Vaar quickly changed his language back to Turkish and spoke to Masory.

Kari shuddered at Vaar's words—it was hard to say what they had done to Doug. She couldn't help but feel sorry for him, even after his betrayal.

She anxiously gazed out the window while Vaar, Masory, and Sahre talked. She focused on the setting; she needed to remember the direction they were heading.   When they did

83

get a chance to escape, she wanted to be able to find her way back to the airport.

Kari was amazed how tall the buildings were. Most of the houses and apartment buildings were five stories high, and there wasn't any kind of space between the buildings—they were built right next to each other.

Masory turned a corner, and they were suddenly driving alongside an immense sea. Kari wasn't sure what ocean it was. She glanced at Jill with a puzzled look—Jill shrugged her shoulders. They drove past a long, massive stretch of sand that looked to be the local beach area. It was nearly vacant, with the exception of a couple snuggled up lovingly, walking down the shoreline. Kari imagined the beach was packed during the hot summer days.

After a few miles, Masory took another left-hand turn. Kari hoped Jill was also trying to keep track of the number of turns they made. The houses slowly thinned out as they approached the downtown area of the city. The sun was now shining vividly. There were clusters of people setting up tables with new merchandise alongside the road. The stores were all lit up, and many of them were setting some of the merchandise outside. The street was lined with vendors selling jewelry, carpets, antiques, leather, and spices.

Kari stared at a small dark-haired boy—he was slicing cheese and wrapping it up.

She was surprised to see that most of the women were not wearing veils. She had always heard they covered their faces.

They drove further through the city, passing restaurants, hotels that looked like Bed and Breakfast Inns, and a huge cinema.

Masory made a couple more turns to the right, taking them to a dissimilar part of the city. The further they drove, the more poverty materialized. They passed a few rough blocks that convinced Kari they were in crime vicinity—there were numerous nightclubs with posters of nude women tacked on the walls. Several scraggly men were hanging out on a corner smoking and laughing. A dirty-faced guy on a bench huddled under a soiled blanket. Another old man in ragged clothes and tattered socks, staggered down the street, clutching a bottle in a paper sack.

Kari felt Jill's body stiffen next to hers. She glanced at her—Jill's eyes grew hazy as she chewed nervously on her bottom lip. If only she could speak to Jill to comfort her. But she was too scared to say a word, for fear of what Vaar would do. She quietly slipped her hand into Jill's and squeezed it tightly. Jill's cold, delicate fingers quivered in Kari's hand.

Kari was relieved that Vaar and Sahre were continuing with their own conversation, and not paying any attention to her or Jill. She couldn't stand it when Vaar looked at her—he sent chills up and down Kari's spine. She knew she had to get Jill away from these horrible people as soon as possible.

After a few more miles, Masory took another left turn, down a trashy, deserted street. Kari cursed silently. She had lost her sense of direction, as well as the number of turns.

She stared at the neglected buildings along side of the street; they had shattered windows, broken shutters, faded paint, and looked to be vacant. Kari didn't see a single soul anywhere.

Suddenly, Masory slammed on the brake and the car came to a screeching halt in front of a large structure that looked like a deserted apartment building.

Kari was more confused than ever. *There's no way I'm going into that rat hole with these people,* she thought. She grasped Jill's arm to keep her from climbing out of the car.

"Get out," Vaar ordered.

Kari reluctantly climbed out of the car after Jill, and they followed Sahre up the sidewalk to the entrance of the building. Vaar trailed close behind them.

Sahre knocked on the door and shouted some words in Turkish. The door swiftly opened, and a rough, longhaired bearded man holding a rifle stood aside so they could enter.

Kari stepped into the hallway and huddled close to Jill. She glanced into the front room; it was disgustingly gross. Trash was scattered on the floor, and plates with dried-up food were stacked on the dusty end tables. Kari cringed at the sight of a roach crawling across one of the empty plates. She glanced

85

toward the stack of dirty clothes lying against the back wall of the room.

By the sound of Vaar's voice, he wasn't happy at the way the place looked either. He shouted angrily at the grungy man. The Turkish guy hung his head and kept repeating evet every few minutes.

Vaar finished cursing at the man, and turned toward Kari and Jill. "Follow me."

Kari and Jill reluctantly followed Vaar up the stairs and down a long narrow hallway, to a room in the middle of the hall. Kari had heard female voices from the other rooms as she passed by the closed doors. For a split second, she could have sworn she heard a girl's voice whispering in English.

Vaar grasped the handle of the door and turned the knob. He led Kari and Jill into a small room with two cots. The room was in worse shape than the one they had stayed in back in the States. The dirty paint was peeling off the walls, and the wooden floors were stained with dark splotches. There was absolutely nothing else in the room except for the two cots and a blanket and a pillow on top of each one of them. There weren't any dressers or tables, not even a pitcher of water or a toilet. If it weren't for the sunshine radiating through the two bare windows, the room would be completely dark.

"Don't get too comfortable, girls—you will only be here a short time. Your meals will be served to you in here." Vaar pointed down the hallway in the direction they had come. "The restroom is down the end of the hallway on the right hand side. It won't be as luxurious as you rich American girls are used to. We do things differently in this country. The toilets will look quite different." Vaar chuckled. "You may only go to the restroom. Stay in this room unless you are told otherwise." Vaar glared from Kari to Jill, "This door won't be locked, but there are guards all though this building, so I wouldn't try to escape if I were you. The guards have permission to shoot you, if you try." He grinned heartlessly. "Are there any questions?"

Kari and Jill shook their heads.

Kari just wanted the horrible man to leave, so she could sort through all the misfortunes that kept occurring.

86

Vaar leaned the top half of his body toward Kari's. He brushed the back of his hand against her cheek. "You are a prize to me—you know."

Kari flinched and bowed her head down to the floor.

"We don't have redheads in this country." Vaar gently slid his hand down the back of Kari's shining red hair. He wrapped her hair around his hand and suddenly, tugged on it, jerking Kari's face up toward the ceiling. "You look at me when I am talking to you."

Kari remained silent, although the pain brought tears to surface.

Vaar instantly released Kari's hair and shoved her toward the wall. "Get the fuck out of my sight." He turned toward Jill and his eyes lingered on her chest. "Do you know how to make a man happy?"

Jill's body trembled. "No," she whispered.

Vaar patted Jill on her rear. "You will learn real soon—or you will be sorry." He glared at Jill before turning to leave and slamming the door behind him.

Kari's dazed eyes remained on the closed door. The back of her head was throbbing against her skull. She broke her trance and glanced toward Jill, who was shaking hysterically. She rushed over and wrapped her arms around Jill's shoulders. She didn't know how much longer Jill could go on. "Are you okay? Calm down, he's gone now." Kari stroked Jill's head softly. "I won't let him hurt you."

Jill sobbed, bowing her head down on Kari's shoulder. "I hate him!"

"Come on, honey, pull yourself together."

"Why, Kari? Why?" Jill slowly cocked her head up. "Why is this happening to us?"

"I don't know, sugar, but we'll make it. Just be patient." Kari held Jill close to her while she sobbed. "We'll just have to wait until the right time to make our escape."

"But what if we can't?"

"I won't let you down. I will get us back home—one way or another. You have to believe me." Kari didn't know if she could convince Jill to trust her, but she knew she had to try, although

87

she was skeptical herself. "I have to go to the restroom. Do you want to go with me?"

"I'm not staying here alone." Jill clung to Kari's arm as she stepped out of the room.

As they crept by the rooms, Kari again, thought she heard English chatter behind one of the doors. She stopped to pause in front of the closed door. She spun quietly around to face Jill. "Listen. Do you hear English in there?"

Jill nervously glanced up and down the hall before pressing her ear up against the closed door. "Yeah, I do. But let's go before we get in trouble."

Kari listened a few more seconds and then continued down the hall.

A young, dark-haired girl wearing a slightly bloody bandage over her left cheek was walking out of the restroom just as they were coming in. The girl's somber black eyes met Kari's; she quickly looked away and hurried down the hall without speaking.

"What was that all about?" Kari asked Jill as she closed the restroom door.

"I don't know. She couldn't have been over twelve years old."

"Yeah, I know. I started to speak to her, but she took off before I could get a word out." Kari walked over to the stall and swung the door open. "Oh my gosh, what is this?" Kari stared at a round ceramic hole in the floor where the toilet should be.

Jill walked over and stood behind Kari to gaze at the hole in the floor. "So that's why Vaar started laughing earlier when he was telling us about the restroom."

"How the heck are you supposed to use it? And where's the toilet paper?"

Jill glanced around. "There's a roll of toilet paper." She pointed at the sink counter. "And I guess you're supposed to squat over the hole."

"Hand me the paper." Kari reached for the toilet paper from Jill and hesitantly slipped inside the stall.

Kari finished and explored around the restroom while waiting for Jill. She noticed that there were two separate stalls—each of

88

them had a hole in the floor. She walked around the corner and spotted a large shower room with four different shower faucets. There weren't any curtains to dress behind, just a big open space with a small, faded white bench to lay your clothes on. A high-up window was covered with a ragged yellow flowered curtain.

Kari figured there wouldn't be much privacy when they showered. She had always been modest, and the thought of taking a shower with a bunch of girls appalled her. Even in her physical education classes, she would avoid taking a shower until all the other girls were finished. She stared at the vacant space—if she did decide to take a shower she would have to be sure to get down here before anyone else. Kari rolled her eyes—she couldn't believe she was fretting over taking a shower in front of a bunch of girls when she should be more concerned about what Vaar's intentions were.

Jill came out of the stall carrying the toilet paper. "Maybe we should leave this where it was." She sat the roll back on the counter.

"Hey, come here." Kari motioned Jill into the shower room.

"Shouldn't we get back to the room?" Jill asked, glancing uncertainly toward the door.

"Don't worry." Kari slid the bench over against the wall and climbed up on it to peek out the window. "Wow—I don't think we should jump from here. We've got to be twenty feet up."

Jill cautiously crept over and climbed upon the bench to peer outside. "You're right—we are far up. There isn't a thing to climb onto out there either."

Kari pointed toward the door at the back of the house. "That must be the back door."

Just then, the back door flung open, and the same man who had let them in the front door stepped out, carrying a bucket full of garbage. He trudged over toward the alley, lifted a lid off a metal trashcan, and dumped the garbage inside. Kari and Jill quickly ducked as he spun around toward the house. Kari slowly lifted her head to peek over the ledge of the windowsill.

The man was stooped over next to a towering tree. Suddenly, he glanced up and down the alley, reached inside a circular hole in the tree, and pulled out a brown pouch. He quickly pulled a wad of bills out of his pants pocket and stuffed the bills inside the pouch. He again looked uneasily around the vicinity before placing the pouch back in the tree.

Kari quickly bowed down as he turned back toward the house. She peeped again just as the back door slammed shut.

"What did you see?" Jill asked, wide-eyed.

"See that tree?" Kari pointed to the tree. "He has a pouch hidden in there, with money in it."

"Really? I wonder why."

"I don't know, but when we escape—if we have time, let's grab it."

"Yeah, that might come in handy!"

Kari climbed down off the bench. "Come on—we better get back to the room before they come looking for us."

Kari and Jill hurried back down the hall, pausing briefly in front of the door they had heard English behind. This time it was silent. They quietly slipped back into their own room.

"What do you think they are going to do with us?" Jill asked as soon as she closed the door.

"I'm clueless." Kari sat down on the cot. "I can't seem to make heads or tails out of any of this."

"Do you think there are more girls here that are going through the same thing as us?"

"Maybe. I do know one thing; I'm sure that young girl we almost ran into knows something."

Jill brushed a few tears off her cheeks with the back of her hand. "Kari, I'm so scared."

"I know you are. So am I, but have some faith." Kari patted the cot. "Come sit—I think I'm going to hang out in the restroom this evening and see if I can find out something from the other girls. You probably should stay in the room in case someone comes to check on us."

"And if someone comes—then what am I suppose to say?"

"Just say I'm in the restroom and after they leave, come and get me."

"Oh, please be careful. If something happens to you, I'll kill myself."

"Jill, don't say things like that. You wouldn't do something like that."

Tears continued to ooze from Jill's eyes. "Oh, yes I would, too. I am not staying in this dump and letting that monster touch me."

Kari stood. "You're just emotionally drained. I want you to lie down for awhile." She gathered the cover in her arms.

"What are you going to do?" Jill lifted her legs upon the cot and laid her head on the pillow.

Kari gently spread the blanket over her. "I need to think about our escape. Go to sleep, okay? You'll feel better once you have rested."

"Thanks, Kari. You're the best friend in the world." Jill's tears ceased as she closed her eyes.

"And you're mine. Now, get some rest." Kari patted Jill's head.

Kari wandered over toward her own cot, pushed it up against the wall, and climbed upon it. She laid her head down on the pillow and stared up at the ceiling. She stared at a small black spider as it crawled across the ceiling and disappeared into a web in the corner. She closed her eyes, trying to shut out the repulsive room and the horrible situation they were in. But she couldn't quit thinking about the reality of it all. She let the tears flow freely, rolling off the side of her face and splashing onto the pillow. She didn't have a clue how they were going to escape or if they even could. She just knew she had to keep telling Jill positive things or she would freak out.

Kari thought of Kelli and her parents. She was sure they were frantically worried by now. If only Kelli was here with her, she would know what to do; she had always been able to figure a way out of the toughest situations.

Kari's mind wandered to the time that she broke her mother's jewelry dish that her great grandmother had given her, and Kelli was the one who bailed her out. Her mother had told both of them to stay out of her jewelry, but Kari and Kelli didn't abide. They had been playing dress-up, and Kari had wanted to wear her mother's flowered brooch. She'd snuck into her mother's room and lifted the lid off the glass jewelry dish to sneak the

91

brooch out, but her hand slipped, knocking the dish off onto the floor. It broke into four different pieces. Kari had tried to glue it back together, but the glue wouldn't stick. Kelli came up with a brilliant idea: they would tell their mother that they wanted to surprise her by cleaning the house, and they accidentally knocked the dish off the dresser when they were dusting. It worked—their mother believed them, and they didn't get into trouble.

Kari smiled, reminiscing the comical day. When she and Kelli had returned to their room they had laughed until they were crying.

"Oh Kelli, I need you more than ever," Kari mumbled miserably.

After several drowsy blinks, she finally closed her eyes, and drifted off to sleep. A vision of Kelli when they were younger floated through her head. Kelli was in the swing at the park, and Kari was pushing her.

"Push me higher, Kari, please…" Kelli whined.

"But mommy says not to go too high."

"C'mon Kari, I want to touch the clouds with my toes."

"Okay, here I go." Kari pushed the swing higher.

"I did it! I did it, Kari! I can feel the clouds with my toes," Kelli squealed.

"What does it feel like?"

"It feels soft, like cotton candy. Push me higher, Kari. I want to go higher."

Kari pushed the swing even higher. Suddenly, Kelli disappeared into the sky. The swing returned back to Kari and it was empty.

"Kelli, where are you? Come back. Please, come back, Kelli. I want to go with you," Kari cried. "Kelli, you can't leave me. You promised we would always stay together. Come back, Kelli, so we can go through the clouds together. Please, Kelli—through the clouds we'll go…"

Kari slowly stirred awake; sweat was dripping off her forehead. She rose up and threw her legs over the side of the cot, visions of the dream still fresh in her mind. The dream had seemed so real. The loneliness she had felt in the dream all came rushing back to her as she glanced around at her surroundings, realizing how far away from home she actually was.

CHAPTER NINE

Kelli rubbed the sleep out of her eyes and rolled over to check the time—it was already 8:00 p.m. She had only meant to rest her eyes, but must have fallen asleep. It was so strange—she had been dreaming of her and Kari playing at the park when they were little. The dream had left her feeling unbearably lonely. She missed Kari more than she ever thought possible.

She threw the blankets off and jumped out of bed. She was eager to see if her parents had heard any more news. They had been sleeping earlier when she returned home, so she hadn't bothered them. She had called Hank, but he didn't have any new information—he did inform her that Doug's car was a black Mustang, though. Kelli told him about the car that had been following her again, but she purposely left out the part about her visit with Jay.

Kelli ran down the stairs and into the kitchen.

Frances and Bill were sitting at the kitchen table. Frances was clutching tightly to Kari's coat, and Bill was doodling on a notepad.

Kelly instantly sensed something was wrong. "What's going on?" She glanced from her mom to her dad.

Frances gazed down at the blue wool coat. "She forgot her coat." Tearful sobs escaped her throat. "Now, she probably won't need it."

Bill reached across the table and squeezed his wife's hand. "Calm down, honey. Let's not jump to conclusions." He reached

94

over and pulled the other empty chair out. "Sit down, Kelli." He waited for Kelli to sit. "Hank called—they found Doug Parker and his car." Bill hesitated. "Unfortunately, they found him dead in his car, at the bottom of a pond."

"Oh, no!" Kelli was flabbergasted. "And Kari and Jill?"

"They weren't in there with him. But..." Bill's quivering voice lowered, "They did find Jill's purse in the car. It was stuck under the seat."

"No, please, don't tell me that! That means they were with him." Kelli threw her head back. "This isn't right!" She beat her fists on the table. "It isn't fair! Kari and I are supposed to go through life together. I don't want to go through life without her. I can't live without her. I can't do it, Dad!"

Kelli stood and Bill embraced her. He glanced at Frances as he comforted Kelli. "Come on, ladies, let's not get discouraged yet." He reached over and stroked his wife on the head. "They haven't found the girls. We have to believe that they're alive until we hear different." Bill lifted Kelli's chin up so her eyes met his. "Understand?"

"Yeah, I guess." Kelli cleared her throat, "What happened to Doug? Did he wreck?"

"No, he didn't." Bill glanced uncomfortably toward the floor and then met Kelli's gaze. "He was killed first. They think he was strangled, although they found an abrasive spot on his head where he had been hit, too."

Poor Jay, Kelli thought silently. "Have they told Doug's roommate yet?"

"Hank didn't say, but I'm sure they probably have notified Doug's parents by now."

Frances glanced up from her tissue in alarm. "What if they're torturing Kari right now?" She grimaced. "Bill, we've got to go down to the pond and look around. Maybe we can find some clues that will lead us to Kari and Jill."

"I've already suggested that, honey, and Hank said there wasn't a thing we could do, and we would just be in the way. He said they have the place blocked off and no one could get through anyway. He promised to call us if anything else shows up."

95

"I feel so useless." Frances's snivels ceased as she stared helplessly out the kitchen window.

"I need to go." Kelli hurriedly grabbed her jacket off the coat rack.

Frances glared at Bill. "Bill, tell her she's not leaving this house."

"Where are you going?" Bill asked as Kelli grabbed her keys out of her purse.

"I don't know. I just need some fresh air. I think I'll just drive around awhile. I promise I won't be gone long."

Bill shook his head. "I don't think you should be driving while you're so upset."

"I'm fine, Dad. I was shocked at first, but for some reason, I believe Kari and Jill are okay. I just need to get out for a little bit—I'll be fine.

Bill glanced toward his wife's pleading eyes. "Honey, she'll be okay." He patted Kelli on the back. "Don't forget to take your cell phone with you in case we need to get hold of you."

"I will." Kelli kissed her dad on the cheek and bent down to kiss her mom. "I'll be fine, Mom—don't worry." She rubbed her mother's hand gently, and then hurried out the door.

Kelli was actually surprised it had been that easy to get out of the house. Hank must have not told them about the car following her earlier. She was thankful, because they probably wouldn't have let her leave if they had known. She hated to lie to them, but she couldn't shake the urge to see how Jay was doing. He must be devastated. She prayed that she wouldn't get the same dreadful news about Kari and Jill.

Kelli pulled up in front of Jay's house and parked directly behind a patrol car. She figured the police would have already been there—maybe this wasn't a good time to come. But she had already parked, so she figured she might as well go up to the door.

After a short time, Kelli finally climbed out of the car. She pondered a few minutes longer, and then shuffled up the sidewalk and pushed the doorbell.

Surprisingly, Hank opened the door. "Kelli? What are you doing here?"

Kelli fiddled with her keys. "Oh, hi—I was just worried about Jay and thought I would stop by and check on him.

Hank looked puzzled. "You know Jay?" He looked accusingly at Kelli. "I didn't think you knew Jay and Doug."

"I didn't know Doug, but I met Jay earlier this afternoon when I stopped by here." Kelli wished she would have driven on by—she didn't suspect Hank to be the officer with Jay. "I know I shouldn't have come here by myself earlier, and I apologize for interfering with police business, but I was frantic at the time.

Hank frowned and dropped his arms to his sides. He hesitated, and then held the door open. "Well, come on in." He waited for Kelli to step inside. "Jay's not doing so well. He went to the restroom to see if he could find some aspirin. He should be back any minute."

Kelli could tell Hank wasn't at all thrilled about her showing up uninvited. She entered the living room just as Jay staggered toward them from the hallway. She could tell he had been crying. "I'm so sorry. Is there anything I can do?"

"Kelli, I'm surprised to see you. Thank you for stopping by." Jay grasped Kelli's hands and hugged her. He released her and reached for the package of cigarettes on the counter. "I can't believe this is happening. I keep thinking I'm going to wake up from this horrible nightmare any moment."

"I know, I keep thinking the same thing," Kelli said.

Hank pulled a pocket-sized notebook and pen out of his pocket. "Would you two mind sitting for a few minutes? Kelli, I was getting ready to call you and your folks but since you're here now—I can fill you in on the details."

Kelli quietly sat down in the center of the couch.

Jay grabbed an ashtray, started toward the couch, and then abruptly stopped, stubbed out his cigarette, and set the ashtray back on the counter. "It's still hard to break old habits." He took a seat next to Kelli.

Hank was silent as he reviewed his notes. He finally looked up at Kelli. "Well, we followed up on that car that was following you earlier, and we think we located it. There was a silver Porsche rented from a car rental place in Glendale. It had been rented out for the last three weeks and was returned today. A

Turkish gentleman using the name of Ivan Mahalan was the man who rented it." He tapped his pen in rhythm against his leg. "We're in the process of tracking him now."

"Do you think he is involved with Kari and Jill's disappearance?" Kelli glanced sympathetically toward Jay. "And Doug's death?"

"It seems to be leaning that way, but we're not certain yet." Hank stopped tapping and used the pen to itch the tip of his nose.

"I guess you haven't found any more clues on Kari or Jill, have you?"

"I'm sorry to say we haven't, but I have almost every man in the unit working on this case. It's just a matter of time now." Hank's cell phone rang. "Excuse me, I'll be right back. I'll take this outside."

Kari and Jay sat silently until Hank returned.

"Well, we just got some more information. They found an old warehouse that we believe Doug's car was parked at earlier. They also found a pair of girl's socks that might be your sister's or Jill's." Hank returned his cell phone to his jacket pocket and wiped the drops of perspiration off his forehead with the back of his hand.

Kelli's heart pounded. "I would know if they're Kari's if I saw them. May I please go look?"

"They will have them back at the station shortly. I hate to leave you two, but I really need to get down to the crime scene and help out."

"Please, let me go with you," Kelli pleaded.

"I'm sorry, Kelli—I can't let you do that." Hank returned the notebook to his pocket. "Why don't you go on down to the police station, and I'll call Jack and give him permission to show you the socks. I will call you just as soon as I know anything else." He glanced at his watch. "I will have one of my men go by your house and fill your parents in."

"Can you least tell me where this building is?" Kelli asked.

"You wouldn't remember it—it's before your time; it use to be called the old Laughlin Shirt Factory. It's a few miles past Jericho Creek."

"I've heard of that place before." Kelli paused—she was uncertain how much she could trust Hank. "Hey, could you not tell my parents that you've seen me?"

"Any certain reason why?" Hank's eyes narrowed. "You're not hiding anything from me, are you?"

"No, it's just that my parents are worried about me, and I didn't tell them I was coming by here. I told them I was just riding around. My mom would be furious with me."

"Well, I can't lie to them, Kelli. They have every reason to be worried, and I don't blame them." The warning look in his eyes was stern. "Did you tell them about the car following you earlier?"

"No, I didn't—only because they were sleeping and then I forgot," she lied.

Hank shook his head. "I think you need to go home as soon as you leave the police station and stay there until we notify you." He shook his index finger at Kelli. "I won't go out of my way to tell your parents I've talked to you, but if they ask—I'm not going to lie. But you have to promise me that you will stay home where it's safe until we can trace down all the evidence we need to figure out this mystery."

"Okay, I will." Kelli rose from the couch.

Jay, with slouched shoulders, followed her to the door. She turned to hug him. "I'm so sorry. If you need anything, give me a call."

"I might just do that. I'm going to be climbing the walls without anyone to talk to. I already miss him so much; I can't even bear to look at his picture." Jay bowed his head toward the floor.

"Well, you can call any time." Kelli stood on her tiptoes and kissed Jay on the cheek. Her heart ached for him. She called out, "Bye Hank," and hurried out the door. She had to get out of there before she burst into tears.

The drive to the station was wearisome. She struggled to eliminate the negative presumptions that were building up. She couldn't let her mind fill with unconstructive thoughts now. She massaged her temple with one hand while she steered with the

99

other. She knew she needed to stay focused. She wanted so much to believe that Kari and Jill were still alive.

"Kari, look, there's a falling star," Kelli said aloud, glancing up toward the sky. *I am losing my mind,* she thought, as she shifted her eyes back on the road. *My God, Kari, I was only kidding when I told you that you drove me crazy!*

Kelli had been waiting in Hank's office for fifteen minutes when an officer marched through the doors, carrying a clear plastic bag containing the socks. Kelli stood motionless, staring in disbelief at the socks. She instantly recognized the blue striped socks because they were hers. Kari had borrowed them from her yesterday morning because she didn't have any clean ones.

Kelli squeezed her eyes shut to fight off the tears burning behind her eyelids. She was half-scared to open them in fear she would fall apart. She finally opened her eyes. The officer, Jack, was holding a glass of water. She took a sip before informing him that she recognized the socks. She again fought back the emotions building inside of her until the officer had dismissed her. When she was finally returned to her own car in the parking lot, she couldn't hold back any longer—she let the tears come, not caring about the cars passing by. She folded her arms over the steering wheel and laid her head on them. She couldn't believe this was happening!

After awhile, Kelli slowly raised her head and stared out the window. She whirled some strands of her hair around her finger as she tried to fit the pieces together. For some peculiar reason, she still believed Kari was still alive. The officer had told her the socks were found under a bed, between the mattress and the box spring. Kelli thought it almost sounded like someone purposely hid the socks there—it had to be Kari who hid them, hoping someone would find them. Kelli could vaguely recall watching a movie with Kari when they were younger, and a woman in the movie who had been kidnapped had done almost the exact thing. Suddenly, Kelli truly believed that Kari was still alive and was leaving clues for them to find her.

Kelli had a sudden urge to find Hank to see if he'd found out any more information on the Turkish guy. She was sure that that particular Turkish man could lead her to Kari and Jill's

100

whereabouts. She was torn whether to go home or try to find the old warehouse. She figured if Kari and Jill were still alive, they weren't anywhere near the warehouse now. She could always call Hank on his cell phone. Besides, her parents were probably getting worried about her. She pulled away from the curb and drove toward home.

Frances, with a flushed face and angered eyes, confronted Kelli as soon as she walked through the door. "Where have you been? We've been worried sick about you!"

"I haven't been gone that long." Kelli dumped her purse on the kitchen table. "I stopped by the police station. Did anyone come by here and tell you guys about Kari's socks?"

Bill stopped pacing the floor and faced Kelli. "Yes, Hank sent an officer over here to fill us in. However, at the time they weren't sure if the socks even were Kari's or Jill's." He shoved his fidgety hands into his trousers pockets. "They're supposed to call, and we're supposed to meet them down at the police station." His eyes remained on Kelli. "Did you get to see the socks?

"Yes, I saw them and they were definitely mine—I lent them to Kari yesterday."

"Oh no!" Frances covered her mouth. "What does this mean?"

"Listen Mom, I think Kari put the socks there. They found them between the mattress and box frame. I think she was trying to leave us some sort of sign that she's still alive."

"I sure hope you're right," Bill shifted his weight from one leg to the other as he ran his hand over his unshaven chin.

The phone rang, startling everyone. Kelli quickly reached for the receiver. "Hello."

"Is this Kelli?"

"Yes."

"This is Hank. I know it's getting awful late, but I wanted to let your parents know the latest. Do you think they would want to drive down here?"

"I know they will. Could you tell me if you heard any more on Ivan Mahalan?"

101

"Not yet, Kelli. I have had most of my men searching the warehouse for clues. But it's getting too late, and it's hard to see much with flashlights. They might come up with some more evidence in the morning."

"What are you searching for? You don't think you're going to find..." Kelli couldn't bring herself to say it.

"We're just looking for any little clue that will help us find your sister—that's all."

"Okay." Kelli wasn't sure if Hank was being sincere or not. "Well, my parents will be down there shortly."

Kelli, dazed, placed the receiver in the cradle and stared into space.

"What is it, Kelli—was it Hank—what did he say?" Bill asked.

Kelli broke her trance and turned toward her dad. "Hank wants you and mom to drive down to the station, and he'll fill you in on all the latest details. But there's still no sign of Kari and Jill."

Bill was already reaching for the jackets off the coat rack. "Aren't you coming with us?"

"No, I don't think so. I'm starving. You can fill me in when you get back."

Frances slipped her arms through the coat Bill was holding out. "I'm sorry, Kelli, I didn't cook anything for dinner. I haven't felt much like doing anything—there is a package of ham in the refrigerator if you want to make a sandwich."

"That's fine. I'll find something."

Frances kissed her daughter on the forehead. "Be sure to lock up."

"I will." Kelli stood in the doorway as her parents hurried down the sidewalk. She waited for her dad to depress the button on his electronic key ring to unlock the car doors. She waved, slammed the front door shut, and locked it. She immediately grabbed the phone book off the counter and hurried into the living room. She decided if nobody else was going to look for Ivan Mahalan then she would do it herself. If Ivan had already returned the rental car—that probably meant he planned to leave town. She couldn't believe the police hadn't thought of that.

More than likely Ivan was flying off to somewhere. She skimmed the yellow pages under "Airports".

Kelli dialed several of the nearby airports. But after several attempts and repeatedly being told that they couldn't give out personal information, she gave up.

She kicked her shoes off and sighed. She was sure there had to be a connection between Ivan, and Kari and Jill's disappearance.

The phone rang, interrupting Kelli's thoughts. "Hello."

"Kelli, it's me. Are you doing okay?" Bill asked.

"I'm fine. Is something wrong?"

"Well, Hank has received some more information. Some Turkish men were using the warehouse. The police have figured out all their real names, and they have located all of them purchasing airline tickets back to Turkey."

"You're kidding."

"No. But they didn't all fly at the same time—they took separate flights. The latest one, the name you mentioned earlier, Ivan Mahalan—actually, his real name is Ivan Berlin—he took a flight out just a few hours ago. They think he is working for a man by the name of Vaar Roami."

"Really? So what else did they find out?" Kari glanced up at the clock on the wall; it was 11:30 p.m.

Bill hesitated. "Well, Kel, there's more bad news—none of them were flying with any female passengers."

Kelli froze—those were the dreaded words she had feared. She swallowed—her throat was suddenly dry. "So what does this mean?"

"Hank's not sure. He's asking for some help from the FBI. He assures us they will immediately start tracking these guys." Bill paused to cough. "But they are sending another search team out in the morning over by the warehouse." Bill covered the mouthpiece for a few seconds. "Kelli, as much as I hate to say this, we're going to have to be prepared for the worst. If we know they were with the Turkish men in the warehouse, and now they're not with the Turkish men..." Bill's voice trailed off.

"Don't think that way, Dad. I know Kari and Jill are still alive. Let's go to the Drury Airport and ask around to see if anyone has seen them there."

"Now?" Bill asked surprised.

Kari glanced back at the clock—it would be midnight soon. "Well, I guess we do need to wait until there are more people working. Let's go in the morning."

"I don't know, Kel, if we should do that. I don't think Hank would agree. Maybe we should let the FBI handle this."

"Dad, I know Kari's alive, and she's waiting for us to find her—I can feel it in my bones. She intentionally left the socks—I know she did! Can't we just go and look around? We won't be hurting anything by just asking people if they have seen her," Kelli said, her stubbornness not waning.

"I don't know, honey. I sure hope you're intuition is right. I pray your sister is still alive." Bill's voice quivered. "Let me think about it." He paused. "Your mom's not doing so well— we'll be on our way home shortly. Let's try not to talk about this until I can get her to take some sleeping pills and lie down. There's a nurse with her now."

"What happened?"

"They think she might have had an anxiety attack. She'll be fine; she's just stressed out."

"Okay, I'll get some coffee started."

"Have you eaten anything?" Bill asked.

"Not yet. I'll make us some sandwiches."

"That sounds great, honey. We're going to need our strength over the next few days."

Kelli was definitely confused about Kari and Jill's whereabouts. She had been almost certain that they were with Ivan. Now, she didn't know what to think. She fought off the direction her mind was drifting. She couldn't let herself consider anything so appalling.

"God, please let Kari be okay," she prayed aloud as she started the coffeepot. Kelli suddenly found herself on her knees. She held her hands in a praying position, closed her teary eyes, and prayed for a miracle.

CHAPTER TEN

Kari and Jill sat silently as they watched the man roughly place the tray of flat unleavened bread and water on the floor. Kari could smell the stench of the bearded man across the room. It was the same guy who had opened the front door for them and who had hid the money in the tree. He never once looked up at them, and he seemed to be in a hurry to leave.

Kari's stomach rumbled at the smell of the bread. She was beginning to wonder if Vaar had decided not to feed them. They hadn't eaten anything since the flight, and it was already growing dark outside.

She waited until the stinky man left the room, and then she scampered over toward the food. "I was hoping we would get more than bread this time, but it's better than nothing." She handed Jill a slice.

"Thanks." Jill reached for the bread and waited for Kari to pour the water. "I'm starving." She stuffed a huge portion into her mouth.

"Me too." Kari chewed hungrily and then reached for another piece. "I'm going down to the restroom in a bit and hang out until someone comes in there."

"You're going to leave me all alone, aren't you?" Jill snarled up her nose.

"You'll be fine. Hopefully, someone will come in there and tell me what the hell is going on around here."

Jill reached for the pitcher of water and filled her glass back up. "What do I do if that grimy man comes back here to get the tray?"

"Just tell him I went to the restroom—if he even understands English. If he doesn't—just point down the hallway."

"What if he decides to wait here until you come back?"

"I don't look for that to happen. Not if he has all these rooms to tend to, delivering food and picking up the trays. You worry too much!" Kari finished eating and brushed the crumbs off the front of her dress. "Now stay put. I'm going down there."

"Kari, please be careful...and don't leave me for too long."

"I won't." Kari cracked the door open and glanced up and down the hall before stepping out. She hurried down the long haul not pausing to listen to the closed door this time. She didn't want the man catching her in the hallway, or she wouldn't get to linger in the restroom like she planned.

The restroom was empty—she used the so-called toilet and then plopped down on the bench to wait. After ten tedious minutes, Kari pulled the bench over toward the window and climbed upon it. She peeked over the window ledge—the bearded man was hurrying toward the tree. He again acted restless as he glanced up and down the alley. He reached inside the tree and pulled out a brown sack that contained a large, oddly shaped bottle.

He unscrewed the lid and lifted the bottle to his lips several times, each time glancing up the alley. He finally screwed the lid back on, patted his stomach, and set the sack back inside the tree. He suddenly spun around, stumbling clumsily over a branch. Kari quickly ducked. She was certain he had been drinking alcohol. He must have left the money in the tree for someone to deliver him the booze. She would have to remember that—it could be an advantage for her and Jill when they made their escape: they could wait until the evening when he got drunk and passed out, and then sneak out of the house. Of course, they would have to watch out for the other guards, Kari thought. Vaar had said there were more.

Suddenly, the restroom door flew open, and Kari jumped off the bench. Two young girls marched into the room. Kari guessed

106

the thin, tall blond-haired girl to be close to her own age while the petite dark-haired girl looked to be a few years younger. They both had on dresses similar to the ones she and Jill wore, with the exception that the younger girl's blue flowered dress was soiled with dirt. Kari thought the blond was exceptionally pretty, with high cheekbones, a slender nose, and pale blue eyes—she looked like a movie star.

Kari smiled. "Hi. My name is Kari."

"You speak English. I don't believe this. My name is Renae." The blond grinned and motioned the dark-haired girl to go ahead into the restroom stall. "She doesn't speak English, but I can understand her pretty well."

"Where are you from, and how did you get here?" Kari detected a British accent.

"I'm from London, and I got here probably the same way you did—unwillingly."

"Do you know what they plan on doing with us?"

"Well, the best I can make of it from the others here..." Renae spoke softly while glancing over her shoulder toward the door. "They auction us off as slaves."

"What?"

Renae's eyes grew misty. "Yeah, I guess they sell us to men that don't have wives, and we become their slaves in any way they please."

"Oh my God, that's sick."

"I know; it makes me nauseous just thinking about it." Renae pointed to the stall the other girl was in. "Una told me the different things we will be expected to do such as cooking, sewing, and scrubbing." She nervously looped her fingers together and glanced down toward the floor. "And even other reluctant acts, such as sex—if they demand it."

"How does Una know all of this?"

"She's from here, and it's just something she knows about, I guess."

Una walked out of the stall and turned the faucet on to wash her hands.

"Una, this is Kari." Renae pointed toward Kari.

107

"Hello." Kari smiled warmly at the young girl. She looked similar to the girl who she had seen earlier with the bloody patch on her cheek—but this one seemed much friendlier. The girl grinned and nodded her head.

"Don't stay in here too long, or Scrooge will come looking for you." Renae disappeared into the stall.

Kari waited until Renae came out. "Did you say that nasty guy's name is Scrooge?"

"No, I just started calling him that, and now the others have picked up on it too."

"How long have you been here?"

"A little over a week." Renae brushed away a few fallen tears. "They took my friend Chandra away a few days ago."

"You mean you were captured with a friend and they separated you two?"

"Yes." Renae tore some toilet tissue off the roll and blew her nose.

"I'm with a friend, too. She won't survive if we're separated. We've got to get out of here, somehow, fast!"

"You mean—try to escape?" Renae motioned Una to wait for her.

"Yes. Has anyone else tried to escape?" Kari asked.

"Not to my knowledge, and I don't know why—they're probably too scared."

"Well, me and my friend Jill, we're going to try. Do you want to come with us?"

"I don't know." Renae glanced over at Una. "I don't want to leave her alone, and if we all try—we might get caught. I know; I'll help you and your friend, and if you succeed—you can tell the police where we are."

"I can do that. How many men are there here?"

"The only one I've ever seen is Scrooge, although Vaar said there were more—I don't think there is. Maybe that was just Vaar's way of scaring us."

Una sauntered over next to Renae and tugged on her dress.

Renae nodded to Una. "Okay, Una, we'll go now." She turned toward Kari. "We'd better go—Scrooge will be coming to pick up the trays. Meet me back here in an hour. Which room is yours?"

"The one in the center on the left side of the hall."

"I'll tap gently on your door twice to let you know I am on the way in here." Renae opened the door and glanced up and down the hall. She whirled back around to face Kari and whispered, "Wait a few minutes before you leave, so it doesn't look like we were talking."

"Okay, thanks Renae. Bye Una."

Una grinned and followed Renae out the door.

Kari quickly climbed back up on the bench to see if Scrooge was still outside anywhere, but she didn't see any sight of him. She waited a few more minutes and quietly went back to her own room.

Jill was sitting on her bed in an Indian position, staring at the wall. Kari decided it was probably best not to tell Jill everything that she'd learned. She knew if Jill found out that they were going to be separated, she would go berserk.

"Are you sleeping with your eyes open?" Kari asked.

"Almost." Jill's eyes shifted upwards toward Kari. "Well, what did you find out?"

"We were right. There is an English girl here; she's from London. Her name is Renae, and she was with a Turkish girl named Una."

"You really got to talk to them?"

"Yeah, and that's not all. Renae is going to help us escape."

"How?"

"I haven't figured that part out yet. But I'm working on it." Kari glanced at the floor and noticed the tray still in place. "So, he hasn't been here yet?"

"Nope, not yet. What else did Renae say?"

"She calls that man Scrooge, so that's what we'll call him."

"Scrooge?"

"Yeah. She also thinks he might be the only one here. She said that he's the only one she has ever seen."

"Did she know what they planned on doing with us?"

109

Kari shifted her back toward Jill and ambled toward her own cot. She could lie better if she wasn't looking Jill in the eyes. "No, she didn't know." Kari crawled upon her cot.

The door suddenly opened, silencing Kari and Jill. Scrooge glanced from Kari to Jill before picking up the tray and slamming the door shut.

"Boy, he sure is a friendly one," Jill said.

"No kidding. I saw him at the tree again. He has a bottle of booze hidden there."

"I wish he would bathe." Jill squeezed her nostrils.

"No joke!" Kari glanced down at the dress she had on. "We'll probably smell like that in a few days."

"Oh, I would love to take a shower. Do you think we could?"

"Why not? We'll just have to put dirty clothes back on." Kari didn't really care if they showered or not. Why should she get cleaned up if she was going to be sold to some brute? Maybe if she stunk badly enough the man wouldn't want her.

"Do you think they have any towels or soap?" Jill asked.

"I don't know. Renae is supposed to come and knock on our door in about an hour, so I'll meet her back in the restroom—I will ask her then."

"What are the girls like?" Jill asked.

"Una is from Turkey, so she has a dark complexion. She looks like she might be twelve or thirteen. She has long, silky black hair down to her waist—she resembles the girl we saw earlier, but she's a lot friendlier." Kari flipped to her side, facing Jill. She propped her elbow on the pillow and rested her head on her hand. "Renae is not only nice but beautiful. She looks like a model, tall and thin, blue eyes, curly blond hair."

"Are they both scared?" Jill's eyes shifted to a roach crawling across the floor. She leaped up to grab her shoe and smashed it. "Yuck, I hate those things."

Kari shuddered at the sight of the crushed roach. "Me too." She waited until Jill had climbed back upon the cot. "If the girls are scared, they don't show it."

"Well, they're braver than I am." Jill laid her head down on the pillow.

Kari gazed toward the window; the sun was setting and orange shadows were seeping through. All of a sudden, she had an idea—to slip downstairs to see where Scrooge was and to see if there were others. She figured that they should try to make their escape tomorrow night. They couldn't wait any longer than that and risk being auctioned off. "I think I need to sneak downstairs somehow." Her heart hammered in her chest at the thought.

"Oh Kari, no! That's too risky." Jill sprang to a sitting position.

"But if we plan on escaping, we need to know what we're up against."

"But what if you get caught? He might hurt you!" Jill drew her knees up to her chest and wrapped her arms around her legs.

"I know, I'll go back down to the restroom and wait for him to go back out to the tree, and then I'll rush downstairs and take a quick look around."

"What if there are more of them downstairs?" Jill shivered, grabbed the blanket, and threw it around her shoulders.

Kari's eyes widened. "I'll hold my stomach and pretend to be sick. I'll act like I was just looking for help." She smiled, proud of her speedy cleverness.

"I don't know." Jill stuck her thumbnail in her mouth and gnawed nervously on it.

"We have to try." Kari playfully pulled Jill's thumb out of her mouth. "You better save those nails. You might need them for self-defense." She instantly wished she could take back her words. Jill's eyes watered. "Hey, it's going to be okay." Kari hugged Jill and then stood.

"You're really going to do this, aren't you?" Jill asked.

"I have to! I'll be fine."

"Do you want me to go with you?" Tears slid down Jill's cheeks.

"No, you stay here. I'll be back shortly."

"Kari," Jill grabbed Kari's hand and gazed up at her. "Be careful."

"I will, I promise." Kari hurried out the door before Jill could change her mind. It was going to be tough when they actually

111

made their break. She knew Jill was going to be frantic, and it could mess up the whole plan.

***

Kari had been waiting only a few minutes when she spotted Scrooge back at the tree, nursing the bottle of booze. She immediately hopped off the bench, ran out the door, and down the hallway. She hesitated briefly at the top of the stairs, as she considered what would happen if she were caught—now wasn't the time to be having doubts. She covered her stomach with her hand just in case someone was at the bottom of the stairs. Kari gripped the rail to the stairs with her free hand to help steady her shaking legs.

She tiptoed slowly down the stairs, keeping her eyes alert. The silence consumed every move she made. The overhead light in the hallway shone brightly, making the living room completely visible. Her eyes darted from the front door to the living room and then to the room back past the living room—where the back door must be. There was still no sign of anyone.

She quickly glanced toward the front door, noticing a dead bolt and two chain locks. *That should be easy enough to get out of,* she thought. Kari shifted back toward the living room. It looked completely different from the way it looked this morning—it was actually clean. The floor had been swept; there weren't any dishes lying around or dirty clothes. Although the furniture had recently been polished, it still appeared worn-looking: the tan flowered couch's cushions were torn and soil-stained. The only other chair was a brown leather recliner with rips and white stuffing sticking out of it. There was a small rectangular coffee table and three square end tables. An old-fashioned radio sat on one of the end tables, and a small thirteen-inch TV sat on the other one. The yellowish-white wallpaper was flaking off the walls, and the green area rug was faded and stained.

Kari took a few steps toward the kitchen; she thought she should check out the back door locks, but sudden footsteps approaching the back of the house startled her. She speedily sprinted back up the stairs, skipping every other one. She heard the back door slamming just as she reached the top of the stairs. She quickly darted across the hallway, out of view. She quietly slipped down the hall and into her own room.

"That was close." Kari collapsed on the cot.

"What happened—did someone see you?" Jill shot to her feet.

"No, but I heard the back door opening, so I took off." Kari carefully explained all the particulars that she had witnessed. "We can easily get out of here tomorrow night."

"But Vaar said we would be killed if we get caught."

"Yeah, and he also said there was more guards downstairs, too." Kari paced uneasily beside her cot. "Why would he kill us? If he did that, then he wouldn't be able to auction us off, and he would lose money," she blurted out.

"What? Auction us off? What are you talking about?" Jill covered her mouth in surprise.

Kari's mouth dropped opened as she realized what she had said. She wanted to kick herself in the butt for the slip-up. "I'm sorry, I didn't tell you earlier because I didn't want to upset you."

"That was so wrong. You should have told me, Kari. Please, don't keep things from me."

Kari hung her head. "I'm really sorry." She quickly told Jill what Renae had actually said. "See why we need to escape as soon as we can?"

"Yeah, I do now."

"Renae should be coming soon. I'm going to rest my eyes and concentrate on our escape plan." Kari laid her head back on the pillow and shut her eyes.

She knew she didn't have much time to come up with a strategy. She wondered what Kelli would do if she were here now. She visualized Kelli driving the car around and around the mall, looking for her and Jill. How sad she must be, or perhaps she was glad. No, Kari was sure that deep down Kelli would be miserable without all of the joking they shared.

Kari recalled as young children how they were always trying to read each other's mind. They always thought if they

113

concentrated hard enough that they would be able to tell what the other one was thinking, but it never seemed to work.

Kari squeezed her eyes closed. She pictured Kelli in her mind and repeatedly told her where she was and that she needed help. Just like she imagined—nothing happened.

After a few minutes, Kari rolled over on her side so she was facing the wall. She felt like she was wasting her energy—no one was ever going to find them. And even if they did escape, they would probably be lost in Turkey forever. She was feeling desperately hopeless; she imagined that some of Jill's negative views were rubbing off on her.

The sudden tapping on the door made her jolt. It must be Renae. Kari knew she had to somehow reinforce her courage. She knew she couldn't give up now—she owed that much to Jill. She shook her head as if to finalize her decision—no way was she going to let Vaar defeat her; she was too determined to see her parents and Kelli again.

Kari sat up on the edge of the bed and spoke firmly to Jill, "Don't worry, Jill. We're going to get out of here! Vaar doesn't realize what he is up against," she said with a new kind of strength. She knew she had to believe they would survive, and she had to act fast before it was too late.

CHAPTER ELEVEN

Hank poured coffee into his prized Packers mug and moved toward the window. He sipped the steaming coffee while gazing up at the dark sky; the glinting morning sun was just starting to emerge through the foggy clouds. He placed the hot cup down on the file case, raised his arms above his head, and stretched his fingers toward the ceiling. He then bent forward, touched his toes, and raised his arms back up toward the ceiling and stretched again. He'd had only four hours of sleep the night before. It had been after midnight by the time Kari and Jill's parents left his office. By the time he had climbed into bed, he was wide awake; he couldn't seem to unwind from the day's events. It was after one before he had fallen asleep, although he knew he had to be at the office early because of the search party they had planned at sunrise.

Hank wished he could have worked out or ran a mile to ease his troubled mind. He knew working out did more than just condition his body; it was his escape from the downside of everyday tribulations. When he ran he was in his own little world: he didn't think about his job or financial problems—he would just let the wind hit him in the face while he took in nature's surroundings. He would daydream about future trips with his wife or the past night's lovemaking, but never would he let his mind drift back to his job. He always felt such immense strength after a good run.

Hank did a few more toe-touches and then reached for his mug. He walked over to his desk and glanced down at the pictures of Kari and Jill. He kicked the trashcan with the side of his foot and swore under his breath. He was almost certain they would find the bodies of the girls today. All the training he'd had never left him prepared for such tragedies. After the condition they found Doug's body in, Hank was scared of what they would find today. He never could comprehend the violent acts of such sickening criminals.

Hank dropped down into the swivel computer chair and spun around so he was facing the window again. He extended his hands out in front of him and popped his knuckles. He didn't understand why he always managed to get so emotionally involved in these cases. Most of the police officers he knew didn't seem to have this problem—or maybe they just didn't want to admit it.

He thought of Kari and Jill's parents. They were such nice people, and Kelli reminded him a lot of his own niece. Hank's stomach knotted as he realized how easily this could have been Leila they were looking for. He shuddered at the thought—no parent should have to go through such torture.

He hadn't been able to tell the girls' parents last night what he was suspecting they would find today. They were still hopeful, and he hadn't been able to bring himself to crush their expectations. Hank was sure the time would come soon enough when he would have to confirm his doubts to them.

The knock on the door snapped him back to the present. He wheeled his chair around so he was facing the door. "Come in."

Mike O'Donnell marched into the room. "Sir, I think we're about ready to go."

"How many do we have going, O'Donnell?"

"All of us, plus about fifty volunteers."

"Did you double check to make sure we've got everything?"

"Yes sir."

"Have you already briefed all of the volunteers?" Hank asked.

"Yes sir."

"Okay, I'll be out in a second."

116

Hank contemplated what the intentions of the Turkish men were. *Why would they purposely single out Kari, Jill, and Doug?* he wondered. *Had they planned it out, or were they randomly selected? Was it the thrill of the kill—and rape, perhaps? Why were there so many men involved; and why the separate flights back to Turkey?* There were so many unanswered questions. He was relieved that the FBI would be helping with the case.

The more Hank thought about the situation, the more he thought that it seemed to be premeditated. Kari and Jill's disappearance had to be planned ahead of time—he was almost certain of it. The questions continued to stumble through his head: *If the Turkish men planned to kidnap the girls and Doug— what did they want? Ransom? Did things go wrong? Maybe Doug tried to escape and they had to kill him—in which case, there still could be a chance that the girls were alive.*

Hank picked up the pictures on the desk again to study the young naïve faces closer. He wasn't quite sure what he was looking for. They were both attractive girls—*was it a kidnapping or rape?* He was sure it had to be one or the other, and if it was a kidnapping—then there was still a chance that they were alive.

He dropped the pictures back on the desk and grabbed his jacket off the coat rack. At least now, he had a bit of hope. Hank prayed he wasn't just building himself up to be let down, but he didn't think he could go out there looking for those girls if he didn't have something to encourage him.

***

Kelli finished drinking her juice, picked up the empty glass, and carried it over to the sink. "Let's go, Dad."

Bill glanced toward Frances. She was staring quietly out the window. "Honey, are you sure you're going to be okay?"

"I'll be fine." Frances continued to gaze outside.

"Now, remember to call Kelli's cell phone if Hank calls about anything, and we will come right home. Don't try to go down to the station without us. Okay?"

117

"I'll be fine." Frances casually glanced at her husband inexpressively and then back out the window. "Just bring me home some good news."

"We're going to try." Bill bent down and kissed Frances' cheek. "I love you."

Kelli gently stroked her mother's hair and then reached down and kissed her on the forehead. "I love you, too. We will call."

"Don't worry about me." A watery film coated Frances' eyes as she gazed up at Kelli. "Just bring your sister home."

Kelli hated leaving her mother alone. She looked ghastly: her usually rosy skin was pale, and she had dark circles under her once-bright eyes. She had been too depressed to eat, and Kelli was worried that she was getting weaker.

However, Kelli knew her mom wasn't in any condition to go with them either. Her mother had wanted to stay close to the phone anyway just in case Kari called. Kelli wished they had some relatives that could sit with her, but there weren't any. Both sets of Kari and Kelli's grandparents had already passed away. They only had some distant relatives in Wisconsin.

At first, Kelli's father was convinced that they should stay home. Kelli had to use a lot of her expertise to persuade her dad into driving down to the airport. He didn't think they should interfere with the investigation. However, after endless pleading, Kelli finally coaxed him into it. She had told him that they might find something out that the police might overlook. Her mother had insisted that they go; she claimed there wasn't anything any of them could do at home. Kelli was relieved because she had already made up her mind that if her father didn't go with her, she was going to go anyway.

Kelli and her father drove in silence most of the way to the Drury airport. It was a tedious two-hour drive.

Bill found a parking place near one of the entrance doors. "Don't forget the pictures," he said as he crawled out of the car.

Kelli grabbed the pictures of Kari and Jill out of the glove compartment and followed her dad into the airport.

They first stopped at the information desk, and Bill anxiously held out the pictures for the young, clean-cut gentleman to look out. "We need your help. These two girls are missing—could you please tell us if you have ever seen them before?"

The young man studied the pictures briefly. "They don't look familiar right off hand, but I see a lot of people every day. It's possible I could have seen them and don't remember. I'm sorry."

"Thanks anyway. Maybe you could help me with some flight information from yesterday. Could you tell me which flights went out to Turkey yesterday?" Bill asked.

"Well, they would have to go through JFK first. Let me see..." The man pushed some keys on his computer and wrote some gate numbers and departure times down on a piece of paper. "Here are the different flights that flew to JFK yesterday."

"Thanks a lot." Bill reached for the piece of paper. "We appreciate your help. If you do see them or even think you might have seen them—here's a number you can reach me at." Bill handed the young man one of his business cards.

"Sure." The man smiled, took the card, and bowed his head back over the computer.

Kelli and her father ventured to all the different gates on the list, and asked the various employees if they had seen Kari or Jill. Unfortunately, no one had. They even asked people waiting in the lobbies, the clerks at the bookstores, and the restaurant's waitresses.

Kelli sighed—her hopes were slowly diminishing. "Dad, I'm going to the restroom. I'll be right back."

Kelli politely smiled at the cleaning lady sweeping the floor in the restroom. "Hi. Could you tell me if you have ever seen these girls before?" Kelli held up the pictures.

The woman's eyes darted from Kari's picture to Kelli's face. "If that's not you, she must be your twin. Yes, I saw her yesterday." The lady glanced at Jill's picture. "Yes, she was with her—and another attractive lady."

"You're kidding! Are you sure?" Kelli was dumbfounded.

"Yes, they came in and used the restroom while I was filling the paper towels up. I never forget a face. The girls were very pretty, and the lady was extremely striking with all the diamonds she had on."

"Oh my! Could you tell me what she looked like—the lady?"

119

"Sure. She was tall, dark tan skin, dark eyes, and silver frame glasses—I think." She paused. "I believe she was wearing a tight-fitting black suit over her full-size bust." She giggled and held her hands up to her chest to emphasize the big size. "She had on a sparkling diamond necklace with matching earrings and some flashy rings on her fingers. Her hair was pulled into a bun—she definitely was a classy-looking lady—that is why I remember her so well.

"What about the girls? Were they okay? Did they look hurt or anything?" Kelli's breath ceased as she waited anxiously for a reply.

"No, not at all, they looked fine. They smiled at me as I went out the door."

"Oh wow, you see, they disappeared a couple of days ago, and we've been looking for them. Would you mind stepping outside and telling all of this to my father? He's waiting for me. He'll be thrilled to hear..." Kelli hesitated and then continued softly, "That they're still alive."

"I would be happy to." The sweet lady followed Kelli out the door.

"My name is Kelli Raker."

"I'm Barbara Hayes."

"You don't know how glad I am to meet you!" Kelli pointed toward her father sitting across the aisle in the waiting area. "There's my father." Kelli rushed toward her dad. "Guess what. Barbara, here—she saw them."

"Thank God!" Bill held out his trembling hand to shake Barbara's. "I'm Bill Raker."

Barbara repeated to Bill what she had told Kelli.

Kelli could easily relate to the tears glistening in her father's eyes. This was the best news they had received since Kari and Jill's disappearance. Kelli had been right after all—following Ivan had paid off. Everyone in town was searching in the wrong places—thinking they would find the girl's bodies like they had Doug's, but they were all wrong. Kari and Jill had boarded the airplane with another female. These Turkish men were clever—no one had considered Kari and Jill being with a female. Kelli was thrilled to learn that they were still alive.

She couldn't imagine why a female would want to be involved in such an appalling crime as kidnapping, though. It all seemed awfully suspicious. There was no doubt in Kelli's mind, though, that Kari and Jill had flown to Turkey, for whatever reasons, just as this mysterious lady and the Turkish men had.

Kelli waited while her dad jotted down all the information from Barbara so the police could contact her, and then they graciously thanked her.

After Barbara had left, Kelli turned and threw her arms around her dad's neck. "I knew they were still alive." Kelli and her dad embraced as they shared their emotions.

"I need to get hold of Hank right away." Bill glanced down at his watch. "We might as well drive back to his office."

"Dad, I know Kari is in Turkey. I wish we could go there."

"We can't go to Turkey, honey. We don't even know for sure if that's where they are. Maybe these men are just trying to mislead us."

"I'm sure that's where she is! They had a woman fly with them to lead us in a different direction. Why can't we go?"

Bill stared down at the piece of paper with the information that Barbara had given him while nervously shifting his weight to the other leg. "We just can't." He paused and then continued, "I'm sure Hank and the FBI will find them."

"I want to help find her. I don't want to wait—it could be too late then," she whined. "And we still have our passports from our London trip." Kelli stayed right on her dad's heels as they exited out the door.

"Kel, I know how devastating this is, but we just can't take off to Turkey. I want to find Kari more than anything. We have to trust that the police and the FBI will do everything in their power to find them. Let's go home and tell your mother the news." Bill wrapped his arm around Kelli's shoulders. "You know we can't leave your mother in the shape she is in anyway. I just don't think it would be in the best interest for any of us to fly there."

"Mom could go with us. No—someone needs to stay here just in case Kari tries to get hold of us."

121

"I do agree, though, if Kari and Jill are over there, I feel useless sitting over here doing nothing." Bill massaged his temples. "The thought of those girls in a foreign country by themselves makes me nauseous." He unlocked the car door and Kelli climbed in. "I do wish we could go over there and help search for them. I just don't see any way..." his voice trailed off.

"What do you think they're doing with Kari and Jill?" Too many ugly thoughts had already crossed Kelli's mind.

"I can't let my mind think about that, Kel—or I'll be of no use to anyone. So help me, though, if they have hurt Kari in any way—I don't know what I'm capable of doing."

Kelli was glad that her dad hadn't totally ruled out the possibility of going to Turkey. She could tell by the way he cocked his head sideways, protruding his creased forehead over his eyes that he was deep in thought. Although he acted as if he was engaged in watching the road, Kelli knew better.

She grew solemnly quiet and stared out the window. She said a silent prayer to God, thanking him for answering her prayers and leading them in the right direction to Kari. She was certain they were going to find her now. She closed her eyes and dozed the rest of the way home.

***

Hank unwrapped the paper off the end of a candy bar and bit into the tempting chocolate. He took a long sip of Coke and flipped his computer on. He couldn't believe that Bill and Kelli had actually found someone that had seen Kari and Jill. He had been more than relieved this morning when they hadn't found any dead bodies, but he hadn't been prepared for the news Bill had delivered. He hadn't even known they were driving up to the airport. Any other day he would have been furious with them for meddling with the investigation, but in this case, he couldn't be upset.

Hank was irritated at himself, though, because he had been pursuing the wrong trail—but at the same time, thankful that Bill and Kelli had come upon Barbara Hayes.

He was surprised to hear Bill say that he and Kelli were seriously considering booking tickets to Turkey in the morning—if it were permissible. *The guy must be nuts,* Hank thought. But then he quickly realized he would do the same thing if it were his niece missing.

Hank finally convinced Bill to at least wait until the FBI did some investigating to make sure that that was where the girls were. Bill had been persistent in going, though. He had informed Hank that he had already talked it over with his wife, and she desperately wanted him and Kelli to go.

Hank finished his candy bar, rolled the paper up in a ball, and tossed it in the trashcan. He had been too distracted to take a lunch break earlier. His mind was too wrapped up in the missing girls. He had already finished typing the report on finding Doug's body, and now he was suppose to do a follow-up report on the morning's investigation.

Doug's parents had stopped by the office earlier. They confirmed what Hank had already suspected—that Doug was gay. Jay had already hinted enough for Hank to assume that. *So Kari and Jill were seen with Doug—a gay man—having a soda,* he thought. *All three disappeared at the same time. They had to have left the mall willingly, or someone would have noticed a struggle. It didn't make sense! If the girls left with Doug, where were they headed? To the warehouse? Or were they forced to go there by someone else?*

The question kept running around in Hank's head—*was Doug involved somehow?* Why else would he be with Kari and Jill—whom he didn't even know before that day? So says Kelli, anyway. And Kelli did seem to know her sister inside out, and Hank had no reason to doubt her.

He had already considered someone holding all three of them at gunpoint and making Doug drive his car to the warehouse. But then again, someone would have witnessed something. For some reason, that scenario didn't make any sense either.

The more he thought about it, the more he was sure that Doug was involved. He flipped his computer off and quickly stood up and grabbed his jacket. There was only one person that knew Doug better than anyone—Jay.

123

He knew Jay was upset about the whole ordeal, but there were a lot of gaps in the case that needed clarification. Hank felt an urgency to talk with Jay. He knew he wasn't going to have a peaceful moment until these girls were found.

CHAPTER TWELVE

Kari turned and tossed all night. She dreamed she was locked in a dark, isolated room with thousands of spiders and man-eating mice. She finally awoke in a frightful state.

Scrooge brought their breakfast of bread and water up to them before the sun even peeped through the windows. He was in his usual state of mind—distant and unsociable.

Kari spent the rest of the morning discussing escape plans with Jill. They rotated trips to the restroom to meet with Renae or Una.

Una and Renae coached her and Jill on some of the basic words that might be useful when they made their break. Kari learned that yesterday when Scrooge was saying evet, he had been saying "yes" to Vaar.

Renae carefully explained to Kari what she had learned from the other girls about the black market and the selling of young girls to single Turkish men. She informed Kari to be cautious whom she asked for help from because there were many involved in the coalition.

Shortly before lunch, Scrooge threw some clean clothes onto the unswept floor of Kari and Jill's room. He disappeared, and then returned carrying fresh towels. He quickly tossed them on the floor before spinning back toward the door, muttering words under his breath, and slamming the door shut behind him.

Kari hesitated at first, but finally decided to take advantage of the opportunity because she was afraid there wouldn't be another chance to bathe for a while. They hadn't showered the night before because there weren't any towels.

She thought it was rather suspicious, though, that Scrooge wanted them to be cleaned up. Kari was sure Vaar had put him up to it. Maybe Vaar was planning to sell her and Jill off as slaves today.

Kari was glad that they had decided to flee right after Scrooge went out to the tree to hide the money. They had decided that they would try to snatch the money if they had time.

She knew they had more likelihood of escaping if they waited until Scrooge started drinking, but she figured they might need the money, not knowing what lay ahead of them.

Kari and Jill quickly showered and dressed.

"Are you sure you understand everything?" Kari asked Jill.

"You haven't any faith in me whatsoever, do you?"

"Of course I do. I'm just getting nervous."

"I'm more worried about you being caught when you sneak back to get the money," Jill said.

"I'll be fine. You just stay put until I get back to you. If by chance Scrooge does catch me—it will be up to you to run ahead and get help."

"Don't talk like that, Kari, it scares me!"

"Well, we've got to plan ahead in case something does go wrong."

Renae poked her head into the restroom. "Well, you don't have much longer to go. Scrooge should be bringing up our lunch any time. Don't forget, I'll be here waiting and when I hold up my thumbs that means Scrooge is coming upstairs to get the trays, so that should give you enough time to grab the money."

"Thanks so much." Kari hugged Renae.

"You're welcome. Just be careful and don't forget us." Renae glanced nervously over her shoulder. "I better get back to the room."

"Thanks for everything." Jill clasped Renae's hands in her own and squeezed them.

"Tell Una bye for us," Kari said.

126

"Okay. Wait a few minutes before you go back to your room so Scrooge doesn't expect anything." Renae hurried down the hall.

Kari ran her fingers through her tangled hair; Scrooge hadn't bothered to give them a brush. "Well, let's get back to the room. He should be coming soon."

Kari and Jill slipped into their room just as Scrooge reached the top of the stairs with a tray of bread for the first room. Kari knew he would have to make three more trips before she and Jill got their tray. They then would have to wait for him to bring the last tray to the far room, and then they could sneak back down to the restroom to start watching for him to go to his spot.

Kari let her mind drift as she paced back and forth in front of her bed. She hadn't thought of any what ifs before, but now a ton of them were racing through her head—like what if they were caught. Kari quickly dismissed the pessimistic notion—she couldn't afford to start thinking negatively.

She quickly glanced around the room, making sure they hadn't forgotten anything, and then recalled she didn't have anything to forget.

Kari glanced toward Jill, who was sitting on the cot, nervously biting on her fingernails.

"I think I hear him coming." Kari rushed to her own cot to lie down while listening for the door.

The door quickly opened, and Scrooge nonchalantly walked in, set the tray of bread and water on the floor, and then hurried out of the room.

Kari quickly jumped to her feet and tiptoed to the door. She motioned to Jill while pressing her ear firmly against the door. She could hear Scrooge's footsteps fading back down the stairs. "Okay he's going down to get the last tray, so when he goes back down after that—we'll go to the restroom," Kari whispered.

"Okay," Jill said weakly.

Kari pulled her ear away from the door and stared at Jill. "Are you okay? You look pale. You're not going to pass out on me now, are you?" Kari placed the back of her hand on Jill's forehead. "You're not running a fever."

"I'll be fine just as soon as we get out of here," Jill said in an unstable voice.

"Try to stay calm. Remember that as soon as we get out the front door, we'll run down the street until we're out of sight of the house. We'll find a hiding place, and then you stay put while I sneak back to get the money. Shhh here he comes." Kari pressed her ear back against the door as she listened to Scrooge opening the door across the hallway. She waited until she heard his footsteps descending the stairs.

"Okay, let's go." Kari glanced one last time around the room before opening the door. She walked softly toward the restroom with Jill at her heels.

Once inside, Kari scooted the bench over to the window and climbed up on it. Jill stayed near the door listening.

Kari repeatedly glanced from the tree toward the back of the house, patiently waiting for Scrooge to come outside. Five minutes later, the back door opened, and Kari saw him casually walking toward the tree, glancing uncertainly up and down the alley.

"Okay, he's out. Let's go." Kari's heart skipped a beat as she flew off the bench. She hurriedly threw open the door and ran down the hallway with Jill right behind her. She paused briefly to knock on Renae's door to let her know they were leaving. She rushed down the stairs at full speed, skipping every other one. Kari had just reached the front door when she heard a loud thud behind her. She spun around to see that Jill had fallen on her knees.

"Ouch, I missed the last stair. Oh, it hurts." She grabbed her knee with her free hand and wiped at the blood oozing out.

"Come on, get up!" Kari was already unlatching the chain locks. "Hurry, we got to go."

Jill tried standing but fell back down on her good knee. "I can't make it." Her eyes flooded with tears. Her legs quivered as she tried to stand.

Kari unlatched the dead bolt, pulled the door open, and ran back to Jill. She grabbed Jill's arm and threw it around her neck. "Please, Jill, try to walk. We are going to have to run if we're going to make it."

128

Jill's wobbly legs started to cooperate with Kari's help. "Maybe you should go without me. I'll just slow you down," she said in a frantic whisper.

"Don't be silly." Kari quickly led Jill out the front door and quietly pulled the door shut. She thought she had heard Scrooge walking toward the back of the house. "Come on, please try to run." Kari grabbed Jill's hand and started jogging slowing, pulling Jill alongside of her.

Kari was glad they had decided to run in the opposite direction of Scrooge's view from the back of the house. Fortunately, the street was deserted; there wasn't a soul visible anywhere.

Kari jogged two blocks away from the house before slowing to a fast walk; she glanced at Jill, who was panting heavily. "Look, there's a patch of woods, let's go there." Kari paused to breathe. "Is your leg still hurting?"

"Yes, but not as bad as my lungs." Jill sucked in a huge breath.

Kari trampled into the woods and spotted a huge tree with a soft patch of greenish-brown grass around it that was out of sight from the road. She pulled Jill in the direction of the tree and gently pushed her down into a sitting position against the tree. "Will you be okay? I need to hurry back and get the money."

"I'll be fine. Just hurry." Jill mumbled painfully.

Kari gently patted the top of Jill's head. "I promise I'll be back."

Kari hastily turned and ran back toward the way she had come. The closer she neared the house the more her fears increased. Her stomach was in twisted knots. "Crap," she muttered. She hadn't even considered the possibility of Scrooge seeing the front door unlocked. She couldn't believe she hadn't thought of that earlier. Kari had just assumed that he would go about his duties retrieving the trays upstairs. She prayed he wouldn't notice the front door or the drops of blood from Jill's knee.

She slowly moved toward the back of the house, keeping her eyes fixed on the window upstairs, searching for Renae's "thumbs up" sign.

129

She crouched low behind the rusty picket fence as her eyes darted from the front door to the back door and then back up to the window. She quickly lowered her body onto the ground to crawl. Suddenly, she saw her there—Renae was waving both hands at her and giving her the "thumbs up" sign. Kari immediately stood, waved back, and ran toward the tree at fast as she could. She crammed her hand down into the hollow tree and pulled out the pouch. She lifted her dress up long enough to tuck the bag into her panties. She spun back toward the window—Renae was waving. Kari quickly gestured and ran toward the street.

She raced past the deteriorated vacant buildings. Her eyes shifted toward the broken windows as she passed, and suddenly a chill shot up her back as she imagined hoodlums hiding behind the dark, lifeless windows, staring at her. She quickly dismissed the crazy illusion and increased her speed. The road seemed longer this time, and the houses seemed more isolated. A sense of loneliness overwhelmed her.

She thought it would be great if she and Jill could find an empty building to hide in, but these buildings were much too close to even consider. They needed to get as far away from this place and Vaar as possible, and as fast as they could.

Kari could see only the back of Jill's head slumped forward when she approached the spot she had left her. A rush of panic swept through her until she saw Jill's head bounce up and look her way. "You scared me. I thought you were..." Kari couldn't say it.

"What? You thought I was dead?"

"I just got really scared for a moment, the way you were bent over—well, it did look like you were dead."

"Well, I'm not, yet; and I'm so glad to see you! Did you have any trouble?"

"None yet, but we need to get moving. It's only a matter of time before Scrooge realizes we aren't in the restroom or sees the front door unlocked." Kari nervously glanced back toward the way she had come. "It's hard to say how many men will be out looking for us then."

Jill quickly stood. She placed her hand against the tree as she tried to regain her balance. "Where do we go now?"

"I have no clue. I just know we need to move as far away from this place as we can. Can you walk okay?" Kari bent down to inspect Jill's knee. She had an ugly scrape on it, but the bleeding had ceased.

"It's not hurting as bad. I can walk okay." Jill winced as she took a step.

"As soon as we find some water, we'll have to clean it well, so it doesn't get infected. Come on, let's cut through this patch of woods and see where it takes us."

Kari edged her way into the woods as the silence surrounded her and fear engulfed her. The woods were exceptionally quiet; not even the birds were chirping. Even the stiff air around them was soundless, and the suspended branches remained motionless. The air was chilly but since the wind wasn't blowing, Kari didn't think it would become a problem as long as they kept moving. The socks that Scrooge had given them were knee-high and made of cotton, so the bottom half of their legs would at least be kept warm.

Kari sighed; she couldn't believe they were still alive. She pushed her way through the sticker bushes and fallen branches, hurdling back every now and again to miss a spider web. She kept her eyes and ears alert as she cautiously moved forward. She glanced back over her shoulder to check on Jill and noticed that she was wheezing; Kari immediately slowed her pace.

After a good twenty minutes, the woods thinned out, and they eventually came upon a dead-end street. There were two newer-looking gray brick buildings on each side of the street; both of them were busy with women and children.

Kari hesitated and turned around to face Jill. "Just follow me and don't talk."

"Okay," Jill whispered.

Kari walked briskly past the young children playing in a sand pile, and past the ladies hanging up clothes on the clothesline. A small black dog ran alongside her, barking. She ignored the dog and kept her head bowed. The dog finally gave up and ran toward some boys playing ball.

131

An elderly lady sitting in a lawn chair knitting held up her cane and waved it at Kari and Jill. *"Selam."*

Kari recognized the word immediately—Una had told her it meant "hello." Kari waved back. *"Selam,"* she called out, and then arched her head back down toward the sidewalk; she sped up her pace before the woman had a chance to speak again.

The next few blocks were similar to the neighborhoods back in the states. It seemed like the women were engaged with some kind of outdoor activity. A few of the women working outside stopped and stared at Kari and Jill as they passed. Kari was sure they were gaping because of her red hair and Jill's blond hair—it was obvious that they were the foreigners in this country. She was certain if any of the women were asked if they had seen a blond or red-haired girl, they would easily remember them. Kari wished she had something that they could have worn over their hair so it would have been less noticeable.

The further they walked, the busier the streets became and more shops appeared. A row of clothes shops and deli stores swarmed with customers while other vendors continued to do their business selling from stands.

Kari paused in front of a bakery window, eyeing the donuts. Her stomach rumbled since they had missed lunch earlier. She leaned toward Jill. "We probably need to get some food to take with us before we find somewhere to hide."

"We've got money, get us some doughnuts." Jill's keen eyes pleaded as she glanced nervously up and down the street.

"We need to hurry and get away from all these people before someone recognizes us," Kari whispered, debating whether to take the time to get food. "Besides, the pouch is in my panties."

"Oh." Jill hurriedly looked around and then pointed to a small gap between two buildings. "Look—in between those buildings. I'll cover you while you get the money out."

"Okay, let's hurry." Kari and Jill squeezed in between the two narrow buildings, and Kari quickly removed the pouch. She opened it up and pulled out a bill. She knew it was called a lira, but she wasn't sure how much one bill would buy. She decided to take out another bill just in case one wasn't enough.

132

Kari quickly closed the pouch and they rushed back toward the bakery. The sweet-smelling aroma filled the air as soon as Kari opened the door. She smiled at Jill. "These will taste so good, but remember, we must hurry."

Kari grinned up at the lady waiting to take their order. She pointed to the glazed donuts and held up six fingers. She kept glancing toward the front door as she waited for the lady to bag up the donuts.

The lady handed Kari the bag of doughnuts and held up a can of soda.

Kari glanced toward Jill, who was nodding her head. Kari held up two fingers. The lady dropped two cans of soda in another sack and handed them to Kari.

She handed the lady the two bills and waited while the lady got change. Kari couldn't remember the word for "thanks," so she just nodded.

They scampered outside. Kari scanned the area and pointed to a less lively street. "Hurry, let's go this way and see if we can find somewhere to hide."

They had to jog for a few blocks before the buildings finally dwindled down. They were now out of the shopping area and approaching a less populated area where the houses weren't as adequately developed.

Kari motioned for Jill to stop. She pulled her hair behind her ears as she scrutinized the remaining houses on the block. Kari's eyes came to rest on a faded red brick, three-story structure. It sat isolated, back off the main street. It was run-down with several cracked windows. The bushes around the front of the dwelling were brown and dead-looking and the yard was unkempt. Kari was certain it was deserted. "Hey, look. Do you think we should try going in there?" She peeked around the side of the building.

Jill pointed to quaint hand-painted sign posted in the window. "What do you suppose that says?

"I don't know. But we need to hide somewhere! Scrooge has to know by now that we are gone. Vaar is bound to come looking for us." Kari meandered up the sidewalk toward the front door. She glanced uneasily up and down the street before turning the brass doorknob; the door was locked. "Damn! Let's go around to the back." Kari quickly jogged toward the back of the house; she immediately spotted a large glassless window. She nudged Jill. "Hey, I'll lift you up into there, and you can come and let me in the front door."

"How about I lift *you* up there?" Jill said, grinning.

"Do you think you can?"

"Of course not. I haven't a muscle in my arm." Jill sighed. "Okay, put your hands together." Jill stepped into Kari's folded hands and pulled herself up through the gap in the window.

Kari heard a big thud on the other side of the window.

"I made it. Yuck, right into a spider web too." Jill peered back out the window at Kari and shook her hands vigorously.

"What's it like?" Kari asked.

"You can see for yourself. Meet me at the front door."

Kari ran back to the front door and waited for Jill to unlock the door. She nervously glanced around before eagerly stepping into the building; she quickly pushed the door shut and locked it. One quick look down the long narrow hallway was enough to tell Kari that the building was unquestionably abandoned. The ceiling was slanted and looked like it could cave in at anytime. The flowered wallpaper was flaking off the dirty walls. There were stairs leading up but some of the steps were missing boards. The building looked like it once might have been an apartment building.

Kari followed Jill into what might have once been one of the apartments. The front room was spacious. There were still worn green drapes hanging over the windows. An area rug had been pulled up and a large square mark had been left where it had lain. The wooden floor was dusty, and cobwebs dangled in the corners of the room. The ceiling had water stains from some sort of leakage.

Kari wandered into the bedroom. She ran her hands over the goose bumps emerging on her arms. The room was colder than the front room. The only furniture was a dresser with a broken leg sitting in the corner of the room. She called to Jill in the front room, "Come in here, there's a dresser in here. Maybe there's something in the drawers." Kari hurriedly pulled out the drawers, but they were empty.

"Well?" Jill asked as she entered the room.

"Nothing." Kari pulled open the closet door. "But look up there." She pointed to the top shelf. "That looks like warm blankets to me."

"Yeah, it does. Can you reach them?"

"I'm not sure." Kari stretched on her tiptoes until her fingers were touching the fabric. She jumped and pulled on the textile, and the blankets tumbled to the floor, dust flying everywhere. She picked up one of the blankets and shook it out. There were three large holes in the center of it. "Well, it's not the best, but it will keep us warm." She brought the blanket up to her nose. "Yuck, it doesn't smell too great either, but it'll do."

"How come we can't just ask someone to help us?" Jill's asked as she glanced around the room.

"We will in time, but not yet. We don't know who we can trust."

Jill moaned and picked up the other blanket to spread out. "I don't think we should wait too much longer." She sat cross-legged on the blanket. "How about some doughnuts? I'm starved."

Kari lowered herself down beside Jill and handed her a doughnut and a soda. "We won't wait too long. Maybe tomorrow we'll ask for help." She snarled up her nose as she scanned the room. "I know this isn't too comfortable, but I do think we should stay here tonight."

"It's going to be cold."

"We'll be okay." Kari tossed her head back. "Oh my God, Jill—I can't believe we escaped." She clasped her hand over Jill's. "We actually did it! I know we're not out of the clear yet, but I know we're going to make it!"

"I hope you're right." Jill stuffed a sizeable bite of the doughnut in her mouth. "Oh wow, this is heavenly."

"I forgot what real food tasted like." Kari chewed the doughnut. "I still can't believe we tricked Vaar."

"I know—me neither. Thanks, Kari."

"Well, you did as much as me." Kari sipped her pop. "Can you imagine how furious Vaar is going to be when he finds out?"

135

"I know." Jill rolled her eyes and reached for another doughnut. Suddenly she froze as her eyes widened. "Do you think he will still hurt our families?"

"I've already considered that, but remember Sahre telling him that he ought to tell his men to get out of Leewood? I think they know it would be too dangerous for them to stick around there. Everyone in town is probably looking for us."

"You're right. Vaar might have been bluffing all along. I hope so, anyway." Jill's eyes darted to the curtains. "Why don't we use some of those old drapes for our bedding tonight?"

"That's a great idea. We might find some more stuff elsewhere, but I don't think we should attempt to go upstairs; it looks dangerous."

"Yeah, it does." Jill paused. "Do you really think we'll make it home?"

"I hope so, but we are going to have to be really careful, so Vaar's men don't find us. It's hard to say how many men he has over here working for him." Kari brushed the crumbs off the blanket. "You know, we should try to make some scarves to cover our hair."

"Yeah, that would be smart." Jill stuffed the rest of her doughnut in her mouth.

Kari grew silent as memories of an ordinary weekend at home filled her head. She imagined her mom in the kitchen, sitting at the table, filling out the bills while a casserole dish baked in the oven, and her dad in his shop, building another birdhouse for the back yard. She could see Kelli sitting in front of the TV, laughing at the Cosby Show, munching on hot buttered popcorn. Homesickness overwhelmed Kari as she thought of her family. She knew she had to make it home soon. She wanted that more than anything in the world.

CHAPTER THIRTEEN

Hank sat comfortably on Jay's sofa listening while Jay spoke endlessly of Doug's qualities. It was obvious that Jay had tremendously strong feelings for Doug and was having a hard time dealing with his death.

Hank glanced down at his watch. An hour had already passed since he arrived at Jay's house. It felt like he wasn't making any progress. Although he felt sympathy for Jay, he knew that Doug hadn't been completely honest with his roommate. There were still too many pieces of the puzzle missing.

"I know this is hard for you, Jay, and I hate to ask you this. I don't have a search warrant, but would you mind if I looked around in Doug's personal things?"

"No, of course not. Doug hadn't anything to hide, and Lord knows I want to find who did this to him as much as you do."

"Thank you."

Jay stood and led Hank down the hallway to the bedroom. "Here's our bedroom." He pointed to the oak dresser against the wall. "That's Doug dresser." He strolled over and slid the closet door open. "This is his side of the closet." He glanced around at the rest of the room and pointed toward the desk. "That's his computer."

Jay wandered over to the bed, bent down, slid his hand under the bed, and pulled out a shoebox. "Here are some of his personal things and photos." He hesitated and stared lovingly down at the box and then handed it to Hank. "You can help

137

yourself to any of it. I will leave you alone now. I'll be outside smoking a cigarette if you have any questions."

"Thanks." Hank waited until Jay had left the room, and then immediately dumped the shoebox's contents onto the bed. Some old photos, letters, marbles, and lighters fell out. He picked up a faded picture of Doug's mother and father. There were more photos of Doug at different stages in his life and numerous pictures of him and Jay. Hank picked up a folded piece of paper and unfolded it. He read a few lines before realizing it was a love letter from Jay. He folded it back up and searched the contents of the other letters. They were all the same—letters from Jay professing his love for Doug. Hank studied the collection of lighters and marbles. Hank assumed the old marbles were left over from when he was a kid. He looked at the different lighters; they all seemed to have a name of a city on each of them. Hank imagined that Doug had started the collection to remind him of all the places he had been.

Hank sighed—there wasn't anything in the box that looked unusual. He carefully arranged the items back in the box neatly and placed the shoebox back on the bed. He ventured over to Doug's dresser and pulled out the top drawer. There were only the usual boxer shorts and t-shirts, arranged in a tidy manner. He pulled out the remaining drawers only to find clothes neatly organized in each one. He checked the closet and all the pockets of the pants hanging up but didn't find anything.

Hank casually glanced around the room, his eyes settling on the computer. He hurriedly pulled out the chair, sat down, and booted up the computer. Once he had connected to the Internet, he located Doug's email. He slowly read all of Doug's recent emails; most of them were spam. Reluctant to give up so easily, Hank kept reading.

After fifteen minutes of continuous reading and not finding anything of value, Hank groaned as discouragement set in. He was just about to exit the mail system when he noticed there were emails in Doug's "deleted messages" folder that hadn't been emptied. Hank quickly clicked on them and started reading. Suddenly, an email caught his attention—the subject line read: *Don't be late!*

Hank continued to read.

Doug
Be at the location we discussed by noon. I will be patiently waiting.
V

Hank checked the date and noticed it was sent on October 31—the day before the girls and Doug had disappeared. He wiped his sweaty palms on the side of his slacks and inhaled a deep breath. *Could it be?* Hank wondered. *Could the V be from Vaar Roami? It had to be! And the location had to be the warehouse. So, Doug was involved with these men somehow,* Hank thought. He wasn't sure how much involved Doug had been, but he was sure Doug had known something. He quickly printed out the email, folded it up, and slipped it into his shirt pocket. He scanned the rest of the deleted emails; not finding any more evidence he exited out of the mail.

Hank took one last look around the room. Satisfied by what he had found, he hurried into the living room where Jay stood staring into the aquarium.

"Well, did you find anything that would be helpful to you?" Jay turned to meet Hank's gaze. He dabbed at a single tear escaping from his eye.

"I'm not sure, yet. I wish I was in a position to tell you more, but I'm not. I do appreciate you letting me look around, though."

"No problem. If I can help out in any way just let me know." Jay followed Hank to the door.

"Thank you." Hank held out his hand to shake Jay's. "I'm sorry for your loss. Take care of yourself." He fastened his jacket and hurried out to his car. He was eager to get back to the office and figure out the intent of the new lead.

He climbed into his car and fired the engine. He felt sorry for Jay; he was a nice kid. He knew it would crush Jay when he found out that his roommate was involved.

Hank pulled away from the curb while wondering what had gone wrong with Doug's participation in the crime—had he done something wrong, or did Ivan and Vaar backstab Doug? And what did these Turkish men have planned for the girls? Hank was almost certain that the thugs somehow seized Kari and Jill, and now had them confined in Turkey. He had already heard the stories of the many different black-market schemes using prostitutes, drugs, and other illegal acts that go on in other parts of the world. And this could very well be the course to such behavior.

More than anything, Hank wished he were flying to Turkey in the morning with Bill and Kelli. He was already deeply involved in the case and solving the mystery would be a rewarding experience. Besides the pleasure he would have witnessing the blow-up of a huge illicit ring.

Hank drummed his thumbs impatiently on the steering wheel while waiting for the stoplight to change green. He did already have a passport. However, Betty wouldn't be too happy about him leaving, although she had been an extremely understanding wife for the last twenty-two years.

He thought back to the time, twenty-one years ago, when he found out that he couldn't give her children. She had been devastated at first but after the shock diminished, she had told him, "I must have not been meant to have children. God must have other plans for me. This way I can devote more of my time to teaching." And that was what she had done all of these years. Hank never loved a woman more for her devotion. He knew she could have easily left and found another husband to give her children, but she had stayed with him.

He recalled all the nights he had come home late from work, and all the times he had been called out on related cases. Yes, she was definitely the most patient woman he had ever met.

Hank was almost certain she would understand his yearning to go to Turkey. She had, after all, been equally upset when he had told her about Kari and Jill missing. Hank thought, perhaps, he could take her with him but immediately discarded the notion—she wouldn't be able to leave her fourth-grade class during this time of the year, not with quarter grades coming up.

He pulled the car into his normal parking space at the police station. His mind was made up; he was going to take some vacation time and fly to Turkey. He knew he wouldn't be allowed to do any police work there but a little snooping could go unnoticed. Besides, maybe he could persuade the FBI into letting him tag along with some of the investigations. Something was going down in Turkey, and Hank was determined to find out what it was. He glanced at his reflection in the rearview mirror and ran his hand over his hair. "These losers thought they could run out of the country and hide—boy, are they going to get a rude awakening." Hank mumbled.

He hurriedly gathered his belongings and climbed out of the car. He anxiously jogged toward his office, whistling as he went. He had many phone calls to make before he left. First, he would call Betty at her school to make sure she didn't object to him going, and then he would call Bill and Kelli and fill them in on his plans, so they could arrange to fly together.

***

Kelli lay in her bed staring at the TV, not really paying any attention to Lucy and Ricky on the screen. She was thinking of the trip they were about to take in the morning. She had spent most of the evening washing clothes and packing. She had packed extra clothes because she wasn't sure how long they would be gone. She had also slid Kari's favorite jeans and sweater in the suitcase just in case they were fortunate enough to find her and Jill.

Kelli surfed through the channels and then flipped the TV off. She lay on her back and stared up at the glittering ceiling. She had been shocked during dinner when her dad had told her Hank had called and would be making the trip with them. She was glad he was coming just surprised that his job and family would allow it.

Kelli knew she would get a little behind in her school work, but she was so much more advanced than the other students, she was certain that she wouldn't have any problems catching back up.

She glanced at the radio clock. It was after ten already—it had been a long day. She yawned and closed her eyes. Almost instantly, Kari and Jill's images popped into her head—it was

141

the day they had disappeared, and Kelli was driving them to the mall. They were all laughing, and Kari was teasing Kelli as usual. The only difference was when Kelli let them out at the mall she got out with them and went inside, too. Kelli's eyes suddenly flew open. If only she really could go back in time, she would never have let them go into the mall by themselves. She would have gone with them and then none of this would have ever happened, because she wouldn't have let it.

***

They had been on the plane for over nine hours, and Kelli couldn't have been more relieved when the pilot came on the intercom and said they would be landing shortly. It had been a long, boring flight. She had tried watching movies, reading magazines, sleeping, and eating to pass the time. However, the time had still dragged by.

Her father had spent most of the time carrying on a conversation with Hank. Although she found their discussions monotonous, they seemed to have a lot in common.

Kelli stretched her arms above her head; she was anxiously waiting for the plane to land. She was preparing herself for disappointment—she had secretly hoped she would get off the plane and immediately see Kari and Jill, but she knew that wouldn't be the case. She was told that this was going to be a difficult search, especially since they didn't know how to speak Turkish. However, Hank told them that he was familiar with a few words only because he was in the Army years ago and stationed in Turkey temporarily. Kelli thought that could be beneficial for them; it was more that Kelli and her dad had to offer.

They had already booked hotel rooms in Istanbul. They were told a taxi would be waiting for them to take them to the hotel. Hank had made many of the arrangements ahead of time. He even had some names and address of the guys that were linked to Kari and Jill's disappearance.

Hank had told Kelli that they wouldn't be able to come with him when he went to interrogate the Turkish men. Kelli smiled

142

silently; she decided she would use her intellectual charisma to persuade him otherwise.

The sudden jolt of the plane landing interrupted Kelli's thoughts. She waited until the seat bell light went off, and the flight attendant told them they could stand. She gladly followed her dad and Hank off the plane.

As they waited for their luggage, Kelli studied the variety of people rushing to get their bags; most of them were Turkish nationality. She glanced toward the skylight ceiling; she thought the airport was classy looking.

Hank and her father snatched the luggage off the conveyor belt. Kelli clung to the back of her father's jacket as they headed out the exit doors. A young Turkish gentleman immediately jumped out of a faded white taxi and opened the trunk to load the luggage into. Hank handed the driver a card with the name of the hotel.

Kelli gripped the arm rail in the back seat tightly as they rode. She thought the drive was extremely rough. The driver had a bad habit of darting in and out of traffic, cutting off the other drivers. She caught herself covering her eyes several times. After several minutes, the driver pulled up in front of a towering hotel with an elegant waterfall. Hank handed him some money. Kelli was glad that Hank had thought ahead of time to convert their dollars into lira.

She tagged close behind her dad as they entered the hotel lobby. "Thanks, Dad, for letting me have my own room." Her dad had agreed to share a room with Hank and let Kelli have her own room.

"Well, I thought you might appreciate the privacy," Bill said.

"I'll go check us in. I'll be back in a minute with the keys." Hank left them standing in the lobby.

"Dad, can we start looking for Kari and Jill right away?"

"Well, let's wait and see what Hank suggests we do. I'm thinking we ought to grab a bite to eat before we get started. It's going to be a long day; jet lag will set in before you know it."

Kelli glanced at her watch. It was already morning here, and she would just be getting ready for bed if she were back in the states. She felt wide-awake; she had slept for hours on the plane.

143

A few minutes later Hank returned, carrying keys to the rooms. Kelli followed her dad and Hank down the long narrow hallway. They passed several dark-skinned men in navy uniforms, who were either carrying luggage or pushing carts of food. Kelli was glad Hank had asked for the rooms on the bottom floor. She wasn't too fond of riding in elevators—not since she and Kari had been stuck on one in a hospital when they were eight years old. It had taken the maintenance men an hour to get them out. It had been a horrible experience; she'd had a terrible time trying to coax Kari into not crying. They both tried to avoid elevators as much as possible since then.

Hank stopped in front of a room and handed Kelli a key. "Well, Kelli, this is your room."

Kelli took the key and unlocked the door. She peeked inside, sat her luggage down, and turned back toward her dad and Hank. "Okay, what's the scoop? What are we going to do now?"

Hank glanced from Bill to Kelli. "If you two don't mind, I would like to take a quick shower, and then maybe grab some food before we start searching."

"That's fine with me," Bill shifted his eyes to Kelli. "I don't want you leaving this room without us."

"Not even to get ice?" Kelli asked.

"Not even to get ice." Bill rested his luggage on the floor.

"But, Dad, I'll be fine."

"No, Kelli—your father is right. We're in another country, and we don't know how safe it is here yet. It is best that you do as your father says."

"Okay." Kelli sighed. "Come and get me when you guys are ready to go eat."

"Be sure to keep your door locked too," Bill added.

"Sure. See you later." Kelli rolled her eyes and pushed the door shut. Usually her mother was the one that treated her like a baby—now her dad was starting to do the same thing.

She casually roamed around the room, inspecting it thoroughly. It didn't look much different from hotel rooms back in the states. She plopped down on the bed and bounced up and down. Tears abruptly sprung to Kelli's eyes—this would be her first time staying in a hotel room alone—without Kari.

144

She leaped up and marched into the restroom. After examining the restroom thoroughly, she decided a shower might help her feel better. She grabbed some clean clothes and spread them neatly out on the bed. She eagerly slid out of her dirty clothes and stepped into the shower. Kelli squeezed her eyes shut while the hot water spilled over her head. The steaming water seemed to relax all of her tight muscles. She let the hot water beat down on her body as the tension slowly crept out of her.

She still couldn't believe she was actually in Turkey. All of a sudden, a stinging sensation shot up her spine as fear besieged her: what if they were too late to save Kari and Jill—could they already be dead? Or, worse yet, what if they never found them at all? Kelli didn't try to fight the tears from spilling down her cheeks—she realized the harsh reality that Kari and Jill could already be gone forever.

CHAPTER FOURTEEN

"What was that noise?" Jill asked, scooting her shivering body closer to Kari.

"Probably just the wind," Kari said soothingly. *Poor Jill.* She had been restless all day; every little sound initiated emotional anguish. Jill was convinced that it was just a matter of time before Vaar and his men found them. It had taken Kari the entire day to reassure Jill that they were safe.

Kari had been relieved to find out they had water in the house, but unfortunately, there wasn't any electricity. Earlier, before it had grown dark, they had made a pallet on the floor of the bedroom with the heavy drapes from the back rooms.

After a while, Kari's eyes grew accustomed to all the daunting shadows in the room.

Jill sat up, fluffed the folded curtain under her head, and lay back down. She tucked the covers neatly underneath her body. "I'm so cold and scared!"

"It is cold in here," Kari began in a hoarse voice. "Keep close to me; our body heat will keep us warm."

Suddenly a disruptive crash from the kitchen frightened Kari and Jill to their feet.

"Someone's in there," Jill whispered as she grabbed Kari's hand.

"I know, I heard." Kari held tightly to Jill's hand as she tiptoed toward the door. She glanced at Jill. "Be quiet." She released Jill's hand, leaned forward, and strained to see if she could see into the adjoining rooms. She couldn't make out any unusual shadows, but she couldn't see into the kitchen because it was on the other side of the living room.

Kari hurriedly grabbed the broom that they had found on the back porch. She grasped the handle tightly and lifted it above her head. "I'm going in there." She could feel Jill's quick, rasping breath on the back of her neck.

"I'm going with you." Jill huddled close behind Kari.

Kari inhaled a deep breath and cautiously moved forward, keeping her eyes focused on the various shadows flickering across the wall. The forceful pressure from Jill's terrified body caused Kari to stumble against the wall; she whirled around and motioned Jill to stand still. Kari stalled for a few seconds while regaining her courage, and then she gradually crept toward the kitchen. She could feel her heart throbbing irregularly against her ribcage. She considered Jill's fears—the possibility that one of Vaar's men had found them, and now he was going to kill them. She shuddered and prayed for strength. And then, with all the courage she had, she stepped into the chilling dark kitchen.

An unexpected swift movement from the corner of the room startled her. She screamed and swung the broom fiercely into the air as her eyes darted from side to side; she couldn't see anything of form. Suddenly, a black ball of fur pounced off the counter and landed at Kari's feet, causing her to lose her balance and tumble forward onto it. She screamed just as an injured cat shrieked.

Jill appeared shaken in the doorway. "Are you okay?" She grasps Kari's hands to pull her up.

"I'm not sure." Kari slowly stood. "That freaking cat scared the crap out of me." She gaped at the scrawny black cat licking his paws. He was small but slightly larger than a kitten. Kari assumed he had just recently been weaned from his mother's milk. "My heart is racing." She placed her hand over her heart and sighed. "I fell on him hard—I hope he's okay."

Jill's eyebrows creased. "He'll be fine. It's you that I'm worried about." She scanned Kari's body from head to toe. "You took quite a fall. I saw the cat just as you swung the broom, but everything happened so fast, I couldn't get a word out."

147

The cat purred softly. Kari and Jill exchanged serious glances, and then suddenly, they both giggled.

"I can't believe it was just a cat," Kari said.

"He's probably looking for something to eat."

"Well, if he finds something he'd better share." Kari bent down to stroke the cat.

"Do you think anyone heard you scream?" Jill's teeth chattered, and she cradled her body against the wall.

"I hope not. It's got to be late—I didn't see any lights on in any of the houses earlier except a few porch lights."

The cat meowed and stretched his paws out in front of him as if he was enjoying Kari's petting.

Kari carefully swept the now-composed cat up in her arms. "I think he's okay." She nudged Jill. "You're freezing. Come on, let's go back to bed." She snuggled the cat up against her chest. "He might as well keep us company."

Jill led the way back into the bedroom. "My first thought was that it was Vaar."

"I wasn't thinking that—I thought it was a wild animal of some sort!" Kari lied, not wanting to admit her fear to Jill. She gracefully lowered herself on the pallet, positioning the purring cat between her and Jill. She wished she had something to feed him, but they hadn't gone to get any food since the doughnuts that morning. Kari thought it would be too risky to go out so soon; she was sure that Vaar and his men were patrolling the streets steadily.

She and Jill had spent the day creating scarves to wrap around their heads when they did go out. Kari's stomach rumbled hungrily; she knew they would have to go out in the morning for food.

She glanced toward Jill—her eyes were closed. Kari quietly laid her head down on the folded curtains. Her mind raced; she wondered how long they should stay in the eerie building before going for help. She couldn't remember which direction the airport was or where they could go to find police officers. And if they were fortunate enough to find help, Kari didn't know Turkish well enough to explain their predicament. She moaned softly; she didn't have a clue what their next move should be.

148

She didn't want to make any foolish mistakes and risk being captured by Vaar again.

Kari listened quietly to Jill's heavy breathing; she was glad Jill had relaxed enough to sleep. She cuddled up close to the cat and closed her eyes, keeping her ears alert to all the eccentric noises traveling through the house. For some reason, she felt a little safer with the cat beside her. She figured if he had slipped through the broken window, she was sure other wild animals could, too—this way if one does, at least, the cat would protect them; she hoped, anyway. After a while, she couldn't fight the fatigue any longer; she finally drifted off into a restless sleep.

***

The loud commotion outside the building vibrated through the walls like a severe thunderstorm. Kari froze as she listened warily. Her head cleared as the recent dream vanished and the reality of where they were returned. The sun was already shining vibrantly through the windows. She shook Jill's slender shoulder. "Jill, are you awake?"

Jill pulled the cover up under her chin and yawned. "No."

"Listen." Kari shifted toward the window. "What's that racket?"

"I wish it was a furnace kicking on." Jill shivered and flipped to her side; she pulled her knees up to her chest. "You go find out what it is and then come back and tell me."

"Are you going back to sleep?"

"Not if you keep talking." Jill leisurely stretched her arms above her head. "Well, I'm awake now." She sat up and immediately covered her ears with her hands. "Wow, that is head-splitting; I can't believe I slept through it.

"I'm going to peep out the window." Kari was glad they had decided to keep the curtains hanging in the bedroom and living room. They had taken the older drapes out of the back rooms to make their beds. She guardedly tiptoed toward the east window and slowly pulled the drape back to peek out. Two middle-aged bearded men dressed in gray coveralls were busy drilling into the sidewalk. Kari slowly released the curtain. She tiptoed back

149

toward Jill and bent down to whisper, "It looks like they might be pulling up the sidewalk out front."

"What for?"

"Well, how am I supposed to know?" Kari snapped. "I'm sorry—I'm cranky." She paused. "Now I don't know how we are going to get food as long as they are out there. If we try to leave, they might see us climbing out of the window."

"Well, maybe we can go when they take their lunch break."

"That's an idea, but I'm starving now."

"I know—me too. I could eat eggs right now, and I don't even like eggs."

"I could eat spinach right now and I hate spinach!" Kari tried to smile, but frowned instead. She was tired of pretending that everything was going to be okay. The fact was they were stranded in an unfamiliar country, hiding out in a freezing neglected building, and they were starving to death. Kari was certain her parents didn't have a clue where they were; they were probably still circling the mall. And to top it all off, an appalling mobster and his followers that possibly dominated the whole city were out right this second, circling the blocks, planning his revenge for Kari and Jill's daring act. Kari grimaced; depression was settling in.

The black cat strolled into the room. He had silently disappeared sometime during the night. The sight of the gaunt cat comforted Kari somewhat. "Where have you been, Mister?" Kari reached down to stroke the cat. He purred and rolled over onto his back. "You're a sweetie." Kari swooped up the cat and cuddled him. "Come on, Mister, we might as well get back under the blankets because it's going to be a while before we get to go anywhere."

Kari and Jill spent the rest of the morning under the blankets, taking turns napping and listening to the outdoor activity. It seemed like hours before the men stopped working.

"Listen, I think they're gone now." Kari stood. "We'd better hurry." She strolled to the window and glanced out; the men were gone. "Hey, why don't you stay here, and I'll go." Kari quickly bundled her hair up and tied one of their homemade scarves around her head.

150

"I don't know. I'm scared, Kari." She nervously interlocked her fingers together. "Shouldn't we stay together?"

"It'll be okay. Besides, Vaar will be looking for two of us, not one. I'll be less noticeable. I'd better hurry, though, before the men come back. I'm going to take that bucket out that we found and put by the window so I can get back in."

"Oh Kari, please be careful." Jill tried to stand but staggered. She immediately sat back down.

"Are you okay? What happened?" Kari had a sudden disturbing feeling. "You don't have the strength to stand, do you?"

"I'm not sure. I just got really dizzy." Jill lay down and pulled the covers back over her. "I'm not feeling too well."

"How's that leg doing?" Kari pulled back the covers so she could examine Jill's knee; it was red and swollen with yellowish puss leaking out. "I think it's infected. I'll pick up some medicine."

"But we don't have much money left, and I would rather have food. I'm sure that's probably all that's wrong with me; I'm just really hungry."

"We don't have much left, but I will get what I can. I have to go. Don't try to get up," she said firmly. "I'll be back shortly,

"Be careful," Jill called out.

Kari jogged the few short blocks to the downtown area. Although the winds were sharp, the vivid sun had crept out from behind a cloud, casting welcoming warmth on Kari. The streets and sidewalks were busy with a mixture of vendors and shoppers.

She was glad she had covered her hair; she now blended in with the majority of the crowd. All the same, she kept her head bowed and her eyes and ears alert.

She immediately spotted a diminutive, cramped market on the right side of the road that looked like it could have a variety of foods. She quickly crossed the street and hurried inside, glancing back over her shoulder to make sure no one was following.

The store was nearly empty with the exception of a short broad lady, wearing pointed cat-eyed glasses and dragging two

151

whining youngsters through the store. Kari quickly grabbed a loaf of bread, a package of lunchmeat, a box of crackers, and some slices of cheese. She studied the racks of medicine, but was unable to read the directions. She finally decided on a small tube that looked like salve.

After paying for the items, she still had money left, so she carefully examined the remaining shelves in the store—settling on a big bag of potato chips, a bottle of juice, and box of doughnuts for her sweet tooth.

Kari hurried and paid for the remaining items. She snatched the brown paper sack off the counter and turned to exit out the door. Suddenly she froze; her eyes widen, as her hand remained motionless on the doorknob—walking directly in front of the store was Masory. Her heartbeat increased as her fear escalated. *Oh my God, I'm dead now,* she thought. She started to duck, but realized any sudden movement might cause him to shift his head and look in her direction. She held her breath for what seemed like eternity as he heedlessly passed by—he was staring straight ahead. Kari knew if he had turned his head, even slightly, he would have seen her.

She waited a few more minutes, giving him time to continue up the street. She slowly opened the door, stepped softly outside, and pulled the door quietly closed behind her. She tiptoed to the corner of the building and peeped around the edge of the wall. Kari could see Masory ahead, crossing over to the other side of the street. He had his hands shoved in his pockets, revealing the spare tire around his midriff. Kari was sure his hand was grasping a polished pistol. She was relieved he was heading in the opposite direction from the street that led to her hideaway.

Suddenly a firm hand touched the back of Kari's shoulder. She gasped; a stab from a switchblade in the center of her back couldn't have frightened her more. A horrific dread besieged her; she feared the worst—Vaar. She was afraid her life on the run was finally over. Kari shuddered; she was too petrified to turn around. She inhaled deeply and with all the courage she had, spun around. She was ecstatic to see the clerk from the store mumbling loudly in Turkish and pushing change into her hand.

Kari had been in such a rush to leave the store she had completely forgotten about the change from her last purchase. She smiled gratefully and nodded to the woman.

She quickly dropped the change into the sack and took off running as fast as she could down the street. She continued to glance uneasily over her shoulder to make sure Masory wasn't anywhere near. Kari ran at full speed all the way back to the building.

Luckily, the men hadn't started back on the sidewalk, and she had time to slip through the window unnoticed.

She rushed into the bedroom panting and dropped to the pallet on her hands and knees. "Guess who I saw?" She didn't wait for Jill to respond. "Masory." Kari gulped for air. "I about died! I was in the store getting ready to go out the door and he walked right in front of the store."

"You're kidding!" Jill squealed.

"I wish I was. I was so scared he was going to turn his head and see me. I ran all the way back here as fast as I could." Kari quickly explained to Jill the whole story.

"I would have just died if he would have caught you, and I was left here by myself." Jill's eyes grew misty. "I wouldn't know what to do. You mustn't leave me alone again!"

"We better not leave here for a day or more. At least, long enough for them to go looking in another area." Kari shrugged. "I hope I got enough food for us. I only got us one big bottle of juice since we have water."

"Yeah, but remember what that water did to our stomachs yesterday?"

"We should be getting used to it, though." Kari dumped the groceries from the sack. "Look at all I was able to purchase. We had more money than what I thought we did."

Kari opened the bag of chips and shoved a handful in her mouth.

Jill glanced at the contents scattered across the pallet. "It looks good, but I don't think I feel much like eating right now." She leisurely laid her head back down on the folded drape.

"You're kidding me, right? You have to be starving." Kari reached over and placed the back of her hand against Jill's forehead. "You're burning up. Oh no, please don't tell me you're getting sick."

"I'm sorry, Kari, I just don't feel good."

Kari quickly pulled the ragged covers off Jill's leg, grabbed the ointment, and rubbed it thoroughly over Jill's injured knee. She wasn't sure what was causing Jill's fever; she didn't know the slightest thing about medical procedures. She wished, though, they hadn't waited so long to clean her knee. They had been so busy exploring the building that she had totally forgotten about Jill's leg until she had complained about it hurting her late in the afternoon yesterday. "I know you don't feel good, but you're going to have to make yourself eat, or you're going to get worse."

"I don't think I can."

"Here, I'll help you." Kari elevated Jill into a sitting position and handed her a sandwich. She unscrewed the cap on the juice and sat it next to Jill. "Here, you need to drink too."

Jill raised the sandwich to her mouth and nibbled on the crust. She grimaced. "I'm just not hungry right now. Can't I eat this later?"

"Come on, Jill, please try to eat it." Kari lifted the bottle of juice up to Jill's lips. "Here, take a drink. Maybe it will help."

Kari's eyes remained on Jill as she gradually ate the sandwich. It looked like every bite was a never-ending effort for Jill. She had never seen Jill so feeble before and it terrified her. "Do you feel any better?"

"Maybe if I sleep, I'll feel better." Jill slid back down on the pallet. She pulled the covers over her body and instantly closed her eyes.

"If you need anything, let me know."

"Okay," Jill mumbled softly.

Kari ate, gave Mister some scraps, and watched Jill sleep. She occasionally would hold her hand up to Jill's mouth to make sure she was breathing. She found a piece of cloth in the bathroom, got it wet, and rubbed it carefully over Jill's forehead. Jill never budged.

Kari listened quietly to the men working outside, and from time to time went to the window to peek out and see if they were doing anything different. She prayed they didn't decide to come inside the building. After a while, the men quit working and the neighborhood grew quiet as the dreaded darkness set in. The unsettling creaking noises continued to travel through the aged building, along with an occasional eerie hoot from an owl outdoors.

Kari managed to get Jill up only once; she used the restroom and reluctantly ate a few crackers and cheese. She instantly fell back to sleep—her fever hadn't gone down any. Kari knew she wasn't going to be able to sleep, as long as Jill was so poorly.

The air in the house had grown chilly, and Kari cuddled closer to Jill. She could hear Jill's short, quick harsh breaths in her ear, and her body felt like fire next to hers.

Mister dashed into the room and eagerly stretched out at Kari's feet.

Kari stared up at the ceiling, although all she could see was darkness. A few wet tears slid down the side of her cheeks. She had thought she was brave, but she wasn't. Her hopes for survival were slowly fading. She no longer believed they would be rescued. Jill was terribly sick, and Kari didn't know how to help her. She knew she had no other choice except to go for help in the morning. Kari couldn't risk something happening to Jill, or she would never forgive herself.

If only she would have taken a health class in school, maybe she could help Jill now. She now realized how important an education could be—she wished she had been more serious about it. But she hadn't; she was always more concerned with who her next date was going to be with.

Kari thought of her mom; she was always the one that nurtured Kari and Kelli when they were ill. Kari just always assumed that mom would be around to play doctor. She recalled having the measles when she was six, and her mother rocking her in the rocking chair until she had fallen asleep. And then her mother had slept right next to her all night. Kari had woken up several times crying from itching so much; her mother would quickly stir awake, doctor her sores, and rub Kari's back until she fell back to sleep. Kari longed for her mother's loving arms now.

155

She turned her back away from Jill and sobbed softly. Kari stuck her toes from under the covers, curling them into Mister's fur, trying to find some sort of comfort from the sleeping cat.

She couldn't stop the horrid images from racing through her head. She had a nagging sensation that her life span was going to be reduced significantly. And she was afraid that there wasn't a thing left for her to do about it—and the thought terrified her!

CHAPTER FIFTEEN

Kelli finished her last bite of the Kebabs—meatballs of minced lamb served with rice and breadcrumbs. She sipped her soda, cringing at the syrupy taste; it was much sweeter than the cola she was used to drinking. "Well, I'm done." She wiped her mouth and tossed the napkin into the empty plate. She didn't want to waste any more time—she was too eager to start looking for Kari and Jill.

"I'm ready, too." Hank laid his fork across his plate.

"Okay, let's pay and get started," Bill said with sadness in his voice.

They had chosen an outdoor cafe to eat at, so they could keep their eyes on the lively citizens passing by. Hank had shared the pictures of the men that were connected with the girls' disappearance with Kelli and Bill. Kelli had sat quietly during the meal, observing the men ambling by. However, many of the foreign men looked so much alike; it was hard for Kelli to focus on the dissimilarity. She knew it would be impossible to single out any of the men from just the pictures; she figured she would have better luck just keeping an eye out for Kari and Jill. They would be easier to spot within the crowd, because most of the other girls had dark hair.

The city was much larger than Kelli had anticipated. A mixture of antique stores, dress shops, and food vendors were setting merchandise up next to each other on the sidewalks. The aroma of fresh-baked bread and pies could be smelled throughout the streets.

All the shops and houses were jammed close together, and there seemed to be oodles of people parading throughout the city. Kelli sighed. She wondered how they were ever going to find Kari and Jill.

Hank immediately flagged down a taxi, and they spent the entire day driving up and down the numerous narrow streets. They drove by an assortment of stores, local taverns, unsound slums, along the ocean shoreline, and through the more expensive vicinity in the city. But unfortunately, there wasn't any sign of Kari or Jill anywhere.

Hank finally told the taxi driver to pull into the local police station. He hurried inside while Kari and Bill waited impatiently in the taxi. After a short time, he returned, frowning. "Well, they sure weren't much help. They said they could handle the situation without my help. In other words, it doesn't look like they're in too big of hurry to do a damn thing," he said. "Excuse my language, but it pisses me off! It looks like I'm going to have to check these scumbags out myself, or I'll be waiting forever for these so-called policemen."

"I thought the FBI was helping out?" Kelli asked.

"Yeah, I thought they would have some information about my daughter by now," Bill added, frustrated.

"Well, they're supposed to be working on it, but sometimes they move too slowly, too! I need to contact Charles Naylor, an agent that is supposed to arrive sometime today." He shook the piece of paper in his hand. "But for now, I just want to check out where these addresses are."

Hank mumbled to the driver to take them back to the hotel. He glanced over his shoulder at Kelli and Bill. "I need to go back to the room and grab a few things. Sorry, but you two will have to wait for me there until I get back."

"But I want to go with you," Kelli pleaded.

"I know you do, but its best if you guys wait at the hotel. It will be getting dark shortly. There isn't much else we can do today anyway. We'll just start fresh early in the morning."

Bill wrapped his arm around Kelli's shoulder. "We understand—don't we, Kel?"

Kelli nodded. "Yeah, I guess." Disappointed, she stared out the window. She didn't understand why she couldn't ride with Hank. After all, she had flown all the way to Turkey to help find her sister. Now he was telling her that they had to stay in their rooms—it wasn't fair.

Kelli reluctantly followed her dad and Hank back to their hotel rooms. Suddenly, she had an idea. "I think I will lie down for awhile," she said, yawning.

"We'll go eat as soon as I get back unless you two want to go ahead and grab something now, and I can eat later," Hank said.

"We can wait until you come back." Bill stopped in front of Kelli's room.

Kelli unlocked the door. "Just come and get me when you get back."

"Okay, Kelli." Hank pulled his key out of his slacks pocket.

Kelli quickly shut the door and stood silently, listening for her dad and Hank's door to close. She scurried over to the bed and dumped the contents of her purse onto it. She had some lire of her own left from earlier in the day, and her dad had also given her more for ice cream. She just hoped she had enough for a taxi.

There wasn't any way she was going to let Hank go without her, especially if there was a chance he might locate someone that was connected with Kari. Kelli decided she had no other alternative; she had to follow him. She just prayed she could pull it off and sneak back into her room without being caught, or her dad would be furious. She quickly stuffed the money back in her purse, grabbed a jacket out of her suitcase, and rushed back toward the door. She pressed her ear up against the door so she could hear when Hank left his room.

After a few minutes, she heard Hank opening his door and telling her father he would see him shortly. She patiently waited until she heard his footsteps fading down the hallway. She quickly slipped out the door, closing it gently behind her. She quietly trailed behind Hank, keeping an adequate distance between them. She sneaked out the front entrance of the hotel

159

and hid behind the multicolored stone waterfall. She peeked just as Hank was waving down a taxi; she quickly copied the same motions.

A dull grayish-white taxi immediately pulled up to the curb. Kelli ducked her head into the window to make sure the man looked trusting enough to ride with. Although she didn't know what a trusting Turkish man should look like, he seemed to have friendly eyes.

"Do you speak English?" she asked.

The taxi driver nodded. "Yes."

Kelli climbed into the back seat. "Please, follow that taxi in front of us."

"Yes."

Kelli concentrated on the various turns and curves the driver was taking. She thought she saw Hank glance over his shoulder in her direction. She ducked. She rose up and spoke sternly to the driver, "I don't want the man in the taxi to know I'm following him."

The driver glanced over his shoulder and winked. "Okay."

Oh great, Kelli thought, *this guy thinks I have something going on with Hank, and that I'm spying on him.*

The driver slowed down to let a few cars in front of him. "Is better?"

Kelli glanced toward Hank's taxi two cars up in front of them. "Yes, this is fine."

For the next fifteen minutes, Kelli rode in silence through the inner city, by the ocean, and past the sections of neglected, run-down homes.

Finally, she spotted Hank's taxi pulling up to a curb in a prosperous neighborhood. The buildings were painted vivid colors, and newly white picket fences surrounded many of the houses. Hank jumped out of the taxi and then leaned back inside the window to speak to his driver.

Kelli told her driver to drop her off a block down. She noticed that Hank's taxi wasn't moving. "Will you be close by?" she asked the driver.

"For a while, I do."

"Thanks." She quickly paid him and quietly crawled out.

160

Kelli closed the door gently and jogged up the street toward Hank, ducking cautiously behind neatly trimmed shrubs. When she was within hundred feet of him, she stooped behind a thick tree trunk that was close to the edge of the road. She watched anxiously as Hank carefully studied the colorful yellow building. It was a stylish three-story brick house with matching yellow flower curtains hanging in all the windows. Inside the front door, there was a luminous chandelier suspended in the hallway.

She glanced back toward Hank; he seemed to be analyzing the gold letters and numbers painted across the top of the building. For some reason, he didn't attempt to go up to the door, which Kelli thought was somewhat odd.

A screen door slammed, and Kelli jerked her head toward the house. An attractive woman in her mid-forties with prematurely gray hair and a pleasant face opened the door and walked out clinging tightly to a toddler's hand. Hank nodded and smiled as the woman passed him. He quickly pulled out his black folder, opened it, and seemed to be reading. Kelli noticed he was shaking his head in disbelief, and then suddenly he slammed the folder shut. He spun back toward the taxi driver and yanked the door opened. He looked to be perturbed. Kelli thought she heard him say something about it being the wrong address.

Kelli was so caught up in trying to hear what Hank was saying that she didn't hear the car that pulled up alongside of the road.

Suddenly, a stiff hand gripped her shoulder and jerked her around. "You really thought you could get away from me!"

"Ouch! What?" Kelli tried to pull away from the loathsome hippie-looking man, but his hold was too tight. Another short, rounded man jumped out of the passenger's seat and opened the back door of the car.

Kelli's adrenalin soared as she realized that the brutal man was planning to throw her inside the car. She screamed with all her might and plunged her body backwards, trying to pull away from the burly man. She briefly caught sight of Hank out of the corner of her eye just as the man shoved her into the back seat of the car and slid in next to her. She plunged her body across the man's lap and pounded her fists against the window as she

161

glared helplessly toward Hank; he dropped his folder and ran toward the car, but it was too late—the driver had already pulled away. The man threw Kelli back up against the seat. Kelli screamed again and pressed her body against the door, but it didn't budge.

The enraged thug slapped Kelli across the face callously, busting her lower lip. "Shut up now, or I will fucking kill you right here." He yanked out a Colt handgun from his coat and aimed it toward Kelli's head. "How dare you try to escape! Did you think you could cut your hair and throw on some jeans, and I would not find your ass?" He viciously grabbed Kelli's hair and pulled her head down on his lap, he continued to jab the barrel of the gun into her head. "Tell me where your damn friend is!"

"I don't know!" Kelli cringed in pain. Everything was happening so fast, she couldn't think straight. What did this bastard want from her?

"Oh, you're going to tell me. Believe me, you're going to fucking tell me by the time I'm done with you." He pulled Kelli's head up and slammed it against the back seat. "You're going to wish you never pulled this stunt. I told you there would be consequences if you tried to escape." He released his hold, pulled a cigarette out of his shirt pocket, lit it, and rudely shouted orders in Turkish to the driver.

Kelli's head throbbed as she tried to recollect all that had happened. She had never been so frightened of anyone in all her life. Drops of blood trickled from her lip down her chin. She wiped at it with the back of her hand, being careful not to touch her swollen lip. She tried to focus her eyes out the window, but the houses and shops blended into a blur. She fought off the dizziness as the urge to puke overwhelmed her. She couldn't imagine what the irate man wanted from her.

Suddenly, the pieces started fitting together. *The idiot must think I'm Kari, and the friend he is talking about is Jill,* she thought. Kelli impulsively glanced his way, and sure enough, she recognized the bottom chipped tooth and the choppy spiked hair. He was definitely one of the men in the pictures Hank had shown her. She glanced nervously out the back window, searching for a sign of Hank—but she didn't see him. Kelli desperately hoped

162

that Hank would catch up with them. The man had yanked her head down so fast she hadn't seen which direction Hank had gone.

Kelli had no other choice but to go along with the charade and pretend to be Kari. She figured if the man found out that she was Kari's twin sister, then he might also realize that the police and FBI were on to him, and then they may never find Kari. She listened carefully to the three men exchanging conversation in Turkish. She frequently heard the driver call the man next to her Vaar. She recalled Hank using the name Vaar Roami several times.

Kelli tried to focus on the direction they were going, but the driver had already distracted her by taking too many turns. She knew she would never be able to keep up; besides, her head was still pounding with pain.

Although Kelli was scared out of her wits, she was thrilled to find out that Kari and Jill had escaped this dreadful man. It was hard to say what he had done to them, but at least they were still alive.

Kelli cautiously glimpsed toward Vaar—he puffed heavily on his cigarette and then cracked the window to toss it out. He had left the top two buttons on his gaudy silver-striped shirt unbuttoned, revealing the thick mass of hair on his chest. Kelli had never seen so many earrings, necklaces, and rings.

She swallowed, tasting the wet blood in her mouth just another reminder of how horrible Vaar was. She knew if she wanted to defeat him, she would have to outwit him. Kelli was determined not to let the creep win the best of her. She would have to fabricate a believable lie about Jill fast.

After a short while, the driver parked in front of a rundown, dinghy brick building. The plump man in the front seat jumped out, opened the back door, grabbed Kelli's arm, and pulled her roughly from the backseat.

Kelli glanced up and down the street, searching for help, but the street was deserted. Not even a cat or dog was in sight. Her eyes shifted back to the massive building in front of her. Her body quivered. The vintage building looked haunting; it was bleak and creepy.

The other buildings on the block looked even worse, with broken windows, peeling paint and trash spread out through the yards. The hefty man tried pulling her forward toward the lifeless building, but Kelli twisted and pulled, trying to break away from his hold. She immediately quit resisting, though, when she felt the point of Vaar's gun in the middle of her back.

"Don't think I won't shoot you right here, little lady," Vaar hissed.

Kelli let the man pull her inside the building. A greasy, longhaired bearded fellow carrying a rifle met them at the door. The stench of the man made Kelli's stomach queasy, and the man glared at her as though he would like to fire bullets through her chest. Surely, Vaar wasn't planning to leave her alone with this character for punishment.

The foul man grabbed Kelli's shoulders and pushed her toward the stairs, yelling stridently in Turkish. Vaar shouted some orders, and the man dropped his hands to his side and backed away from Kelli.

Vaar forced Kelli toward the stairs. "I want to take care of this one myself," he spoke in English and grinned at Kelli.

Kelli reluctantly climbed the steep stairs.

They reached the top, and Vaar nudged the gun into Kelli's back. "You know where to go, back to the same room."

Kelli nervously glanced up and down the hallway at the closed doors, not having any clue which room Kari and Jill might have been in. "I refuse to go back to that dump."

"Oh you do, do you?" Vaar's eye's narrowed as the veins in his forehead protruded.

Kelli feared for her life. He looked angry enough to rupture the vessels in his temples.

Scowling at her, Vaar seized her by the arm and dragged her down the hallway. He led her into a small, dim room and slammed the door shut. He crammed the gun into the pocket of his leather coat, yanked the garment off, and threw it on the cot. He wiped the perspiration off his forehead with the back of his hand. With clenched fists he said, "Okay, I'm going to ask you again—where the hell is she?"

"I don't know," Kelli said boldly, although his rage was frightening her.

Vaar suddenly plowed his fist into Kelli's face, knocking her to her knees. "I'm not playing games. You have really pissed me off, and I'm giving you only one more chance to tell me."

Kelli flinched and grabbed her cheek. She closed her eyes; a tear squeezed through her lashes. "Okay, I'll tell you as much as I know," she said, trying to stall. She rested her hands on her knees. "Just a minute, please, let me catch my breath." Kelli inhaled a deep breath and slowly exhaled it. "I was with Jill when you snatched me. She had just gone inside that yellow building." Kelli dithered. "There was a man that lived there that was going to help us, and she went inside to talk to him."

"And why didn't you go with her?" Vaar asked.

"Because I was suppose to wait for that black man to get there."

"The black man that was chasing our car? Anyway, why would you be waiting outside for him?" he asked in doubt.

Kelli stared at the skull head tattoo on his arm. "I was supposed to wait for the black man because he was a doctor, and he wasn't sure what building we would be in." She glanced toward the coat on the cot—the gun was in the pocket.

"A doctor?"

"Yes." Kelli paused. "The man's wife was pregnant, and she was going into early labor. He and Jill hurried to be with his wife, and I was waiting for the doctor. I saw the doctor and was about to yell to him when you pulled up." Kelli prayed he believed the ridiculous story—it was the best she could come up with.

Vaar eyed Kelli suspiciously. "Are you fucking making this up?"

"No, I swear, I'm not." Kelli glanced toward the coat again; there wasn't enough time for her to grab the gun. Her eyes met Vaar's. She stared at him in silence for a long moment. "Please don't go back there and get Jill. Leave her alone, please." Kelli hoped he would fall for the sham and go back to the spot where they were. Then Hank would catch him, and make Vaar tell him where Kelli was.

165

Vaar paced the length of the small room, growing more and more agitated. He finally stopped and stooped over Kelli, peering down at her with disgust. He reached down, clutched a handful of hair, and yanked her to her feet. He grasped hold of the front of her bloodstained shirt and pulled her within inches of his face. "I am going to check your story out. And if you are lying, I am coming back and killing you! Do you understand me?"

Terrified, Kelli whispered, "Yes."

Vaar let loose of Kelli's shirt and shoved her to the ground. "You'd better not be lying!" He spun around, grabbed his coat, and left the room.

Kelli could hear him locking the door. She remained on the floor, trying to digest all that had happened. Her head ached severely; she ran her hand over the bump on the back of her head and massaged it gently. She had never met such a violent person before. What kind of madman was he, Kelli wondered. She hoped that he hadn't hurt Kari or Jill.

She pulled herself onto her hands and knees and studied the tiny room. There were two cots and nothing more. She thought the room looked poorly, paint flaking and a grimy tarnished floor. She struggled to stand, but got a serious cramp in her calf. She massaged her leg vigorously until the pain subsided.

After a few minutes, she edged her way over to one of the cots. She slowly ran her hand over the pillow as tears surfaced. She wondered if Kari had slept there.

She suddenly froze—she thought she heard tapping on the door. She automatically thought of the creepy guy downstairs and the way he had looked at her.

She tiptoed over to the door and stood quietly. There it was again.

"Kari, it's me. Can you hear me?" A girl said weakly.

After a long pause, "Yes, I hear you." Kelli detected an English accent.

"Are you okay? Did you get to tell anybody where we were?"

The voice sounded sincere, and Kelli wondered if she should risk telling her who she really was. "Is anyone out there with you?"

"No, I heard Vaar yelling at Scrooge. And then when I slipped into the restroom I saw Scrooge hurrying up the alley. So I don't know what happened. We'll probably have a different guard now. I have to hurry and get back to my room before someone comes."

"I'm not Kari."

Silence.

"Are you still there?" Kelli asked.

"Yes, I'm here. I peeked out of my room and saw you coming up the stairs. I know it's you, Kari."

"No, I'm not. My name is Kelli—I'm Kari's twin sister. The police figured out that she and Jill was over in this country, so my dad, a policeman, and I flew over here to find them. Vaar thinks I'm Kari." She paused. "Please tell me if Kari and Jill were okay when you saw them last."

"Oh wow, this is bizarre—maybe we will be found now. Yes, Kari and Jill were okay when they left. They stole Scrooge's money out of the tree out back and went for help. Oh, my name is Renae. I hear someone coming—I need to go."

Kelli listened as the weightless footsteps pattered down the hallway. She heard heavier steps approaching the top of the stairs; a door opened, and then the footsteps faded back down the stairs. She was curious what it was all about.

Kelli wandered over to the cot and sat down. She skimmed her fingertips over her sore lip and winced from the touch. She thought of Hank and her dad. She could imagine how panicky her dad would be when he realized his other daughter was also missing.

She was surprised to learn that there were more girls here. What was Vaar up to? If Hank didn't find Kelli soon, she might not ever know what Vaar's intentions were. When Vaar found out that Kelli's story was fictional, he'd be fuming. There was no doubt in Kelli's mind that he would kill her.

***

Hank doubled up his fist and pounded it against the car's seat. "Damn, which way did they go?" He frantically searched up and

167

down the street, trying to spot the car that had Kelli in it. He couldn't believe this was happening.

"I do not see car, sir," the taxi driver said.

"Damn, keep looking." Hank said, relieved that the cab driver spoke English. He had been looking through his folder when he had heard a piercing scream from a young girl. He had turned just as Kelli was being thrown into a sizeable black car. Hank instantly recognized the man as Vaar Roami, one of the prime suspects in the case. He had read that the man was very wealthy and highly influential in the country.

Hank had chased after the car, but soon realized he didn't have a chance in hell at catching up with it. He grabbed his folder, jumped in the taxi, and ordered the driver to follow the car. They kept on the vehicle's tail for a while, but then the glossy black car made a couple of sharp turns—and that was it— they lost them.

Hank threw the folder down in the seat and folded his arms across his chest. This was a nightmare. "Damn, her father's going to kill me!"

"What?" the driver asked.

"Nothing, just take me back to the hotel." *What the hell was Kelli doing out here?* Hank wondered. *She must have been following me. I should have known she would pull something like this—after all the meddling she's already done.*

Hank was not only furious with Kelli but also disappointed in himself. He wished he could have talked Bill and Kelli out of coming to this unspeakable country. He should have known better than to think it would be safe.

He wondered why Vaar had grabbed Kelli. Did he know she was Kelli, or perhaps he thought she was Kari—with shorter hair—no, not likely.

Hank decided to go back to the hotel and contact the FBI agent. He didn't have a clue how he was going to explain Kelli's' disappearance to her father. He knew Bill would be devastated.

Bill was sitting in the desk chair at the round table, sorting through the pictures of the suspected men when Hank marched into the room.

Hank thought it would be best not to beat around the bush. "I'm sorry, Bill, but I've got some really bad news for you." He sighed, lifting his eyes from the floor.

Bill shook his head and covered his ears with his hands. "I'll be damned! Please don't tell me anything bad. I couldn't bear any more horrible news!"

"I'm sorry. Believe me, I wish I didn't have to tell you this." Hank cleared his throat; this was harder than he had imagined. "Well, it looks like Kelli followed me to the apartment building earlier and..." He wiped at the perspiration forming under his nose. "Vaar Roami grabbed her and threw her in a car. I don't know if he knew who she was or not."

"Oh my God, you're kidding." Bill dropped the pictures he was holding. "What the hell was she doing following you? I told her to stay in her room!" He bounced up, knocking the rest of the pictures off the table. He raced to Kelli's room and banged fiercely on the door. After a few minutes and no response, he drifted slowly back to his own room.

"I'm sorry." Hank patted Bill on the back. Seeing Bill so grief-stricken was heart wrenching. Hank carefully explained the details of Kelli's abduction. "I need to call that Naylor agent." Hank blew his nose. "I'm really sorry, Bill." He pulled out his wallet and flipped through his business cards.

"Shit, I can't believe this!" Bill hit the table with a clinched fist. "We've got to find them!" He ran his hand nervously through his hair and walked toward the window to peer out.

"We'll find them, I promise," Hank said. "I plan on nailing the scumbags once and for all!" He located the business card and silently read it. "I am going to be tied up for a while with this agent."

"What can I do to help?" Bill mumbled, covering his eyes.

Hank knew Bill was close to crumbling. "Hang in there, man. We'll find them." He threw his briefcase on the bed and popped it open. He dug out a map and tossed it to Bill. "I don't want to alarm you, but we need to check out the hospitals in the area. You can start by locating them and showing the girls' pictures." He glanced at the clock on the nightstand. "It's getting late; you might want to wait until the morning." Hank awkwardly walked

169

over to stand next to Bill at the window. He wished he knew the right words to comfort Bill.

Hank stared out into the settling street; lonely shadows seemed to be dancing across the sidewalks. Most of the city had already retired for the night.

"How can I sleep, knowing that some madmen have my daughters out there somewhere—doing—God knows what to them." Bill moaned loudly, followed by a series of uncontrollable sobs.

"I don't blame you—I wouldn't be able to sleep either." Hank gently touched Bill's arm. "I feel awful. This is all my fault." He bowed his head.

"I'm not blaming you at all. I just feel so helpless." Bill reached for the hanky in his pocket. "I'm supposed to protect my daughters, and now they're both missing, and I don't know what the hell I'm supposed to do now." Bill suddenly hurled the map across the room. "I tell you what, though. I'm not leaving this damned country without my daughters, and those bastards better not have hurt them, or I will kill every last one of them!"

Hank couldn't blame Bill for his neurotic behavior. He would be equally enraged if the men had his niece. Leila was the closest thing he ever had to a daughter. The girl had spent nearly every summer with them for as long as he could remember. His brother and wife were decent parents; they just enjoyed traveling a lot. Leila always preferred to stay close to home, so she could be near her friends and participate in the summer activities. She always stayed in the extra bedroom at Hank and Betty's house. It was fine by Hank; he enjoyed her company. He tended to spoil her too much, but he liked doing it. Homesickness stabbed at his heart.

He shook his head and walked away from the window. He made his call to Charles, who agreed to meet him down at the police station.

Hank couldn't help but feel at fault over Kelli. If he were any kind of a reputable detective, he would have realized he was being followed. He slammed his briefcase in frustration. "Hey, I got to get going now. I'll call you later and let you know what we have planned. I'm taking my phone with me this time, so call

170

me if you need me." Hank stuck his cell phone in his jacket pocket. He had called the cell phone company before he left the States to make sure it would function in Turkey. "Everything's going to be okay. We'll find them."

"I hope you're right. I'm going out myself to search. I'll keep my phone on in case you need to reach me."

Hank searched through the pictures that were on the floor until he found the one of Vaar. "This is the man that snatched Kelli."

"Well, if I see him, he's definitely going to find out who I am!" Bill popped his fist into the palm of his other hand. "I think I have been patient enough; I've had it."

"Don't do anything foolish," Hank warned. "Just call me if you come up with anything. I know that's easier said than done, but it's important that we do everything legally. Got to run—see you later."

Hank grabbed his briefcase off the bed and headed out the door. This was, by far, the toughest case he had ever had. He was still puzzled, though, why Vaar had grabbed Kelli. Surely, he didn't know she was in Turkey. Could it be possible that he did think it was Kari? But their hairstyles were so different.

Now he was even more determined to resolve the case since he was partially responsible for Kelli's abduction. Maybe Naylor's respectable authority would persuade the local police to get off their asses and do something. And if they refused to let Hank contribute his knowledge, he would find one way or another to assist in finding the girls—even if it cost him his job.

171

CHAPTER SIXTEEN

Kari shivered as she slowly stirred awake. The room was bitterly cold, and so still that she could hear her chest inflating as she breathed. The sun was just starting to rise, and the outline of the room was barely visible. She listened attentively as Mister noisily cleaned his paws. Although she couldn't see him, she could feel a furry lump nuzzled close to the bottom of her feet. Suddenly the quietness seemed threatening, and panic overwhelmed her. Throughout the night, she'd awakened to focus on Jill's heavy breathing, but now she didn't hear anything.

Kari flipped on her side and jiggled Jill's arm. "Jill, are you okay?" She held her breath as she waited for Jill to reply. After a long silent moment, Kari shook Jill's arm again, more desperately this time. "Jill, wake up." She waited patiently; she thought she saw Jill's chest slightly rise.

Jill's hazy eyes fluttered opened and confusion appeared on her face. "Where am I?" she asked weakly.

"You scared me." Kari sighed. "We're still in the same building we were in yesterday. Don't you remember?"

"I'm thirsty," Jill whispered as her tongue darted over her cracked lips.

"I'll be back." Kari quickly jumped up and grabbed the empty juice bottle. She ran into the rest room, rinsed it out, and filled it with tap water. She hurried back to Jill's side. "Here, take a drink of this." She tried to lift Jill into a sitting position, but Jill winced in pain.

"I can't sit up," she said.

"Where does it hurt?" Kari thought she looked extremely pale and thinner than usual. Her petite frame couldn't afford to lose any more weight.

"I hurt all over."

"Come on, honey, try again." Kari hoisted her gently, as Jill grudgingly pulled herself up into a sitting position. Jill rested her frails hands behind her to hold her weakening body up. Sweat beads dripped off her flushed forehead while her damp hair clung to the side of her face.

Kari placed the back of her hand on Jill's forehead. "You're running a fever." She held the bottle up to Jill's lips so she could swallow. "Do you want to try to eat something?"

"No, I can't. I want to lie back down." Jill eased her body slowly back down to the floor. Her teeth suddenly started chattering. "I'm so cold."

Kari wondered how she could go from sweating to freezing. She wrapped the blanket around Jill and tucked the edges under her.

"Where is my mom? I want my mom," Jill whined.

"Your mom's not here." Kari didn't know if it was her imagination, or if Jill's pupils were dilated. "Do you not remember us escaping from Scrooge yesterday?

"Who? Where is my mom, Kari?" Jill moaned.

Kari decided it was best not to upset her any worse than what she already was. "Jill, honey, I'm going to have to go get your mom. Do you think you will be okay while I'm gone?"

Jill's eyes moistened. "You're going to leave me?"

The last thing in the world that Kari wanted to do was to leave her, but she didn't know what else to do. She couldn't recall ever seeing anyone so ill. Kari feared Jill would die if she didn't attempt to get her help. "I won't be gone long. Here's the bottle of water if you get thirsty." Kari reached down, scooped up Mister, and laid him close beside Jill. "I'll leave Mister with you to keep you company."

173

"Kari, I'm not going to die, am I?" Jill's eyes widened with fear.

"Of course not, sweetie." Kari gently rubbed her hand across Jill's forehead. "You're going to be fine. I'm not going to let anything happen to you. You just lie here until I get back."

Kari quickly bundled her hair up and pulled the scarf over her head. She glanced down at Jill; her eyes were already closed. "Jill, I'll be back soon." Jill didn't respond—she'd already fell back to sleep.

Kari quietly slipped through the broken window; she was well aware of the risk she was taking, but figured the consequences were going to be much worse if she didn't find help. She bent down and pulled her socks up to her knees; the air was clear but the temperature was still frigid. She walked briskly past the rows of inactive houses. She passed only one house that had a light on in the front room. And not a soul was visible on the streets. She figured the sun would be up within the next half-hour and there would be more people commuting to their jobs.

Kari slowed her pace as the headlights of a car blinded her. She bowed her head to the ground, so the driver couldn't see her face. The car zoomed on by. She increased her steps, only to repeat the same actions each time a vehicle sped by. Each time Kari's body stiffened, and she prayed that Vaar's men weren't behind the steering wheel.

After several minutes of continuous fretting, she was relieved to reach the downtown area. The sun was starting to seep out from behind a cloud. Many of the vendors were assembling their workstations. Kari glanced up and down the streets, analyzing the different shops and trying to decide which one might be able to help her.

An attractive young lady, close to Kari's age, stepped out of a cafe to change the lettering on a neon sign. Kari hesitantly approached the girl from behind. "Hello."

The dainty girl spun around and smiled. "Halo."

"Do you speak English?"

"Little." The girl held up a parted thumb and finger to gesture.

174

"I am looking for a doctor." Kari wondered if she should find an American to help her. She quickly added, "Or maybe where the Embassy would be at."

The girl shrugged, puzzled.

"A hospital for someone sick, or the government building," Kari said.

"Hospital?" The girl's face suddenly relaxed with the familiarity of the word. She pointed down the street. "Three stops—turn." The girl motioned her hand toward the left. "One stop—turn." The girl motioned her hand to the right this time. "You see hospital."

"Thank you so much." Kari nodded.

The girl grinned and turned back toward the sign.

Kari scuttled past all the trendy shops toward the direction the girl had indicated. She desperately wanted to run but fought back the urge. She didn't want to attract any further attention. She assumed the girl had meant three blocks, turn left, and then one block, turn right.

Last night, before she fell asleep, Kari had decided that the Embassy might support them after she explained everything that had happened to them. *That is—if Vaar doesn't crookedly work for the government also*, Kari thought. She groaned softly; she was at the point where she didn't know who she could trust. Maybe a doctor for now would be best. Hopefully, he wouldn't interrogate Kari too much.

By the time she reached the final block, the sun was fully visible and the city was buzzing with turmoil. She spotted the enormous hospital as soon as she rounded the corner. It was a huge white brick building with rows of miniature windows on each floor. Kari quickly jogged up to the entrance doors and proceeded inside. The front desk had three older ladies sitting behind it, working on computers.

"Hello. Do any of you speak English?" Kari asked softly.

The three ladies exchanged baffled glances and shook their heads no. The elderly lady with gray streaks rose from her chair and motioned Kari to stay still. She disappeared down the hallway. After a few short minutes, she returned with an incredible, good-looking young gentleman, dressed in a navy pinstriped suit and tie, and carrying a clipboard. It was the first head-spinning guy Kari had came upon since arriving in Turkey.

"Yes Ma'am, may I help you?" The young man smiled warmly.

"Oh, I am so glad you speak English. I need help." Kari hesitated as she recalled what happened to her the last time she trusted a cute guy. She quickly discarded her skeptical theory; she didn't have a choice. "I have a friend that is really sick and needs medical attention."

The young man eyes darted past Kari into the parking lot. "Okay, bring her in."

"I can't. I have no way to get her here. She's back at an isolated building. We are from the United States, and it's a long story that I don't have time to explain right now."

"Do you have money for treatment?" The man thumped his pencil on the clipboard.

"Not with me, but soon as I can contact my parents, I will pay for the treatment."

"I'm sorry, but if you don't have any money, we can't help you here. But I can give you an address where you can go to get assistance." The man reached inside his suit jacket pocket to retrieve a business card.

Kari blinked back tears. "Please, you have got to help me; I don't have time to go somewhere else. My friend is going to die if you don't help her. I promise I will get you the money."

The man studied his watch thoughtfully. "Well, this is against normal policies, but I will help you. Let me see if I can find a doctor, and we will go with you. Please, wait there." The man pointed to the lobby full of empty chairs.

Kari, relieved, sat down on one of the blue flowered cushion chairs and picked up a magazine written in Turkish. *Now I'll have to tell the gentleman and the doctor the truth,* Kari thought. *Maybe they will contact the Embassy and an American consultant will make sure we get home safely.*

Kari skimmed through the pages, not paying any attention to the décor furniture in the pictures. She lifted her eyes to stare at the back of a man who had just entered the room and was leaning against the front desk speaking to the clerk. Something

176

seemed peculiar about the man at the counter. Maybe it was the light brown hair. Up until now, she had only seen black or gray hair since she had been in the country. Even more odd was the familiar plaid blue shirt he was wearing—she couldn't recall where she had seen it before.

Suddenly, Kari remembered where she knew the shirt. She jumped up, dropping the magazine to the floor. *Could it possibly be?* she wondered. She carefully took a few steps closer, studying the back profile of the man. *No, it couldn't be; her dad wouldn't be in Turkey.* She noticed the way the man shifted his weight nervously from one foot to the other just like her dad did when he was upset. The height and lean build of the man was identical to her father's. She glanced down at his shoes and her heart just about hit the floor. There on his feet were the brown golf-like shoes that she and Kelli were always teasing him about. Kari knew that no one but her dad would wear such hideous shoes. "Dad, is that you?" Kari asked in a shaky voice as she pulled the scarf off her head.

Bill spun around, stunned. "Kari! Oh my God, I don't believe this." He flung his arms around her trembling shoulders and gazed up at the ceiling. "Thank you, God." He squeezed Kari tighter as tears flooded his eyes. "Are you okay, baby? We've been so worried!"

"I'm okay." Kari mumbled between sobs. "But Jill—she's real sick, Dad—we've got to hurry."

"Jill? Where is she?" Bill pulled away from Kari and held her at arm's length.

"She's back at an abandoned building. We escaped from those awful..." Kari couldn't utter another word. She clung to her dad as she sobbed. The emotional buildup from the last few days was devastating.

The young gentleman returned with a short, plump doctor. "We are ready to go. Is there a problem?"

Bill pulled away from Kari and slid his arm around her shoulders. "This is my daughter. She and her friend have been missing, and I have finally found her." He squeezed Kari's shoulders.

Kari pulled her bangs behind her ears and wiped at her tears with the back of her hand. "We're ready to go. We need to hurry."

"Yes, of course. Follow me." The young man led the way out into the parking lot toward a tan-colored van. He opened the sliding door for Kari and Bill to climb in. "My name is Ali and this is Doctor Malohi, but he doesn't speak any English. I will be the translator."

"I'm Kari and this is my father, Bill," Kari said in a quivering voice. She still was in shock that she had actually bumped into her father at a hospital in Turkey. How bizarre! She always heard that the Lord worked in mysterious ways, and this was definitely one of those times.

Kari gave Ali the directions to where Jill was. Once they reached the building, Kari hurriedly jumped out of the van. "I'll be right back to let you in the front door." She quickly ran around to the side of the house, ignoring the stares from the men working on the sidewalk. She leaped through the broken window and darted to the door to unlock it. She yanked the door open and hustled back to where Jill was laying. "Jill, I'm back now. I have a doctor with me. He's going to help you." She continued to talk to Jill's closed eyes. "Guess what? My dad is here, too. We're going home as soon as you get well." Kari backed away so the doctor could get near her.

While the doctor was examining Jill, Kari filled her dad in on everything that had happened since Doug had taken her to the warehouse. She suddenly remembered Renae and told her dad about the other girls that needed help.

Bill's stared at the floor for a long moment and then lifted his eyes. "I didn't want to tell you this, but something else bad has happened since we've been in Turkey."

Kari couldn't imagine anything worse than what she had already been through. "What's that?"

"Kelli and a police officer, Hank Catron, who is working on the case, flew over here with me..."

Kari started jumping up and down. "Oh my gosh, Kelli's here." She didn't think she could ever miss her sister as much as she did the last few days.

178

"Calm down—let me finish." Bill hesitated. "Kelli was following Hank last night when I thought she was resting in her room. He had gone to check out a couple of leads on your whereabouts. Anyway, while Kelli was secretly trailing Hank, a man by the name of Vaar Roami grabbed her and threw her in his car."

"What! No way!" Kari covered her mouth with her hand. "Oh my God! Where is she now?"

Bill blinked away a tear in the corner of his eye. "I'm sorry honey, but we haven't found her yet."

"No, Dad, this can't be true! Vaar is the same man that kidnapped me. He's been looking for me." Tears gushed down Kari's cheeks as her voice trembled, "If he has Kelli, he will kill her to get back at me for escaping." She buried her head into her dad's shoulder and cried uncontrollably.

"Hank is trying to find her now." Bill hugged Kari closely.

Kari's head suddenly popped up. "I know where she is. We've got to go get her now before it's too late!"

"I'm supposed to get a hold of Hank—he can go with us."

"We can't wait, Dad. It will be too late. We have to go now! We can call him and have him meet us there" Kari peeked into the bedroom to see what the doctor was doing to Jill. He was lifting her off the floor. Kari puzzled, glanced toward Ali as the doctor passed her carrying Jill. "Is everything okay?"

"I'm afraid it don't look good, Kari. Your friend is very sick and needs to be in the hospital to run more tests. Doctor Malohi can't diagnose the problem without a more detailed examination. He needs to run some blood work on her, and he thinks she may be dehydrated," Ali jotted a memo on his clipboard.

"Will she be okay?" Bill asked.

"I won't lie to you. The doctor can't tell yet. She is very sick. She's not even aware of where she is. We need to contact her parents at once."

"I can give you all that information," Bill said.

Kari had been so elated to see her dad, and now, the heartbreaking news that she had been hit with in the last five minutes about Kelli and Jill was more than she could handle. She couldn't believe everything was okay a few minutes ago, and now it was a disastrous mess. Her whole life was crumpling right in front of her. How could both her best friend and her loyal sister be in such a predicament that their lives were in jeopardy? Kari couldn't control the outrage she was feeling. "Why is this happening? This isn't fair!" she yelled.

"I agree." Bill pulled a clean hankie out of his pocket and handed it to Kari. He locked hands with Kari. "Let's hurry; Jill needs to get to the hospital." They followed Ali out to the van. The doctor already had Jill lying down inside and covered up with a green wool blanket.

Bill waited for Kari to crawl in, and then he climbed in and slammed the door shut. "Honey, you probably should stay with Jill until she is out of danger. You can direct me to the location where you think Vaar has taken Kelli, and I will call Hank and meet him there."

"Vaar is cruel and vindictive, Dad. He would kill you and not think twice about it."

"I know." Bill leaned his head back against the seat. "As much as I want to hurry and rescue Kelli myself—perhaps I'd better wait until Hank gets there and let him and the police handle the situation."

"Do you want me to contact the police for you when we get back to the hospital?" Ali asked.

Bill sighed. "Yes, that would help immensely. Could you be my translator?"

"I'll help all I can. First though, we must contact the girl's parents, just in case..." Ali lowered his voice. "She doesn't make it."

Kari shuddered at his words. Jill, not make it? What a horrible thought. She couldn't imagine her life without Jill—or her sister. Her eyes grew misty as an image of Kelli blurred her vision. The sister whom she adored more than heaven itself, who had always been her mentor, now had risked her own life to try to save her.

Kari knew there wasn't any way she could survive without Kelli; the guilt alone would kill her.

She pulled her hair behind her ears and quietly stared out the window as she concentrated on what to do. As much as she didn't want to leave Jill, she knew she had to go with her dad to save Kelli. They couldn't waste any more time, or it could cost Kelli her life. She figured Jill was too sick to realize that they weren't there with her anyway. And she was safe and in good hands now, Kari told herself, trying to ease the guilt.

The van pulled up to the emergency entrance and a staff of nurses rushed outside to assist with Jill. They laid her carefully on a stretcher and then rushed her inside the hospital.

Kari waited in the lobby while her dad contacted Jill's parents. She wanted to call her mom, but her dad suggested they do that later, after they found Kelli. He hadn't wanted to tell her about Kelli missing yet.

Bill returned to the lobby. "Well, Jill's parents are flying over right away. I asked them not to phone your mom yet. I told them that I would call her after a while."

"Mom will be furious with you for not calling."

"I know, but I just can't bring myself to upset her anymore. She'll be thrilled that we found you, but she will be devastated that we lost Kelli in the meantime. I don't think her poor body can handle much more trauma. So we'll just wait a couple more hours and see what happens."

Bill slipped his address book in his pocket. "I tried to contact Hank, but I only got his voice mail, so I left a message about what had happened and what I'm planning on doing. Ali is calling the police."

"Can I please go with you, Dad? I don't know the address, so I'll have to show you the way."

Bill rubbed his chin with the back of his hand. "I don't know—I don't like the idea of you going." He glanced down at his watch. "But if you don't know the address, I guess you will have to guide me. And once we get there, I'll wait for Hank and the police." He shook his finger at Kari. "And you, young lady—are going in a taxi and back to the hotel. I want you to go straight to the room and lock the door. Here's the key, hide it in your pocket." He handed Kari the key with the name of the hotel and room number on it.

"We won't be able to take a taxi, because I'm going to have to backtrack through the woods to find the place."

181

"Well, I'll just have the taxi follow us the best that he can—they know their way around. I'm sure they can figure out which street the woods come out on. And then the taxi can pick you up while I'm waiting for Hank."

Bill hurried up to the front desk to ask the clerk, "Could I leave a message for Ali?"

The woman pointed to her ear, gesturing that she didn't understand.

Bill spotted a notepad and pointed to it. The lady tore off a piece of paper and handed it to him. He quickly scribbled a note and nodded to the lady.

"Come on, let's go." He led Kari out the exit and flagged down the nearest taxi.

Kari smiled weakly at the driver and spurted out the directions to the building where she and Jill had been hiding. She figured from there she might be able to find her way back to the ghastly place. The thought of going back to the appalling vicinity made her stomach churn. As they drove, Bill explained to the driver what he wanted him to do after they made it through the woods.

The driver's eyebrows creased as he listened to Kari describing the neighborhood where Vaar's building was. "I think I know the place you are talking about, but I'm not sure." He glanced at Bill. "If it's the same neighborhood—I've heard stories—you should be careful." He agreed to drive them as far as he could—to the wooded lot, and then he would try to find the area.

Kari was surprised that the driver spoke English so well. She wondered if he was originally from another country.

She slumped down in the seat and stared out the window. *What have I done to my family and my best friend?* she thought. She accepted the fact that she was the reason for all the chaos—she didn't blame anyone but herself. If she hadn't let her hormones rocket over a hot guy, they wouldn't be in Turkey today.

She grimaced at the thought of Kelli in Vaar's hands. Kari decided even though she couldn't change the past, she could repent by saving Kelli. She wasn't going to let Vaar hurt her sister! She wanted so much to believe that she could prevent Vaar from harming Kelli, but the truth was Kari feared for Kelli's life—and now, her dad's and her own.

CHAPTER SEVENTEEN

Kelli jumped up from the cot as footsteps neared. She shuddered and folded her aching arms across her chest. She had been locked up in the stuffy room all night. She had dozed off occasionally, but never slept soundly. No one had come to check on her since Renae had last come to the door.

She remained completely motionless as the key unlocked the door. Her breath suddenly ceased as the door opened, and Vaar marched into the room. He was wearing sleek black leather pants and a midriff leather jacket with the sleeves rolled up so the bottom of his skull tattoo was visible. A glowing cigarette dangled from his mouth. Kelli didn't miss the rage in his ruthless eyes, and she feared her life was over.

"What kind of fucking game are you playing, young lady?" Vaar reached for the cigarette between his lips, flipped it on the floor, and scrunched it with the toe of his boot.

"Did you really think you could fool me?" He yanked the gun from his jacket and aimed it toward Kelli's forehead. "You know, I could easily shoot you right now."

Kelli cringed; she fought back tears as she nervously chewed on her lower lip. She wasn't sure exactly what he was talking about it. She didn't know if he knew she wasn't Kari, or if he had found out the truth about the lie she had told.

Vaar circled around Kelli, keeping the gun pointed to her head. "Do you want to live?"

Kelli didn't respond.

He shoved the tip of the gun up under her chin. "I said: do you want to fucking live?"

She slowly nodded her head.

"I can't hear you."

"Yes," Kelli gasped.

"How bad do you want to live?" Vaar jostled the gun under Kelli's chin until she was staring up at the ceiling.

Kelli stiffened; she feared he would pull the trigger if she didn't say what he wanted to hear. "Very much."

"That's what I thought. Do you plan to do what I tell you to do?"

"Yes."

"If you make one mistake or try to escape, I promise I will kill you. Is this clear?"

"Yes—yes," she stammered.

Vaar suddenly removed the gun from Kelli's chin. "Bitch, I'm warning you—you better not screw this up. And since I don't have your friend, you're going to make twice as much money for me." His eyes narrowed. "But because you lied about your friend's whereabouts—when we do find her, she's dead and you have only yourself to thank for that." He grinned callously, walked over to the door, and leaned out to motion Sahre into the room. He looked back at Kelli. "Do everything Sahre tells you. Understand?"

"Yes." Kelli stared at the gorgeous woman.

"Have her ready and downstairs in twenty minutes, along with the three other ones." He rubbed his hand seductively over Sahre's hips, winked, and left the room.

Sahre gracefully glided toward Kelli; she lifted a small section of Kelli's hair, letting it slowly fall through her fingers. "What did you do to your hair? This is horrible!" She didn't wait for a response. "You're lucky he didn't kill you. He must think he's going to get a bundle of money out of you." She gazed at Kelli from head to toe. "I don't think he will, though." She turned toward the door. "Follow me."

Kelli followed Sahre down the lengthy hallway to the restroom. She was relieved that Vaar hadn't killed her, but was dreading what lay ahead.

185

Sahre pointed to the restroom. "Use the restroom." She then nodded toward the shower stall. "And then take a quick shower and wash your hair." She laid the towels and shampoo down on the sink counter. "I will be back in five minutes, and I expect you to be done. Don't put any of those funky clothes back on, either." She quickly disappeared out the door.

Kelli decided to do exactly what she was told. She feared if she screwed up one little detail, Vaar would kill her. Her stomach was queasy from the earlier incident; the worse feeling was not knowing if the creep was going to pull the trigger. She could only imagine how scared Kari and Jill must have been. She remembered how frightened Kari had always been of strangers when they were younger; she wouldn't even speak to the mailman. And Jill, the poor thing, was even worse; she'd always been so petite and frail. Kelli recalled the time in fourth grade when Jill had started crying when a teacher had asked her to speak up in class because she couldn't hear her.

Kelli was surprised that they had the courage to escape. She couldn't believe that Kari and Jill would have the nerve to try something so bold. *Good for you, Kari,* she thought. Kelli was thankful that the girls had succeeded in such a complicated task. It warmed her heart to know Kari could survive without her. Kelli flinched—just in case Vaar changed his mind and did decide to kill her.

Kelli finished and wrapped the cotton towel around her body. Goosebumps emerged on her legs as she waited for Sahre.

Sahre returned, carrying a dress and other related articles of clothing. She laid them in a pile on the bench and threw a pair of shoes on the floor. "Get dressed." She tossed a hairbrush on the clothes. "Brush what hair you have left." She then laid a toothbrush and toothpaste upon the sink. "Brush your teeth. I will be back shortly." She snatched up the clothes off the floor that Kelli had had on and exited out the door.

Kelli picked up the kitschy silver silk dress and held it up to examine. It was extremely skimpy—a braless halter-type dress. She sorted through the remaining undergarments to see if Sahre had left her a strapless bra, but she hadn't.

186

She hurriedly pulled the bikini panties on and slipped the lightweight dress over her head. She pulled the thin nylon stockings on and slipped the silver high-heeled shoes on her feet. She strolled over to the half mirror hanging above the sink, and with a critical eye, she studied the inappropriate reflection. Although she could see only the top half of her body, she was well aware of the provocative look she was portraying.

A sickening image flashed through her head. She reminisced the way Vaar had flirtatiously slid his hand over Sahre's backside earlier. Kelli retched and rushed into the restroom stall to throw up. She held her hair back with one hand while waiting for the nausea to diminish. She tried to shake the repulsive thought—she prayed that Vaar didn't plan to have his way with her.

Panting heavily, she made her way back to the sink and splashed cold water on her face. She quickly ran the brush through her wet, tangled hair and brushed her teeth.

Kelli had only been done a few minutes when Sahre returned carrying a duffel bag.

"Sit on the bench!" Sahre ordered.

Kelli wobbled clumsily over to the bench. She didn't wear heels too often, and the shoes were too big; it felt as though she was walking on stilts. Sahre hovered over her and reached for the makeup case out of the bag. She proceeded to apply various makeup to Kelli's face. She grabbed some hair accessories out of a container and brushed Kari's short hair into a spiked bun high upon on her head.

Sahre stepped back to admire the finished product. "You should have left your hair alone." She returned all the supplies back to the bag. "Let's go."

Kelli stood up awkwardly. She glimpsed at the reflection in the mirror as she passed and couldn't believe what she saw. The azure blue eye shadow was caked on up to her eyebrows, and the heavy black eyeliner was smeared thick under her eyes. Sahre had used a bright crimson color lipstick and blush to coat Kelli's cheekbones and lips. There was a sharp pain in the pit of Kelli's stomach as she followed Sahre out the door and down the

187

hallway. She was scared that they were going to make her do something that she had never done before.

Kelli moved stealthily down the stairs, not lifting her eyes from her feet. Just as she touched the bottom stair, Vaar entered the hallway.

His jaw dropped as he gaped lustfully at Kelli. He gradually circled her. "Yes, you shall pay off nicely." He stopped directly in front of her—his eyes hardened. "One false move from you and you are dead. Do you comprehend what I am saying?"

Kelli refused to meet his gaze—she bowed her head. "Yes."

She heard familiar featherlike footsteps at the top of the stairs and glanced up to see a beautiful blond and two younger girls standing at the top of the stairs. A broad-shouldered fellow carrying a rifle shoved them forward.

Kelli wasn't surprised to see that they, too, were clad in dresses and high heels. She imagined the slinky, slender blond was Renae. She reminded Kelli of a high-class super model. She had on a sexy, frivolous black backless dress. Her natural blond hair was bundled neatly on the top of her head, with a few single strands falling around her pale oval face—her makeup was heavy but not too gaudy. Kelli studied the younger girls—even with all the cosmetics and high heels, she knew they couldn't be over thirteen years old. They both had silky-smooth tan skin and appeared to be of Turkey nationality.

Kelli glanced from the girls to Vaar's hungry eyes. The queasiness plagued her again, and she had to choke back the urge to hurl. She couldn't shake the disgusting images out of her head—she knew what Vaar had planned for them all.

Vaar remained near Kelly until the girls were down the stairs, and then he paraded around each of them, gazing at their maturing bodies. He finally opened the front door and spoke harshly, "Follow Sahre!"

Kelli and the other girls followed Sahre out to the full-sized polished black car, with Vaar trailing close behind them. The dutiful driver opened the door, and Vaar pushed Kelli inside the back seat. He slid in next to her. He motioned to the two younger girls to crawl in beside him and pointed to Renae to ride in the front seat with Sahre.

The brawny man who had followed the girls down the stairs exchanged words with Vaar and pointed to a white car parked directly behind them. He then walked back and crawled behind the wheel of the car.

Kelli flattened her body against the back of the seat as Vaar's leg pressed against hers. She quickly crossed her legs and scooted closer to the window. Just the slightest contact from Vaar appalled her.

Her stomach grumbled from hunger, and she had to think when she had eaten last—it was at lunch yesterday with her dad and Hank—it now seemed like so long ago.

The driver pulled away from the curb, and Kelli focused her eyes out the window to avoid Vaar gawking at her. The early sun was shining brightly, and Kelli had to squint to see the surrounding area. Before long, they were out of the slums and driving through the inner city, passing extravagant houses and hotels. They turned on a highway, near the ocean, and traveled out of the city. The further they drove away from the city, the tenser Kelli became. The houses slowly dwindled down as the peaks of towering mountains became more visible.

Kelli fought back tears as she clasped her trembling hands together in her lap. She could actually feel her body quivering— and it wasn't from the nippy temperature. *Death would have been more painless,* she thought. *At least I wouldn't be expected to do immoral deeds.*

She suddenly recalled reading a book once about a kidnapping: the young girl that was snatched had played along with her abductor and then escaped when it was least expected. Kelli's mind raced—she didn't know if she was capable of pulling off the same stunt. She considered the malicious expressions from the faces of Vaar and his men; they all were such hostile creatures.

Kelli stared at the back of Sahre's sophisticated hairstyle and wondered how such a beautiful woman could get involved with such a gruesome man. Kelli gaped at the studded diamond necklace hanging around Sahre's neck and imagined that money was a big part of the reason.

189

Kelli gazed out the window as she tried to concentrate on a structural plan that would aid in getting her and the other girls away from Vaar and his men. She realized time was critical if she wanted to be successful in her escape.

After a good half-hour of driving through the vast country, the driver finally signaled and turned down a dirt road. Each side of the curvy, narrow road was lined with foliage, undergrowth, and trees. Kelli strained to see beyond the greenery, but couldn't make anything out other than a dense forest.

After a few miles, the driver pulled down an adjoining dirt road, which led up to an extravagant two-story brick home with frilly curtains, double French doors, and a marble in-ground swimming pool. Next to the miraculous house was a huge, freshly painted red barn.

Kelli nervously scanned the classy cars parked in the extensive field—there had to be a least fifty. Men of various ages and sizes were walking from the cars into the barn. Kelli glanced toward the front of the barn; vendors in black striped hats and aprons were selling hotdogs and beer. A cluster of men stood in a circle talking and laughing.

Kelli panicked as the driver brought the car to a halt. Her breath quickened as the men in the group stopped talking and stared in their direction.

The driver rushed out of the car to help Sahre and Renae out. He then opened the back door for the rest of them to climb out.

Kelli bit down on her bottom lip as she huddled close to Renae.

Vaar took the lead and motioned to the rest of them to follow him. He stopped in front of the group of men and slid his left hand into his coat pocket. Speaking in Turkish, he gestured toward the girls and laughed.

The men's eyes shot toward the girls as they responded with feisty yelps.

Kelli shifted her eyes to the ground—the dress she had on suddenly felt transparent. She had never felt so disgustingly sleazy before. She didn't know what Vaar's intentions were, but she sure wasn't going to stick around too much longer to find out.

She cautiously glanced around, exploring all of her surroundings, while Vaar continued to chat with the men. She caught a glimpse of a small shack toward the rear of the house that looked like a chicken house. Beyond that was a wooden door in the ground, which she assumed was a cellar. She was surprised it wasn't closer to the house. She did notice it didn't have any lock on it. Her eyes darted past the door toward the woods; the most logical place to hide would be there. However, that was probably where Vaar would look first. She had to hide in a place where he would less likely think her to be.

Abruptly, Vaar shouted, "Let's go, ladies." He headed toward the barn.

Kelli glanced back over her shoulder as the other white car that had been following them parked. The hefty man with the gun got out and trailed behind them. Kelli didn't think it was a wise time to make her escape.

She quickly followed the other girls into the barn. A room full of men that were standing around talking, whistled and hollered as they marched by. A lengthy red velvet curtain was draped neatly across a large platform that went all the way across the width of the barn. Vaar quickly led them behind it, so they weren't visible to the eager men. He then directed them toward a small hallway that led to a huge room with reddish-purple flowered wallpaper and maroon carpet. It consisted of an oval glass table with high-back chairs, a sink, and a stove. On the stylish table was a clear plastic bowl full of apples and oranges.

Kelli impulsively glanced for an exit door and spotted one at the back of the room. There were two cardboard boxes pushed up against it, as if it weren't being used. She noticed a chain lock at the top of the door and hoped that was the only one.

Vaar pointed to the chairs positioned around the table. "You girls sit down and wait for your turn to go on stage. The fruit is from me, to thank you for all the money I am going to make today." He snickered, pivoted toward Sahre, and spoke in Turkish. He then turned back toward the girls. "See you ladies later. Remember to smile pretty when you're up on stage, and you will make some man very happy!" Vaar chuckled ruthlessly. He paused in front of Kelli and brushed her cheek with his

191

fingertips. "You will be going home with one of those hungry men shortly. Did you see any that caught your interest?" His eyes narrowed as his mouth curved into a thin, angry line. "Don't worry, you won't get to choose." He turned on his heels and walked out of the room.

Over my dead body, I am, Kelli wanted to scream. There's no way in hell I'm leaving with any of those filthy men. You'll have to kill me first. Her eyes darted toward the back door, finalizing her decision.

CHAPTER EIGHTEEN

Kari spotted the familiar place where she had left Jill to wait while she ran back to the house to get the money. "This is it, Dad. We're on the right street now." She hadn't had any trouble backtracking though the woods. The recent dry weather helped to prevent the path of broken limbs and footprints that she and Jill had left behind from being destroyed.

"This street looks deserted," Bill said as he glanced uneasily up and down the street.

"Well, it mostly is except the house at the end of the block. That's where he has Kelli." Kari pointed down the street and picked up her pace toward the house. "Let's go closer."

"Whoa, young lady, this is as far as you go!" Bill caught sight of the taxi just as it turned the corner. "Hey, he didn't have any trouble finding us. Go on, get in the taxi, and go back to the hotel. I'll call Hank and let him know where I am."

"But, Dad...." Kari pleaded.

"You heard me!" His tone softened. "Now which house is it?"

"It's the last one on the left-hand side," Kari mumbled.

Bill pulled his cell phone out of his jacket and bent forward to kiss Kari's forehead. "I love you. Now go on, honey. I'll be fine. I'm going to walk a little ways down the street and wait for Hank and the police. Go get in the taxi and go straight to the hotel."

"Okay, I will." Kari leisurely strolled toward the taxi while watching her dad out of the corner of her eye. He was dialing on the cell phone and proceeding slowly down the street.

Bill turned and waved to Kari. "Go on."

"I am." Kari took a few more baby steps toward the taxi. She knew her father meant well, but he wasn't always right. She didn't want to disobey her dad, but she didn't feel comfortable leaving him—she just wanted to wait until the police arrive. Her mind was made up. She abruptly opened the door to the taxi and explained to the driver that her dad had changed his mind, and wanted her to wait until the police arrived. She asked the driver if he would mind coming back by in ten minutes.

The driver hesitated but finally nodded.

Kari patiently waited until her father was halfway down the block, and then she jogged discretely in the same direction. Guilt plagued her, but she couldn't just stand by when something bad might happen to her dad.

She quietly kept her distance, hiding behind damaged fences and shrubbery as much as possible. Her dad approached the sidewalk across the street from the alleged house Kelli was in, and Kari quickly scurried behind a tarnished picket fence and ducked down.

She watched silently as her father dialed several numbers on his phone. A few times, it looked if he was carrying on a conversation. He kept gaping at the house and then glancing nervously up and down the street. He repeatedly paced up and down the sidewalk. Kari couldn't imagine what he was doing. She was worried because he was in clear view of the house and wasn't trying to make his presence undisclosed.

Finally, disgusted, Bill shoved the cell phone in his pocket and marched toward the front door.

Kari gritted her teeth—she couldn't believe he was going to the house alone. She wanted to scream at him to stop, but instead she remained silent. Her mind was racing in several different directions; she didn't know what to do. She thought of Kelli and wondered what she would do. And then Kelli's encouraging words came to mind, 'You do what you have to do.' Kari recalled Kelli quoting those exact words to her when a bully was

194

threatening to take her lunch money. Kelli had told Kari if she had to fight to keep her lunch money than that was what she must do. Kari had taken her advice and stood up to the bully and the tormenter suddenly backed down.

Kari slid toward the edge of the fence as her dad knocked on the front door. After a few minutes of nerve-wrecking silence, and no one opening the door, Kari watched in agony as he slowly twisted the doorknob—and surprisingly, the door creaked opened. She held her breath as her dad glanced up and down the street and then entered the unwelcoming house.

***

"This is the house," Hank told the cab driver as he stared out the window at the poorly maintained house. "Don't leave. I won't be long." He jumped out of the taxi and cautiously headed up the crazed sidewalk with his hand tightly gripping the pistol in his jacket pocket. Suddenly, leaves rustled to the right of him. He crouched low and jerked his head in the direction of the threatening sound. A sudden flicker of red flashed before his eyes as a red head ducked behind a tree. Hank sighed and loosened his grip on the gun. He was sure it had to be Kari. Ali had already told him about Bill finding her. Hank had also received a message from Bill telling him the address they were at. Naylor and the local police were supposed to meet him here any time now.

He darted over to the tree and peeked around it. "Hello there, Miss. Are you Kari?"

He had caught Kari off guard; she jumped up and flattened her body up against the tree. "Who are you?" she gasped.

"I'm sorry I didn't mean to scare you. I'm Hank Catron. I flew over here with your dad and sister."

Kari's eyes grew hazy. "Oh, thank God you're here." She pulled her hair nervously behind her ears and stared up toward the house. "My father went in there. Please, help him. He's been in there too long, and I'm afraid something has happened to him." Single teardrops slithered down Kari's cheek onto her dress.

195

"Okay, wait here. If the police or an FBI agent named Naylor comes, tell them I went on in." Hank pulled the pistol from his jacket. "Go back behind that tree and don't come out until the police get here."

"Okay," Kari wiped at her eyes before ducking behind the tree.

Hank waited until Kari was safely hidden, and then he slowly advanced toward the house. The door was slightly ajar, and a strong, revolting odor filled his nostrils. He held the gun above his head and kicked his foot firmly into the wooden door. The door flew open, slamming back against the wall. He rushed into the house, keeping his gun angled in front of him. He could easily see into the front room, and immediately witnessed Bill tied up and gagged in the corner of the room. Other than the plates of spoiled food scattered across the end tables—the room was empty. Hank didn't see any sign of Bill's assailant, but he had enough experience to know that the foe had to be close by, waiting for Hank to make the wrong move.

Hank moved down the hallway toward Bill guardedly. He hesitated when he noticed Bill's disturbed eyes darting back and forth toward the other side of the doorframe. Hank was sure Bill was trying to tell him that his aggressor was waiting for him on the other side of the door.

Hank held up his thumb to let Bill know he understood. He quietly took a few steps toward the doorway, but suddenly paused—his breathing was too strident, which sometimes happened when his adrenalin escalated. Hank inhaled a deep breath, silently counted to three, and flung himself around the edge of the doorframe. A shot rang out—but Hank knocked the man's arm in time, sending the discharge toward the ceiling. Hank kept his own gun pointed at the man's forehead as he wrestled the gun away from him.

Hank quickly tied the husky man up and freed Bill. "You okay?" He was glad he didn't have to shoot the guy—he held the essential information they needed to locate Kelli.

"Yeah, I think. He caught me off guard." Bill said as he rubbed the back of his head.

196

"Here take this." Hank passed Bill the man's gun. He knew the Turkish police would frown on Bill's involvement, but under the circumstances, Hank didn't have any other choice. He mentally shrugged—he was probably already in trouble for interfering with the situation anyway. "Keep an eye on him. I'm going to check out the rest of the house." He didn't wait for a response—he crept toward the stairs.

Hank paused at the top of the stairs and twisted his head sideways, listening for any inquisitive sounds that might prove there were more assailants on the floor. Not hearing any suspicious noises, he glanced down the hall at the numerous closed doors. He quietly moved toward the first door and gently opened it—the room was empty except for the two unmade cots. He pulled the door shut and preceded on to the next room. It too was vacant. He paused outside the door of the third room; he thought he heard girls' voices. Hank wiped the sweat off his forehead with the sleeve of his jacket and groped for the door handle. He prayed Kelli was on the other side of the door. He tapped lightly on the door and then opened it.

Two young girls screamed and huddled close together on a cot.

"I'm sorry. I am a police officer. I didn't mean to scare you." Hank knew the girls couldn't be more than fourteen or fifteen years old. One of them looked to be Turkish, but the other one had light brown hair and blue eyes. "Do either one of you speak English?"

"I do." The girl with the light hair stood as she spoke.

"I'm here to help you. What is your name?" Hank said kindly. He could tell the girls were scared, and he didn't want to frighten them any more than what they already were.

"I'm Emily and this is Kila. She speaks only Turkish. I was brought here last night—my home is in Paris."

"Do you know why you are here?" Hank asked.

Emily exchanged wavering glances with Kila, but neither one of them spoke.

Hank smiled warmly at the girls as he tried to befriend them. "Believe me, I'm here to help you. I've got the bad guy tied up

197

down stairs. I flew over here to find a girl that was missing from America. Can you help me?

"They took all the other girls away this morning." Emily stared down at the floor. "They didn't take us earlier—I thought you were them, coming back for us."

"Took them away? Do you know where they were taking the girls?"

Emily's voice softened, "Another girl that was here, Renae, she told us that we would be sold as slaves to Turkish men."

"Sold as slaves?" Hank always loathed that word—not because he was black, but because of the gruesome facts that he learned when he had researched the topic in college. Just hearing the word made his skin crawl. But even worse, when it was used in conjunction with young girls—it made him mad as hell. "Do you have any clue whatsoever where they would take the girls?"

"No. I don't know," Emily began in a faint whisper. "What is going to happen to us now?"

"Don't worry, you're both going back home." Hank glanced toward Kila, who was still clinging to Emily. He could easily read the look of terror spread across her innocent face. He glanced back at Emily. "Do you speak Turkish?"

Emily nodded, and Hank continued. "Could you relay to your friend what is going on? My Turkish isn't too clear."

"Yes." Emily smiled proudly. "I'm glad I can speak five different languages; it has come in handy." She quickly turned and spoke Turkish to the young girl.

A wide grin spread across Kila's face as she looked up at Hank with wide eyes. She suddenly ran to him, fell to her knees, and wrapped her arms around his legs.

Hank was speechless. *Poor thing—how scared she must have been!* He stooped down, grasped her hands, and pulled her to a standing position. He placed his hand on top of her head, tousling her hair. He looked back toward Emily. "I need you two to stay in this room until the rest of the police officers get here. They are on their way. Can you do that for me?"

"Sure," Emily shrugged.

"I've got to go find the other girls, so I will see you after a while. Don't worry, you're okay now."

198

Hank waited until the girls had climbed back on the cot before he left the room.

He hurried back downstairs and dismissed Bill, so he could comfort Kari, who was still outside waiting for the latest news.

Hank interrogated the rough-looking guy several times, but the fellow wouldn't bulge; he kept his eyes focused straight in front of him. Finally, Hank tried his specialty—bluffing—he told the guy, in fragmented Turkish, that he would release him if he told him the address where Vaar and the girls were. At first, the guy was skeptical, but as the sirens grew closer, the man panicked and mouthed off an address. Hank smiled—it always worked; the loser fell for the sham. There was no way in hell he was going to let the guy go. Hank was having enough trouble keeping his fist out of the creep's face, but he managed to restrain himself. He figured the authorities were already going to be upset with him for interfering.

Hank quickly jotted down the address on one of his business cards and dashed toward the front door. He just hoped the guy wasn't bluffing himself.

Hank met a Turkish policeman on the way into the house. "Do you speak English?"

"No speak English good," the officer said. He pointed outside toward the street. "Many men here."

Hank assumed he was saying that there were more police on the way. He glanced at his watch and wondered where Naylor was. He knew if he waited too much longer, it could be too late to save Kelli and the others. "Here." He crammed the business card into the officer's hand. "This is where the other girls are." Hank pointed to the upstairs and held up two fingers. "There are two girls up there that need help." He pointed to the man tied up. "He's one of the criminals." Hank stepped through the entrance of the doorway and glanced up and down the street. "I've got to go. Have your men come to that address."

The officer nodded with a confused look, and Hank wondered if he even understood anything he had said.

Hank waved and motioned to the taxi; he didn't have time to explain any more specifics to the policeman.

199

Hank shouted at Bill and Kari, "I know where she is. Go on back to the hotel, and I'll call and let you know as soon as I find her.

Bill rushed toward the taxi. "No way. I'm going with you. Please, Hank, I've got to go—it's my daughter, for crying out loud."

Hank hesitated and rested his eyes on Kari.

"I'll just ride along and wait in the taxi. You won't even know I'm around," Kari said.

"I don't know," Hank began waveringly. He finally sighed. "Okay, but you both must wait in the taxi."

He waited for Bill and Kari to climb in, and then he rambled off the address to the driver.

Hank moaned silently. He knew he shouldn't be taking Bill and Kari with him, but he figured that Bill would probably have ended up following him anyway, and he hadn't wanted to waste any more time arguing with him.

Hank's throat grew dry as he realized the risk he was creating. He knew that this could be his worst decision yet.

CHAPTER NINETEEN

Kelli gnawed on the apple and chewed it hungrily while keeping her eyes fixed on Sahre. She had been patiently waiting for Sahre to move out of earshot, so she could discuss her plan with Renae.

Finally, the overweight man from the white car came to the doorway, and Sahre walked over to speak to him.

Kelli quickly bent toward Renae and murmured, "Do you want to escape with me?"

"How?" Renae asked with raised eyebrows.

"Through that door there." Kelli nodded toward the back door.

Renae covered her mouth to whisper, "I don't know." She wrung her hands nervously together. "I'm too scared. I'll help you, though, if you want. And then you can get help for all of us."

"Okay." Kelli paused to glance from the back door to the entrance where Sahre and the man were talking. "In a few minutes, pretend you are sick and draw as much attention to yourself as you can until I can get out the door. Oh—and be sure to go over toward the entrance, away from me."

"Okay." Renae frowned. "Are you sure you really want to do this?"

Kelli nodded. "I'm sure."

Renae patted Kelli's leg. "Be careful!

"I will, be sure to..." Kelli cut her sentence off as Sahre turned to glare at them. She waited until Sahre had spun back toward the man again. "As soon as the man leaves, go up to her and let her know how sick you are."

"Okay. What if the door won't open?"

"Then I'm going to be in big trouble!" Kelli took another bite of the apple as she cleared her mind. She glanced toward the trashcan. If by chance, she was caught before she could get out the door, she could always say that she was throwing the apple away.

Kelli watched silently as the man waved at Sahre, turned, and left the room. Kelli nodded to Renae.

Renae quickly stood and drifted over next to Sahre. She clutched at her stomach, howled in pain, and suddenly fell to her knees, crying hysterically.

Sahre's face paled as she glanced nervously around the room. She bent over Renae and tried to pacify her.

The other two girls at the table weren't aware of what was going on, and they immediately jumped up to gather around Renae.

Kelli stood, pretending to be interested in Renae's welfare.

Renae's wails increased, and Sahre grew tenser with every shriek. Sahre suddenly stood—she glanced helplessly at the other girls and then down at Renae. "Now what," she mumbled as she threw her hands up in the air, then she turned and ran out the door, yelling for assistance.

Kelli's heartbeat accelerated as she raced toward the back door. She hurriedly knocked the boxes aside and unlatched the chain. She grasped the doorknob and pulled, but it didn't budge. "Oh no! Please God, help me," she whispered. She grunted and gave it another muscular tug, and finally, the door flew open. She glanced back over her shoulder. Renae's muscles in her face relaxed briefly as she gestured at Kelli to run, and then she returned to her frantic bawling.

Kelli peeped out the door to make sure it was clear before stepping outside. She pulled the door shut behind her and ran toward the back of the house in the direction of the cellar. After stumbling a few times, she stopped and stooped over to pull the

202

high heels off her feet. She threw them in the opposite direction and continued onward. She frequently glanced over her shoulder to make sure no one was following. Fortunately, there wasn't a soul in sight. She figured they were all inside, waiting for her to parade across the dreadful stage.

She spotted the cellar and ran to it with full speed. She yanked on the handle and it easily opened. She hesitated as spiders ran for cover. It was completely dark, and the thought of being down there in the dark, with who knows what else, made her quiver. But as she heard men hollering nearby, she didn't give it another thought. She slipped into the cellar, gently easing the door shut over her head. It was pitch black; she slowly edged her way down the vertical stairs, keeping her hands extended in front of her.

She approached the bottom of the stair and turned left, bumping into a dirt wall. She then tried turning right, her hand touched a cobweb, and she jumped back. The room was small; she could easily touch the dirt ceiling with the palm of her hands. She moved a few more feet and ran into a slanted shelf full of canning jars.

Kelli stiffened and listened guardedly. She could hear voices nearby—she ducked under the shelf and moved as far back against the wall as she could, not caring about the spider webs that she encountered. She squatted and remained motionless as she strained to hear which way the voices were going. She could hear men's voices in every direction and was certain that they were looking for her.

After a long five minutes, she heard looming footsteps nearing the cellar. She held her breath and prayed they wouldn't stop. Suddenly, the cellar door lifted up. Kelli froze and covered her mouth to quiet her breathing. She could feel the pulse in her neck beating erratically. A bright gleam from a flashlight flickered, and she huddled closer to the wall. She couldn't tell if she was out of view or not.

She remained utterly still as more footsteps approached. She could hear two men exchanging words. Just as she thought she couldn't hold her breath any longer, the door dropped shut and the footsteps rushed off in a different direction.

Kelli exhaled in relief as her adrenaline ceased. She knew she still wasn't out of danger, but at least for now, she was okay. She wasn't sure what her next move would be. Maybe after a while she would venture out into the woods, or maybe she should just wait it out and stay put until someone rescued her.

Her shoulders slumped—she knew it was possible that no one might ever find any of them. They were so far off into the country; Hank might not be able to track them down. She shuddered—she could sit down in the cellar for days before someone ever found her.

She plopped down on her rear and stretched her legs out in front of her. She decided her best shot would be to wait a few hours, and then take off running through the woods. And hope, by some miracle, she found a kind, compassionate human to help her. Discouraged, Kelli threw her head back against the wall— she suddenly realized that by then it would be too late to save Renae and the other girls.

***

The further they drove the more uptight Hank grew. He clasped his hands together and gazed out the window. Although the aging bald-headed taxi driver had hesitated and stared suspiciously at Hank when he rattled off the address, he still had agreed to take them to the spot. Hank had no doubt, for whatever reason, that the driver knew exactly where the place was.

Hank scanned the settled countryside; they were already twenty miles away from the city. He glanced down at his watch and sighed. He wondered how much further they had.

His cell phone rang and he anxiously drew it from his jacket while keeping his eyes fixed out the window. "Hello, this is Hank Catron."

"Hank, it's me, Naylor. Sorry I didn't meet you back at the house, but I got a lead on where they have Kelli and the other girls, and I'm almost there now. There's more police on the way out there, too."

"Yeah, the head honcho at the house finally coughed up the address, and we're headed there too." Hank glanced at his watch.

204

"I didn't know it was way out in the middle of nowhere. I'm glad you'll be there. Don't scalp these men before I get a chance to!" Hank laughed, although he wasn't joking.

He hung up the phone and glanced at Bill and Kari in the back seat; they were sitting on the edge of the seat waiting for the update. "Naylor and the local police will be meeting us there. I think we have them! I'll have the driver park far away from the scene. It's vital you two stay out of sight."

As they pulled down a second winding dirt road, an extraordinary brick house came into view. Hank noticed a bunch of vehicles parked in a burnt-out cornfield, but he didn't see any police cars. He wondered if he had beaten Naylor and the others there. He gestured to the driver. "Stop here. Don't go any further." Hank was straightforward with the driver about the situation and managed to coax him into sticking around by offering him extra lira. He spun toward Bill, grasping the back of the seat. "I need you two to stay here and don't get out, no matter what."

"If Kelli's up there, I'm going up there," Bill stated flatly as he reached for door handle.

"Hey, I know how you feel, man, but you're going to be no good to your daughters dead!" Hank didn't have time to beat around the bush. "This is police business and highly dangerous. Besides, you will be risking Kari's life if you leave her here alone; you need to stay with her. I imagine when all hell breaks loose these guys are going to be running every which way. I need to trust that you will do as I say."

Bill's eyebrows drew together thoughtfully as he glanced toward the house, and then at Kari. "I guess you're right." He released the door handle. "Yeah, you can trust me. We'll wait here." He glanced back through the rearview window. "Aren't you going to wait for Naylor?"

"I'm just going to hike up the road and hide out until he gets here. That way I'll be close by when they arrive."

"Now who's taking a chance?" Bill tried to grin.

"Trust me. I'll be fine." Hank sensed Bill was having a hard time coping with the situation; his cheeks had reddened and his bottom lip twitched every few seconds. Hank studied Kari. "Are you okay? You sure don't chatter like your sister does."

Kari grinned guiltily and pulled her hair behind her ears. "Actually, I'm the one that usually talks a lot, and Kelli is the shy one. But I guess I'm just really scared right now."

"We'll get your sister back. I promise." Hank winked at Kari as he opened the door. "Now, stay put!" His eyes darted back to the driver. "Remember, if any shooting breaks out drive them back to the hotel."

Hank jogged up the road, hiding behind the bushes and trees. He had just ducked behind a hedge plant near the barn when he recognized Naylor and another agent speeding behind a police car up the dirt road. Hank hoped they didn't sound the siren, that would give the offenders a warning, and then there would definitely be a shootout.

He squatted down as a couple of Turkish men strolled out of the barn; their eyes widened in alarm when they spotted the patrol car. They threw up their hands, cursing in their own language, and spun around to shout back into the barn. It was only a matter of seconds before dozens of men came running out toward the parked cars in the field. More police vehicles pulled up the driveway. The officers jumped out of the cars, pulled out their guns, and shouted commands at the numerous men running.

The events were happening so fast, Hank stood frozen—he didn't know which direction to go. He noticed Naylor already detaining a couple of the men. Naylor then ran inside the barn. It suddenly occurred to Hank that Vaar and his recruits would probably try to escape through a back door.

Hank sprinted toward the back of the barn and immediately spotted a partially secreted wooden door. He didn't think about the consequences he would encounter for his intrusive behavior. He gripped his gun tightly as he groped for the door handle. He momentarily glanced over his shoulder, and then jerked the door open. Sure enough, Vaar was facing the opposite direction with his gun extended toward the front entrance. Three frightened girls and an attractive lady were huddled together near his side. The sound of the back door startled Vaar, and he swung around and fired a shot toward Hank.

Hank instantly dropped to his knees as the bullet flew over his head. He kept his gun aimed at Vaar. "It's over, Vaar. Give it up."

Vaar abruptly grabbed the blond hair girl, yanked her in front of him, and wrapped his arm around her neck. He pointed the gun toward her head. "I'll fucking kill her, I swear!"

"Let her go! There's no way for you to escape. We've got the building surrounded," Hank hoped his bluff would work one more time.

"No way! She's going with me. Move the hell out of my way!" Vaar pushed the girl in front of him as he edged toward Hank.

Hank hesitated, but he knew he couldn't jeopardize the girl's life. He stood and moved aside so Vaar could get through the door.

Vaar dragged the frightened girl toward the door. The fear in the girl's eyes suddenly hardened, and she bent her head forward and sunk her teeth into Vaar's arm. Vaar screamed as he released his hold on the girl; she stumbled forward onto her knees.

"You bitch." Vaar hoisted his gun in anger and pointed it toward the girl. "Your life is over, missy." His finger curled around the trigger.

Vaar was just about to squeeze the trigger when Hank fired his own gun, sending a bullet through Vaar's left leg. Vaar stumbled clumsily backwards over a folding metal chair before hitting the ground with a thud. The other girls in the room screamed while the blond crawled for cover under a table.

Vaar grabbed his injured leg with one hand while twisting his body into a sitting position—he extended his gun toward Hank and pulled the trigger.

Hank leaped to the left, dodging the bullet—he spun and shot Vaar in the arm.

Vaar cursed loudly as he dropped his gun and clutched his bloody arm in pain.

Hank sighed and lowered his gun. All at once, pain sliced through his back as a chair came smashing down on him. He staggered forward but caught his balance by positioning his free hand against the wall. He whipped around to attack his

207

perpetrator and was shocked to see the posh lady holding the chair above her head as if she was going to strike again. Hank had never seen such unruly eyes on a woman before. He was certain if she'd had a gun, she would easily have killed him and not thought twice about it. She indecisively dropped the chair, spun around, and dashed toward the back door.

"I'll have to shoot you," Hank said as he swung his gun back and forth between her wiry backside and Vaar's collapsed body.

The lady's slender legs froze as she glanced over her shoulder toward Hank, and then toward the door. "Sonofabitch." She slung her head back and giggled shrewdly. She turned listlessly and raised her arms in defense. "This was all his idea." She shook her finger at Vaar, who was crumpled on the floor, moaning. "He made me do it."

The front door burst open, and police swarmed in the room. Naylor trailed close behind them. He spotted Hank and eyed him up and down. "Are you okay?"

"Yeah, I'm fine." Hank slowly straightened his back. "She just did one heck of a number on my back, though."

The police ignored Sahre's pleas, handcuffed her, and dragged her out of the room. Hank could hear ambulance sirens approaching from a distance. He secretly hoped Vaar died before they could get him to a hospital.

Hank elbowed Naylor and pointed to the hysterical girls huddled against the wall. "You take care of them, and I'll comfort this one." He nodded toward the blond.

Hank pulled the crying girl up from under the table. "You're going to be okay now. What's your name?"

"Renae Stosberg," the girl answered as she wiped at her nose with the back of her hand.

"You did a very brave thing. You should be proud." Hank smiled warmly. "Now, I need your help again. I'm looking for a girl named Kelli Raker. Have you seen her?"

"Yes." Renae covered her mouth with her hand as she tried to cease the sobs escaping from her throat.

"Do you know where she is?" Hank pulled a hankie out of his pocket.

"She was going to escape and go get help for us but...." Renae paused and reached for the hankie. She blew her nose and then continued. "Vaar was furious when he found out she had escaped, and he sent all the men out looking for her. After some time, Vaar returned and whispered something to Sahre. Sahre waited until Vaar had left the room and then she told us that Vaar had found Kelli and that he had...." Renae bowed her head and lowered her voice to a whisper, "He killed her....Sahre said Vaar killed Kelli." She couldn't stop the tears. "Poor Kelli." She continued hoarsely, "That's why I bit Vaar. That's the least I could do for my friend—if only I would have been brave earlier and escaped with her. Maybe I could have saved her." She leaned her head forward on Hank's shoulder and wept.

Hank was flabbergasted. He had just assumed after finding the rest of the girls that Kelli had to be around somewhere. He had thought that maybe they had locked her in a different room. However, he was unprepared for the news Renae had just delivered to him.

He glanced toward Vaar as the medical team rushed in the room and prepared the stretcher. He wanted more than anything to walk over there and choke the shit out of the bastard. He gently held Renae at arm's length. "It's okay, honey. You did the right thing. If you would have tried to escape, he would have killed you, too." Hank cleared his throat. He didn't want Renae to know how devastating the news was to him. "Go outside with the others. I'll be out in a little bit."

Hank quietly slipped over next to where Vaar lay. Vaar's eyes were shut and he was moaning sluggishly. It took every ounce of control that Hank had not to kick the scumbag. He squatted and leaned over the body. "Okay dirtbag, what did you do to the Raker girl?"

Vaar squinted as he tried to focus his eyes on Hank. "You mean Kari Raker, don't you— that fiery little red head bitch?" He said breathlessly. "She got what she had coming to her. I fucking killed her, but not before my men had a turn with her." He tried to laugh, but instead started wheezing and coughing.

"You bastard." Hank doubled up his fist and rammed it into the center of his jaw. Vaar's groan was acute but that still didn't

209

stop Hank from grasping Vaar's throat and squeezing it as tight as he could.

Hank's grip tightened as he blocked out the shouting commands by the police. All he cared about was watching this man's face turn blue. He wanted to make sure Vaar took his last and final breath.

Hank didn't weaken as the medical team frantically tugged on his arms. He could see Vaar's eyes rolling around inside his sockets. "Die, you sonofabitch!" Hank screamed.

Finally, someone grasped Hank's arms and pulled him with such force he went flying backwards. Hank's head hit the wall before he tumbled to the ground on his backside.

"What the hell are you doing? Do you want to be shot?" Naylor yelled. "You can't be doing that shit in this country." Naylor quickly spoke in Turkish to the police officers standing by and then he extended his hand to help Hank off the floor. "What did the jerk say to piss you off so bad?"

Hank stood up, rubbed his head, and turned to glare at the stretcher as they carried Vaar out of the room. He saw Vaar's chest inflating. "He should be dead!" He turned back to Naylor. "The scum said he killed Kelli after his men raped her."

"Well, we don't know that for sure. Let's hope he's bluffing. The police have been out patrolling the grounds and they haven't come across any bodies yet."

"He wasn't bluffing! Believe me—a man like that is capable of anything." Hank ran his hand over the knot swelling on his head. "I have Kelli's father and sister down the road, and I promised to bring Kelli back to them." Hank swallowed dryly. "Now I have to go tell them that I might not be bringing Kelli to them after all." He grew silent as he stared out the door. He finally shook his head. "This job never gets any easier. I think it's time for me to retire."

With slumped shoulders Hank sauntered out the back door, rounded the corner, and gazed toward the taxi down the street. It was still parked in the same spot. *Damn, this is so wrong*, he thought. He didn't know for certain that Kelli was dead, so he wasn't quite sure what he was going to say to Bill and Kari. He rubbed a tear out of the corner of his eye as he tried to regain his courage, and then he headed toward the taxi.

CHAPTER TWENTY

Kari sat glued to the window when the police zoomed by. She had watched restlessly as men raced to their cars, trying to escape the police. She hadn't been able to see clearly, but she saw well enough to get an obvious picture of what was going on. She had strained to catch a glimpse of Vaar or Sahre, but never did. Her father had a hard time staying in the car. He kept mumbling that he shouldn't have promised Hank that he would.

Finally, Kari caught sight of Hank walking toward them. "Dad, look, here comes Hank." Kari's eyes darted behind Hank, searching for Kelli. "I wonder where Kelli is. Do you see her anywhere?"

"No, I don't, and I'm not waiting in here any longer, either." Bill opened the door, climbed out of the car, and held the door open for Kari to crawl out. "Come on, let's meet him. I think the worst is over with."

Kari clasped hands with her father as they hurried up the dirt road. As they grew closer to Hank, Kari's curiosity rocketed—she released her father's hand and sprinted toward Hank. She instantly detected seriousness in Hank's face that she hadn't noticed before. His shirt was crinkled, un-tucked, and the top button had come unbuttoned. He had sweat beads along his hairline and perspiration stains underneath his armpits. Kari had an overwhelming feeling that something was wrong. "Where's Kelli?"

"Maybe we can find somewhere to sit," Hank said as he scanned the roadside.

"What is it, Hank? Is something wrong with Kelli? Did you find her?" Bill clenched his fists and shifted his weight from one leg to the other.

"I don't know for sure yet. They're still searching the grounds." Hank avoided eye contact by gazing down the dirt road toward the taxi. "We found three of the other girls, though. A girl named Renae says Kelli tried to escape."

"Of course she did! Kelli would never let an arrogant beast like Vaar push her around." Kari grinned and glanced toward the barn. "That's why she's not here, right?"

"Well, that's what we're hoping, but..." Hank glanced at Kari and then gradually shifted his eyes toward Bill. "Vaar says otherwise."

"What do you mean? C'mon Hank, spit it out," Bill said between clenched teeth.

"Vaar's still alive?" Kari asked, disappointed.

Hank crammed his hands into his slack's pockets and rocked on the back of his heels. "He's alive, all right—even after I shot him twice." He paused, inhaled a deep breath, and exhaled it slowly. "He may be lying, but he's claiming he killed Kelli."

"Oh God, no," Bill threw his arms up in the air, twisted away from Hank, and stared helplessly up at the sky.

"Vaar's lying! He's done something with her. I know he has! He's evil enough to kill her, but I know he's lying! He's too greedy—he wants money. He's hidden her somewhere—that's all," Kari shouted.

Hank reached over and grasped Kari's shoulder. "Kari, I'm sorry. I hope you're right. They haven't found any sign of her anywhere yet."

"Well, they haven't looked very good, or they would have found her," Kari snapped. She suddenly turned and ran up the road toward the barn. "Kelli's not dead! I know she's not!" she screamed.

"Kari, come back here now!" Bill hollered through choked sobs.

213

Kari ran faster than she had ever run before. There was no way she was going to accept Kelli being dead—it just wasn't possible. She couldn't go on living if Kelli wasn't a part of her life.

Renae, Una, and another Turkish girl were gathered outside the barn with a Turkish policeman. Kari dashed up to Renae and threw her arms around her neck. "I'm so glad you're okay! Please, tell me if you saw Kelli."

"The last time I saw her was when we were in there." Renae nodded toward the barn. "I pretended to be sick, and while Sahre ran for help, Kelli slipped out the back door."

"Good job! Did she say where she was going?" Kari's eyes shifted toward the house as she anxiously soaked in her surroundings.

"No, she didn't. But did they tell you what Vaar said?" Renae asked sadly.

"Excuse my language, but Vaar is full of shit. Remember, he told us there were more men downstairs, too, when there was only Scrooge. I don't believe he killed her. I think she's here somewhere, and I'm going to find her!" Kari hugged Renae. "I'll talk to you later."

"I hope you're right. Good luck," Renae called out. "I'll be praying."

"Thanks." Kari jogged toward the house.

A heavily built policeman stopped her and rambled off a bunch of Turkish that Kari didn't understand. He wouldn't let her proceed any further.

Hank and Bill had slipped up behind Kari and witnessed the incident.

"You're going to need my help if you plan on scrutinizing around here. They aren't going to let you just take off by yourself snooping around." Hank gestured to the officer that Kari was with him, and the officer smiled, nodded, and marched off in the opposite direction.

"Thanks, Hank." Kari turned and hugged her dad. "I'm sorry that I ran off like I did, but I just know Kelli is here somewhere."

"That's okay, sweetie. I know you're upset." Bill's eyes locked with Kari's. "I hope you're right about Kelli." He sighed. "I'm going to go find Naylor and see if there's any more news."

"C'mon, Kari, let's take a look around the house. I think it's safe now." Hank wiped at the sweat forming on his brow.

"Okay." Kari kissed her dad on the cheek and turned toward the luxurious structure. She gradually paraded around the expensive house, gaping up at it. She kept thinking she would spot Kelli peeking from behind one of the decorative green drapes. She hurried to the back of the house and noticed a newly built-on screen porch leading to the back door. She turned to Hank, who had been letting her lead the way. "Can we look up there?"

"The police have already searched through the house. I'm sure it's locked up and off limits." Hank said.

"Okay—I just want to look on the porch." She trotted up the stairs to the porch and pulled the screen door open. She stood in the doorway, inspecting the area. The porch was exceptionally clean, with fashionable wicker patio furniture and a TV sitting on a glass end table. She moved toward the door leading into the house. She grasped the doorknob and turned, but it was locked just like Hank had said.

Kari met Hank back in the yard and shrugged. "You were right—it is locked up." She scanned the spacious backyard that led into the woods. She tried reversing the situation in her head; she knew if it were herself escaping, she would have run into the woods. However, that probably wouldn't be the most logical thing to do because there wouldn't be any place to hide. Kelli was much more intelligent—she had never once made a wrong decision.

Kari tried to visualize the way Kelly's mind would work. Her eyes shifted to the chicken shed— Kelli might have considered there, but she probably would have thought that it was too obvious.

Kari glanced at the old-fashion tire swing dangling from a thick oak tree. Just past that her eyes lingered on a door leading into the ground; it was a cellar of some sort. Wild weeds were growing along the edges of it. It didn't look like it had been used

215

for years. She slowly moved toward it. "Look," she nudged Hank and pointed toward the door.

She gazed at the faded white wooden door—it was crooked, and the hinges were badly rusted and in need of repair. She pulled her hair behind her ears and then clasped her hands together. Her pulse raced as her hopes soared.

"Stand back and I'll take a look," Hank said.

Kari nodded, swallowed nervously, and took a step backwards.

Hank gradually lifted the door open.

Tiny bugs and spiders darted for safety. The walls were packed tight with dirt. Kari stepped forward to observe the cracked wooden stairs; they looked like they could collapse at any time. She stared down into the spooky dark hole. *Could it be possible?* she wondered. She took a deep breath and then called out, "Kelli, are you down there?"

Kari thought she heard a weak whimper. She squatted and motioned for Hank to do the same. She shifted her ear closer to the hole. "Kelli, are you down there?" She held her breath and waited.

After a very long moment, a flash of red popped in sight, and Kelli stared up at them with wide, terrified eyes. "Is it really you, Kari?"

"Oh my God, you're alive. I knew you were!" Kari shrieked. She ran down the squeaky stairs, grabbed Kelli and twirled her around.

"Kelli, are you okay?" Hank shouted in a stunned voice.

"My legs are a little stiff from sitting, but other than that I'm just ecstatic that you all found me." Kelli beamed.

"Come on up here." Hank held his hand out to help the girls out of the cellar.

Kelli dusted the cobwebs off her legs and glanced nervously toward the barn. "Where's Vaar?"

"You don't have to worry about him ever again—he's going to be locked up for a long time," Hank said.

"I am so thrilled that we found you." Kari jumped up and down excitedly. "Come on, Dad's over by the barn."

Kari grabbed Kelli's hand and pulled her toward the barn.

216

Kelli's expression suddenly saddened. "What about Renae and the other girls?"

Hank slid up next to Kelli's side. "They're all okay, thanks to Renae's brave move. I'll let her tell you about it."

"I don't believe this! I thought you guys were those Turkish men coming back for me. I thought I was hallucinating when Kari called my name out." She suddenly stopped, threw her arms around Kari, and squeezed her tight. "Oh God, I missed you! You'll never know how much!"

"You? Vaar told everyone that he killed you. Can you imagine how I felt?" Kari asked. "Let alone the guilt I would have had to live with—knowing this whole mess was my fault."

"Just answer me one thing—what made you go with Doug that day—did he force you?"

Kari rolled her eyes. "I think you know the answer to that. You know how crazy my hormones get when I see a good-looking guy."

"Well, we're going to have to work on that because I'm not chasing your butt all over the world anymore." Kelli squeezed Kari's hand.

Kari spotted her dad and Naylor standing near the barn. "Hey, Dad, look what I found," she hollered.

"Dad!" Kelli shouted and took off running toward him.

Naylor patted Kelli on the back while she hugged her dad. He strolled toward Hank and extended his hand out. "Good job...partner."

Hank shook his hand and nodded toward Kari. "She's the one that deserves all the credit. She seemed to know right where her sister was."

Naylor held his hand out to Kari. "You're a very bright young lady. Ever thought about going to work for the FBI?" He grinned.

"Thank you, but I don't want to ever go through anything like this again."

"Oh, I got more good news. Ali from the hospital called and wanted me to let you know your friend, Jill, is out of danger. She's going to be okay. She was just dehydrated and picked up a flu bug."

217

"Oh, wow—that's wonderful." Tears ran down Kari's face. She grinned at Naylor and twirled around to hug Hank. "Thank you both so much for all your help. This has to be the most miraculous day of my life." She gazed lovingly at her dad and Kelli. "I'm so grateful!"

Kari threw her arms around Kelli and her dad, and they all cried together.

"I'm so sorry, Dad, that I didn't obey you. I know I shouldn't have followed Hank." Kelli said.

"We'll discuss that later. I am just thrilled you're alive, and I think I'm still in shock!" Bill glanced toward Hank and Naylor—they were chatting while drifting closer toward the barn. "I need to thank them; I'll be right back."

Kari waited until her dad was out of earshot, and then she leaned over and rested her arm on Kelli's shoulder. "So, did you really miss me when you found out I was missing, or were you making arrangements for my room?"

Kelli grinned. "Well, your room is bigger."

Kari smiled and thumped Kelli on the back of her head. Her face grew solemn as she locked arms with Kelli. "I never have prayed so much in my life. I am so thankful that God was with us."

Kari knew it was a true miracle that she, Kelli, and Jill were still alive. She knew it was going to take a long time to get over the whole ordeal. However, she did learn a valuable lesson: although there are a lot of ethical people in the world—there are also a lot of corrupted people—and she now realized that just because someone was handsome or had an honest-looking face didn't mean they could be trusted.

She decided she wasn't going to rush into the dating scene when she returned home. She had all the time in the world to find a boyfriend. Right now, she just wanted to take time to enjoy the one thing that meant more to her than anything—her family.

The End

www.ingramcontent.com/pod-product-compliance
Lightning Source LLC
Chambersburg PA
CBHW031329170626
46807CB00002B/618